"THEY TOOK THAT TRACTOR BEAM OFF US, DIDN'T THEY?"

"Yes, sir." Vale dropped into a seat at the other working console. "But we've still got the guard and the force-field to deal with."

"I hope we can take care of both of them with one torpedo." Picard continued his board, going through the prelaunch checklist, arming and aiming weapons, and finally raising shields. He gazed out the viewport, but the guard in the hollowed-out gunnery position under the nacelle didn't seem to notice their activity.

"We still have full power in the engines, such as it is," reported Vale.

"Don't turn anything on until we fire."

She pointed to the crumpled Jem'Hadar battle cruiser. "Our friend . . . is he going to get the counselor?"

"I certainly hope so," said Picard grimly. "I'm ready. This should be interesting."

The lieutenant braced herself in her seat. His jaw clenched, the captain fired a photon torpedo at a dead ship full of merrymakers less than sixty meters away. . . .

Current books in this series:

A Time to Be Born by John Vornholt
A Time to Die by John Vornholt

Forthcoming books in this series:

A Time to Sow by Dayton Ward & Kevin Dilmore
A Time to Harvest by Dayton Ward & Kevin Dilmore
A Time to Love by Robert Greenberger
A Time to Hate by Robert Greenberger
A Time to Kill by David Mack
A Time to Heal by David Mack
A Time for War, a Time for Peace by
    Keith R.A. DeCandido

STAR TREK®
A Time to Die

JOHN VORNHOLT

Based upon
STAR TREK: THE NEXT GENERATION®
created by Gene Roddenberry

POCKET BOOKS
New York   London   Toronto   Sydney

This book is a work of fiction. Names, characters, places and incidents are products of the author's imagination or are used fictitiously. Any resemblance to actual events or locales or persons, living or dead, is entirely coincidental.

An *Original* Publication of POCKET BOOKS

POCKET BOOKS, a division of Simon & Schuster, Inc.
1230 Avenue of the Americas, New York, NY 10020

A VIACOM COMPANY

STAR TREK is a Registered Trademark of Paramount Pictures.

This book is published by Pocket Books, a division of Simon & Schuster, Inc., under exclusive license from Paramount Pictures.

ISBN: 0-7434-6766-3

First Pocket Books printing March 2004

10 9 8 7 6 5 4 3

POCKET and colophon are registered trademarks of Simon & Schuster, Inc.

Manufactured in the United States of America

For information regarding special discounts for bulk purchases, please contact Simon & Schuster Special Sales at 1-800-456-6798 or business@simonandschuster.com

For John O.

A Time to Die

Chapter One

THE PLEASANT TWITTERING of the birds, the gentle rustling of the breeze through the maple trees, and the rich smell of flowers and freshly turned earth lulled Beverly Crusher into a relaxed state. As the doctor sat in the manicured gardens of Starfleet Academy, she could never remember being happier in her life. It wasn't the lovely surroundings that delighted her; it was the company. Seated on the bench beside her, holding her hand, was a tall, handsome young man who looked a great deal like his father, especially in his piercing brown eyes. After an absence of eight years, her only child had returned to her. With Wesley so close, she couldn't imagine how she had survived his absence and the uncertainty of not knowing his fate . . . or even if he was alive.

The mind is an amazing thing, decided the doctor, *especially the way it can shut out grief, learn to cope, and go on with the obligations of life.* Now it seemed so unfair to have suffered all these years without Wes at her side, when his mere presence brought such bliss. She could almost forget the dark cloud that hung over the *Enterprise* and her shipmates. She recalled her son's words:

"To save the *Enterprise*," he had declared with determination. But this time they weren't being menaced by a failing warp engine or enemy attackers—problems they knew how to handle. They were threatened by the bureaucracy and politics of the Federation.

"Captain Picard is being held at Medical Mental Health," she said in a whisper.

"I know," answered Wes grimly. "I've been here throughout the tribunal and the verdict. You may have seen me assisting Admiral Nechayev . . . I called myself Ensign Brewster."

"Brewster!" she said with surprise. "But how?"

He held up his hand and smiled gently. "Do you remember what Ensign Brewster looks like?"

Beverly frowned in thought, but her stupefied mind felt like mush. "No, I don't remember . . . and I saw him every day at the inquiry."

"It's part of what I can do as a Traveler," explained Wes. "I can be anywhere I want—observing, interacting—but I blend into the background. Five minutes after you've spoken to me, you won't remember me . . . unless I choose to reveal my true self."

The doctor shook her head in amazement and gripped her son's hand, just grateful he was with her in any shape and form. "Then you know about the destruction of the *Juno* and the Ontailian ship, the *Vuxhal.* It wasn't our fault! They're blaming Jean-Luc, but there wasn't anything else he could do!"

"Calm down, Mom." The young man gave her hand a reassuring squeeze. "I didn't see everything that happened at the Rashanar Battle Site, because I hesitated . . . and arrived too late to help. I won't make that mistake again."

"I was there," said Beverly with a heavy sigh, "and I don't know exactly what happened either. According to Data and Geordi, there's a shapeshifting spacecraft in the graveyard, lurking among all those wrecks. It paralyzes a ship with a directed-energy weapon; then it assumes the ship's appearance. Data was insistent that the *Enterprise* was in immediate danger. That's why Jean-Luc fired on the Ontailian craft . . . or what looked like it. He was certain it was a mimic."

"But the tribunal didn't see it that way," muttered Wesley.

Beverly scowled and said, "No, they had to appease the Ontailians, who threatened to pull out of the Federation. They say we can't lose any more members . . . or lose our access to the Rashanar Battle Site. I can't get over the feeling that Admiral Nechayev sold Jean-Luc up the river."

"I disagree," said Wes, letting go of her hand and

rising to his feet. He paced thoughtfully along a flower-lined sidewalk. "I've been with Nechayev through this whole thing, and she took what she was given. Nobody really thinks Captain Picard is unfit for duty. The admiral couldn't let him go to a full court-martial. She didn't have any other choice."

He frowned, looking away from his mother. "But I did. I should have come forward sooner and done more to help. As usual, I just observed . . . I didn't want to give up being a Traveler."

"Oh, Wes!" With a look of motherly concern etched on her face, Beverly jumped to her feet and grabbed her son's arm. "Are you sure you have to give it up? Can't you . . . can't you exist in both worlds?"

He suddenly looked much older than she remembered. "I don't think so, Mom. I'm on a kind of probation. When you're a Traveler, you don't exist in one world—you exist in *every* world. The abilities I have are for a purpose. I've seen enough suffering and joy to last a thousand lifetimes, but to fulfill my mission, I must be like a shadow—never intervening, only watching."

"But you helped Admiral Nechayev," countered Beverly, "so haven't you already broken that barrier?"

"Not really. As long as I don't change the outcome." Wes balled his hands into fists and stopped pacing. "However, I'm about to break that rule. Please tell no one that you've seen me."

Beverly reached for him in desperation as she felt

her baby leaving her again. "Wes! How can I keep it a secret? Don't go away again . . . please!"

"Mom," he said with a quiet smile, "I'm not going to leave you again, not like that. But I can do more and gather information better if I can hang on to my secret a while longer. There is one other I have to tell. I don't know how long I can stay a Traveler, because all of us are sharing this experience even as we speak, but I'm not going to see the *Enterprise* die."

"How long will you have your abilities?" she asked.

He shook his head, collecting his scattered thoughts. "I don't know. All of our minds must be focused—as if through a lens—to allow each individual Traveler to move through space and dimensions. It's like multi-processing. To tell you the truth, I'm not sure anymore if I'm a Traveler or a human . . . or both."

Unable to speak, she hugged him fiercely. Her boy was clearly an adult who had to decide for himself how to now use this extraordinary gift . . . and when to give it up.

Of course, Wesley was always gifted—a prodigy— and we both know the highs and the lows of that status. Was Wes ever really accepted just for himself? Probably not, she decided.

More than anything, her son must have longed to be a real Ensign Brewster. Another face in the crowd, instead of the focus of envy and expectations.

He finally ended the embrace and moved her gently away, but his hands lingered on her trembling fingers. "Mom, you'll be seeing me . . . more likely as this."

Before her loving eyes and bedazzled senses, Wesley turned into the nondescript Ensign Brewster. As the doctor tried to focus on this new face, it disappeared, and she was left standing alone in the tranquil gardens of Starfleet Academy.

Was it just a dream? she wondered. *A hallucination?* Beverly prayed not, because she'd had those delusions before. She felt something in her hand, and opened her palm to reveal Wesley's flight-suit patch from Nova Squadron, the one that had nearly sunk his career in Starfleet.

He really was *here,* she thought, clutching the tattered strip of cloth to her heart.

The Traveler, in the guise of Ensign Brewster, stood on the porch of an elegant Victorian town house in the Russian Hill district. He rang the chime and waited patiently until it opened. Commander Emery appeared—the telepathic aide to the Medusan Commodore Korgan, who had led the prosecution of Captain Picard.

Wesley squared his shoulders and stood at attention while the tall, gaunt human regarded his visitor. "Yes?" asked Emery. "What do you want, Ensign?"

"Don't you remember me, sir? I'm Ensign Brewster."

A small spark of recognition flashed behind the hooded eyes. "Ah, yes. I thought our business with you and Admiral Nechayev was concluded."

"It is," answered the Traveler. "Don't you recall—

Commodore Korgan invited me to tea? I had to decline until the inquiry was over. Now I'm ready to take the commodore up on his invitation."

Emery narrowed his eyes at the low-ranking officer. "I hardly believe this is the time. The commodore is preparing for a new case that starts tomorrow. What's your unit? I'll send a messenger by when the commodore has more time."

"Please ask him," requested the ensign firmly. "I think he'll want to see me as soon as possible."

"One moment," grumbled Emery. He shut the door. The Traveler could see him move a few steps inside the foyer, where he stood perfectly still, communing telepathically with his Medusan superior. After several moments, he opened the door and looked at the visitor with increased respect.

"You were right," said Emery. "Commodore Korgan wants to see you right away. He suggests that I take a stroll while you have tea." He stepped back and motioned the ensign inside.

Trying to look humble, "Brewster" stepped into the foyer. "Thank you for all your help, Commander."

"Will you be able to communicate with him?" Emery asked.

"I think so. It's a nice afternoon for a walk."

Emery sniffed. "I suppose so. The commodore is in the last room down the hall on the left. There's a food slot in the room . . . have whatever you want. Of course, don't open Commodore Korgan's enclosure and look directly at him, or you'll be joining Captain Picard in the mental-health facility."

The ensign bit his tongue at that gibe; however, he knew the warning was well-intentioned and necessary, even for a Traveler. "Thank you, Commander."

"Try not to tire him," said Emery softly on his way out the door.

The Traveler took a deep breath and walked down the hallway. As he neared the last door on the left, he could feel a powerful force probing his mind, but it didn't feel invasive. It felt more like a frank stare from someone who didn't understand what you had just said.

He opened the door and stepped into a brightly lit room with sparse furnishings—a small dining table and two chairs. Built into the wall was a food replicator. The Medusan's protective container rested on the table, along with a few padds and documents. The noncorporeal being occupied an oblong electromagnetic box with four tentacle-like manipulator arms, although the appendages were motionless for the moment.

Welcome, Ensign Brewster. Please take refreshment with me.

"Thank you," he replied, although speaking aloud wasn't really necessary. The Medusan's thought waves were as clear as those of any fellow Traveler. "I am sorry to keep you waiting."

What kind of creature are you? came the impatient query. *You are not human . . . or not entirely human.*

"Not *only* human. I am a Traveler. Have you heard of us?"

Lights on the container blinked excitedly. *Oh, yes,* came the reply. *You have learned to manipulate space, time, thought, and dimension. Most humanoids cannot detect your true nature.*

"We are observers," answered the visitor as he crossed to the food replicator. "Computer, a cola carbonated beverage, chilled."

"Cola, chilled," replied the efficient computer voice as a frosty mug of bubbling soda appeared in the food slot.

The young man grabbed the glass and took a sip, relishing the tingle of the bubbly liquid on his throat. "That tastes good," he remarked. "I've spent too long on dying worlds without any food or drink."

I can sense much sadness in you, replied the Medusan. *You have seen the universe the way it really is. Why did you choose to observe the inquiry into the Rashanar incident?*

"Because I used to serve with Captain Picard on the *Enterprise,* when my name was Wesley Crusher. Dr. Beverly Crusher is my mother." He walked back to the table and sat down across from his host.

You are human, but a Traveler, observed the Medusan. *You are a truly unique individual, yet you wish to remain anonymous.*

"For now," agreed Wesley. "Since you saw through my disguise in the courtroom, I've come to tell you that Captain Picard is innocent. What Data said was true—some terrible entity *does* haunt the Rashanar Battle Site and was responsible for the destruction of the *Juno,* the *Vuxhal,* and the *Calypso.* It might be responsible for the carnage that originally occurred during the Dominion War."

Am I supposed to say I'm sorry for prosecuting an innocent man? The law is not about absolute innocence or guilt, but what can be proven in court.

"I know that," replied Wesley. He took another sip of his soft drink. "That's why I said nothing until the inquiry ran its course. I could have done much more to change the outcome, but I didn't. The letter of the law has been met, and the Ontailians and Starfleet are both satisfied. Now it's time to satisfy the *spirit* of the law . . . to discover the truth."

How do you propose we do that, Traveler?

"You and I have perceptions that others don't have," Wesley answered. "They just see, but we observe. We won't be confused by the chaotic nature of Rashanar. We both have the ability to always know where we are in space. Someone must go back there and confront this threat . . . either to destroy it or to bring back proof of its existence."

I believe you seek revenge, not truth, came the reply.

Wesley sighed. He couldn't entirely deny that. "The damage has been done to the *Enterprise* and her crew," he answered, "not to mention the *Juno.* I only want to prevent it from happening again. Will you go to Rashanar with me, Commodore? Your testimony could make the difference."

After a short painful silence, the Medusan replied, *Do you know, only twelve of my species serve in Starfleet? All but myself are navigators on long-range ships. You once wondered why this was so.*

"That's true," admitted the Traveler with a smile. "I have a feeling you're going to tell me."

The enclosure hummed softly. Its lights twinkled before Korgan gave his answer: *Traveling at warp speeds makes me ill. I nearly died on my first Starfleet training mission. Since then, I looked for and eventually found a more sedentary profession. I travel vicariously through others. So you see, we Medusans are not all alike, just as you are not a typical Traveler or a typical human.*

Feeling defeated, Wesley slapped his palms on his knees and rose to his feet. "I'm sorry to have troubled you, Commodore. Thank you for your hospitality."

But I will do one favor for you, said the voice in Wesley's head. The young man stopped in the doorway to look back at the mysterious container, which blinked cheerfully. *I will file an affidavit saying that the Ontailians were lying. This may be enough to quietly throw out the findings of the inquiry and have Captain Picard released.*

"You *knew* they were lying?"

So did you, Traveler, yet you said nothing.

Wesley lowered his head and listened. *I found out later that they did recover wreckage from the* Vuxhal, *which they chose not to present at the inquiry. I understand that trace elements of neptunium were embedded in the molecular coating, indicating possible proximity to the anomalies found in the center of the site. At any rate, this lack of evidence made them amenable to the resolution offered by Admiral Nechayev. I'm afraid that's the nature of a settlement—someone must shoulder the blame, even if it is lessened.*

Wesley Crusher nodded; sometimes discretion *was* the better part of valor. "Good-bye, Commodore Korgan," he said. "Thank you for your honesty."

Go with speed, Traveler. Please take this parting gift.

The Medusan filled Wesley's brain with the most sublime, blissful thoughts he could ever imagine—birthday parties, puppies, vacations, lullabies—and he was suddenly transported to his past and overwhelmed with happiness. *I'm home! This is home!* Wes began to whistle, leaping down the stairs like a ten-year-old. With a joyous laugh, he found himself skipping up the hill in his beautiful San Francisco.

Jean-Luc Picard sat on bare red stone, gazing out the archway carved in the side of a sheer, deeply striated cliff. His dwelling was about a hundred meters from the top of the bluff. Beneath him floated sulfurous mists which hid a murky river that ran with potable water only a few weeks a year. Above him was a hot, desolate plain. The heat of the day would reach him when the sun struck his level. This humble abode, hollowed from the red rock itself, was no more than a hovel; he had a few clay bowls and utensils and a pile of linen upon which to lie. In the corner sat a large clay pitcher shaped like a *brujgar* horn in which to catch water from the spring just above him. Vulcan tribes had inhabited such cliff dwellings for millennia, dating back to when they had been violent savages. The warrens in the cliff were easy to defend and stayed relatively cool for a village in the Vulcan high desert.

The captain's only nod to modernity was a stack of dog-eared Dixon Hill novels in the corner. He had pens and a journal in which he had yet to write a word. There was nothing in his present circumstances he wished to record for posterity; he wished only to wake up from this horrible nightmare and get on with his life.

As befitting his hermitic lifestyle, Picard had let his beard grow. He wore Starfleet exercise garments, which were more comfortable than the thick Vulcan robes everyone around him wore. Humans tended to sweat much more than Vulcans, and a shower was not available to him, unless he switched to a different holodeck program.

Jean-Luc heard footsteps on the stone walkway just beyond his open door. He wondered if it was a visitor come to see him. A moment later, he was disappointed to see it was just another holodeck character—a wise-looking Vulcan who often stopped to dispense pedestrian platitudes and try to engage him in conversation.

The old Vulcan cleared his throat and said, "Only Nixon could go to China."

"I've heard that already," muttered Picard. "Go on your way."

The Vulcan stood for several seconds, as if the hermit might change his mind and talk, and Picard considered yelling at him to go. No, that would look very bad on his next evaluation, and that one was crucial, whenever it would be. Now it was time to take the kettle off the fire and let the boiling water come to a rest. *And I'm the kettle*, thought Jean-Luc.

"Conditions are favorable for rain this afternoon," remarked the old Vulcan, studying the golden sky.

In response, Picard rolled onto his blankets and stared at the rugged wall at the back of his cavern. He presumed that Counselor Colleen Cabot and her assistants were watching him through the fake wall, if they even bothered to pay attention to him anymore. He supposed that some of this neglect was his own fault, because he had let it be known that he didn't want to see many of his shipmates under these circumstances. They were respecting his wishes . . . thus turning him into a recluse.

He had avoided further proceedings on the Rashanar matter, but now he was beginning to miss the day-to-day interaction with others. The incident was over, as far as everyone else was concerned; for him, it had only prolonged the embarrassment and started an open-ended incarceration.

I have to find some way to cope, he decided, *or I will go mad.*

"Good morning, Jean-Luc," said a friendly voice from the doorway. He turned to see that the Vulcan had finally departed and was replaced by a fair-skinned woman who looked rather youthful, her blond hair blowing gently in the warm breezes of the cliff. As usual, Counselor Cabot wore flattering civilian clothes. He had only seen her in a Starfleet uniform twice, during his inquiry and at the memorial service for the *Juno*'s crew. She made a few notes on her padd. He felt like a zoo animal being visited by the zookeeper. According to Nechayev, Colleen Cabot had done him a considerable favor by allowing more psychological evaluation, but it didn't feel that way to him.

The counselor motioned toward his dingy, austere surroundings. "You know, Jean-Luc, I always figured you would pick the Vulcan room, if left to your own devices long enough."

"It's the most like a cell," he remarked.

"If you say so." She gave him a bemused smile, then ducked her head to step inside his hovel. "People keep making requests to visit you, but you have a very short list of those you approve. You really don't have to be alone, as long as the *Enterprise* is at home port."

Picard sat up cross-legged and looked at his "jailer." "They have repairs and test flights to make, followed by a new mission. Let them get used to Captain Riker without being overly concerned about me."

"That's very selfless of you," said Cabot, sitting down across from him.

"The welfare of the *Enterprise* and her crew is my first concern," he answered. "Always has been."

The counselor nodded. "That's right. If you hadn't been sure the ship was in danger, you wouldn't have fired on the Ontailians."

"They weren't Ontailians," said the captain, his jaw clenched tightly. With considerable self-control, he managed to relax and muster a smile for his keeper. "But you haven't come here to rehash the inquiry, have you? I hope not, because I hate to keep fighting battles I've already lost."

"Isn't that what Rashanar is all about?" she asked. "Fighting that never stops."

"Yes, that's one theory. This doppelgänger ship— or more than one—could explain why the Dominion and Federation vessels fought to the death at Rashanar. They didn't know *who* or *what* they were really fighting. They died at their posts, with surrender never an option."

Colleen Cabot frowned, then asked, "But isn't that how Jem'Hadar and Dominion ships always fought— to the death?"

"No," answered Picard. "If a Jem'Hadar ship becomes too crippled to be effective, they look to board an enemy ship as soon as possible. The Cardassians were never ones to die needlessly—if there was a way to escape to fight another day, they would take it. But not if the whole crew is blacked out with the ship paralyzed. Think about it, Counselor, how can you have a battle with no survivors? You're a psychologist—you know the will to survive is one of the strongest instincts."

Cabot sat forward. "Yes, Jean-Luc, and you went to Rashanar *wanting* to solve this mystery, didn't you? And you *solved* it—you were successful."

Picard narrowed his eyes warily at his keeper. He could see where this line of questioning was going. He had to hand it to Colleen Cabot—she was always working one angle or another.

"I didn't make up the replicant ship just to fit the facts," he said firmly. "Data and La Forge didn't expect to see what they saw—two identical ships—but they did."

"You take me the wrong way, Jean-Luc," said Cabot with disappointment. "This replicated ship is not only at the basis of your defense; it's the basis of your mental state and confidence. As long as you are unshakable in your belief in the mimic ship, your case makes sense to me and everyone else."

He snorted a laugh. "You mean, I'm either right or delusional, therefore it doesn't really matter to you."

"It matters to me a lot," said Cabot somberly. "And it should matter to you, too, if you want to get out of here."

"But how do you prove me right or delusional," asked the captain, "except to go to Rashanar and see for yourself? To me and my crew, Data's word is proof enough. But it wasn't enough for the tribunal, and I can't offer you anything else."

The young blond woman shrugged and rose slowly to her feet, brushing the fake red dust off her pants. "If Data were a humanoid, we could use hypnosis, a mind-meld, or some other process to verify his story. But he's not, and no one else saw the transformation. You're convinced, but you didn't see it firsthand either. I guess you're right, Jean-Luc . . . Starfleet has to go back to Rashanar."

Picard noted darkly, "If we don't stop this threat, more ships will be destroyed."

The counselor sighed on her way out the door. "You attribute too much power to me. What do you want for dinner, Jean-Luc? Something other than healthy Vulcan gruel?"

"I'll stick with the gruel," muttered Picard, lying upon his dusty linens. "It suits my mood."

Strolling down the corridor of the holosuite wing of Medical Mental Health, Counselor Cabot was troubled. She couldn't fulfill the charge given her, because there was no more information to be gleaned from Captain Picard, or any of the others connected with this incident. He was as sane as anyone in Starfleet. Keeping him here was unnecessary. Rather than hold him here, they should just give him a medical discharge and be done with it. The Ontailians had all left Earth to return to their own space, so dragging this out seemed pointless . . . unless there was something to be gained.

The young counselor was still deep in thought when she opened the door to her office and walked toward her cluttered desk. A hulking figure whirled around in the chair, startling her. He was a formidable presence indeed.

"Admiral Nakamura," she said, catching her breath. "What are you doing here?"

"I thought it was time to talk," the distinguished officer answered crossly. "We don't have much of it before we have to decide what to do."

Colleen tossed her padd onto her desk. "I've reached a dead end. He doesn't know any more about the mimic ship than he's already told us. If you send Picard to Rashanar, he'll only try to destroy it."

"You must have ways to influence him," pressed Nakamura. "Drugs, posthypnotic suggestion—there must be a way to get him to capture this weapon, so we can study it."

Cabot felt resentful toward Nakamura's patronizing attitude. She no longer cared about the promised fast-track promotion. "Why not send a fact-finding mission?" she asked. "A whole task force to study it or capture it . . . or whatever you want to do."

"No. The Ontailians are too touchy now. Remember, they control Rashanar. It has to be a covert mission. My department has been collecting and studying Dominion technology, and a shapeshifting spacecraft—what a coup that would be!"

Cabot seethed at the unfairness of the whole situation; however, she still had one big card to play in this game—Jean-Luc Picard. He was her property until she chose to let him go, but now the captain wasn't foremost in her thoughts.

"I've heard something," she asked, trying to hide her worry, "that Beverly Crusher might end up in charge of Starfleet Medical?"

The admiral shrugged his brocaded and bedecked shoulders. "Oh, that's just a rumor. Whenever Dr. Crusher is in town for a few days, you always hear that."

"She holds no love for me, not after the way I've treated Picard. If that should happen, I'll have no future in Starfleet, no matter *what* you do to help me."

Nakamura straightened his tunic and stared pointedly at her. "Forget Crusher and concentrate on the task at hand." He stopped as an idea hit him. "Data! He would be more pliable than Picard. At least there are ways to program the android. He's malfunctioned twice in recent memory—at Rashanar and at the Ba'ku planet, so he is due for reprogramming."

The imposing admiral rose from Cabot's desk and strode toward her, headed for the door. "Just make the captain comfortable, but not *too* comfortable, so he'll be happy to get out of here when the time is right. I know you can do *that* without any problem."

She cringed as Nakamura passed her. Colleen had begun to dislike her chief benefactor intensely. Colleen had known his backing wouldn't come cheap, but this was not how the young counselor wanted to succeed in Starfleet. However, like Beverly Crusher, Nakamura would be a bad one to cross.

Either way, I'm screwed, she mused.

Chapter Two

ON THE BRIDGE of the *Enterprise,* acting captain William Riker stood over La Forge's shoulder and watched readouts dance across the auxiliary engineering console. This was their first warp trial since making repairs in orbital dock over Earth, and Riker wanted the test to go well. On the other hand, going *too* well might mean an early departure for their next mission . . . and leaving Captain Picard and Data behind.

"The deuterium slush is running a little rich," said Riker. "What do you think, Geordi?"

"Hmmm? What?" The engineer blinked his ocular implants at his captain, his mind light-years away.

Riker acted as if he hadn't noticed the lapse. "The deuterium slush looks rich to me. That might indicate the matter reactant injector needs to be replaced, which ought to be good for another day in dock, shouldn't it?"

La Forge mustered a smile. "Yes, sir, I believe the injector does look a bit off. We'll have to take it apart and see." Then he frowned anew, distracted by more than repairs to the warp propulsion system.

"I'm sure Data will be all right."

"Why did they need him again?" demanded La Forge. "They took away his emotion chip and ran him through a battery of tests and diagnostics. There was nothing wrong with him! Now they have to do it again? I just don't get it."

Riker paused to phrase his answer to Data's best friend. "Geordi," he said slowly, "not everyone knows Data as well as we do. To us, he's a loyal friend and colleague. To them, he's an exotic lifeform, a walking computer, or at worst . . . a machine. Starfleet is just trying to find answers for what happened at Rashanar."

"They're looking in the wrong place," countered La Forge. "Data wasn't convicted of anything. He can't even tell a lie. If I were a sighted person, the tribunal would have taken *my* word for what happened."

"Data saw more than you did," answered Riker, shaking his head in frustration. "Listen, I can't change what's happened to us. I've got a ship to run. We're all upset about this; however, we have to get over it and do our jobs. You can worry about them on your own time, La Forge. Just shake it off when you're on duty."

The engineer Scowled and rose to his feet. "Captain, I'd like to request a leave . . . to help Captain Picard and Data."

The words kicked Riker in the gut like a hobnailed boot. He instantly wanted to retract what he had said. Of course, they were all worrying about Picard and Data every minute of the day, whether they were on duty or not; it was pointless to pretend they weren't. La Forge looked so determined, his jaw set so firmly. He wasn't the type to fly off the handle like this.

Seeing Riker's perplexed expression, La Forge softened his features. "I know you've got to run the *Enterprise,* so you stay," he said. "Let me see if I can do any good."

Riker felt a delicate hand on his back, and he saw another hand reach for La Forge's shoulder. He turned, thinking he would see Deanna, but it was Dr. Crusher. Unlike the rest of them, she wore a smile that was confident and content.

"Reconsider, Geordi," she said in a low voice. "I can tell you that we have help coming from an unusual source. I know it's hard to be patient when you feel so helpless, but Captain Picard and Data have other allies besides us. If you get involved, you'll just butt your head against a wall. We need patience more than anything else, we need to have the whole crew ready."

"Ready for what?" asked La Forge, sounding

unconvinced. "Ready to survey the Jupiter asteroid belt? That's a mission for third-year cadets. I don't think I can just stand around and wait for Starfleet to come to their senses."

"Are you planning to break the captain out of a secure psychiatric wing?" asked Crusher. "Are you going to storm the S.C.E. and rescue Data? We need to have Starfleet's blessing when we go back to Rashanar, not more of our crew under lock and key."

From the corner of his eye, Riker caught sight of a relief bridge officer hovering a bit too close, possibly near enough to hear their conversation. "Back to your post, Ensign," he barked at the young man, whose name he could not place.

Beverly Crusher gave him another smile. "Don't worry, Will, nothing we say will go beyond the bridge. We're all in this together."

"That won't be so easy," said the acting captain. "In the officers' club, I've heard people whispering about us behind our backs. I've heard them repeating the accusations against the captain, saying it was only a matter of time before he cracked up. You know, I think some people in Starfleet are glad to see the *Enterprise* brought down a notch or two."

"Human nature," replied Crusher. "It's okay, our mystique can survive. Please, Geordi, hunker down and ride out the storm. At least see what another week will bring. We've got a friend who will keep an eye on both Picard and Data."

The angry engineer gritted his teeth and returned to his seat, studying the data coming from the warp propulsion system. Riker let out a sigh and silently thanked Crusher; he wished he had half of her confidence that all of this would work out. Even if it did, they would have to spend a long time repairing their reputation. Crusher left his side and had a few words with the nondescript ensign he had noticed before. Riker was suddenly very glad for the doctor's levelheaded presence. Since she was closer to Picard than anyone, her calm meant a great deal to the crew.

"Conn," he said, "set a course back to Earth, warp two."

Footsteps sounded across the spotless floor, and all conversation in the Starfleet Corps of Engineers' laboratory ended a moment before a familiar voice said, "Hello, Commander Data."

Lying upon a workbench, Data turned his head to see Admiral Nakamura peering down at him. The admiral was dressed in a lab coat and was pulling on thin cotton gloves, as if he were about to go to work.

"Hello, Admiral Nakamura," answered the android. He was glad he no longer had his emotion chip, because Nakamura's presence would definitely inspire a twinge of fear. "Does your visit have something to do with the inquiry?" he asked.

"Of course," answered the admiral. "We also had a chance to take a look at your emotion chip. We feel that the socket on your neural net could be used for other purposes."

Data considered the possibility, then remarked, "It is true that other enhancements could be added via that particular socket, but I doubt if anyone other than my creator, Dr. Soong, could reliably program such a chip."

Nakamura smiled. "I see you don't have much faith in the S.C.E. They've reverse-engineered lots of unusual devices. They think they can do the same with your emotion chip. At any rate, we've got a test chip we'd like to install in that socket—it doesn't do anything but see if we've guessed the right pathways and algorithms. It will be functionally neutral—you won't notice a thing."

"I would prefer not," said Data honestly. "That socket is not intended to be used with interchangeable devices."

The admiral's cheerfulness changed in a flash. "Remember, we still want to know if your emotion chip affected your judgment in Rashanar. So this is an order."

Data nodded thoughtfully. "In which case, I cannot prevent you, Admiral. You may proceed."

"Very good." Nakamura turned to the lab's chief engineer, a Bolian named Moroz, and said, "Give me the new chip."

The Bolian looked quizzically at him, then hesitated before he answered, "We gave it to your aide just a few minutes ago."

"My *aide?* I sent no aide down here. Where is this person?"

"Well, he was just here." Commander Moroz looked around, and he glared expectantly at his assistants.

"He was standing over there," said one, pointing to a corner. "A slight man, a lieutenant."

"I thought he was a commander," said another. "Stout and older."

"Stout?" queried another. "He was Andorian, and they're not stout."

"Andorian? No, he was human!"

Bickering broke out among the assembled technicians, who could not agree on one single detail.

"You *gave* that chip away to somebody?!" thundered the admiral. "Just somebody who walked in?! You don't even know *who?!*"

Data stared at the blustery man, who was shaking his fists at the terrified engineers.

The admiral stomped around the laboratory, waving his hands. "It was a prototype! I can't just walk down the hall and get another one. This is insane!"

"Am I free to leave?" asked Data, sitting up on the workbench and swinging his legs over the edge. "I have duties aboard the *Enterprise.*" He didn't have to admit that they were rather mundane duties since he had not been directly questioned. But he didn't see the need to be completely honest with Admiral Nakamura, as Data assumed the ranking officer was not being completely honest with him.

"Wait here a few minutes!" ordered the flustered admiral, storming toward the door. "I'm going to check with security and run the vid log on this laboratory. We'll find out who got that chip!"

After Nakamura left, Commander Moroz let out a relieved sigh. "I'm sorry, Data, but you know how orders are. Now it looks like we'll be in as much trouble as you are. Do you remember what that aide looked like, or his name?"

"Inexplicably, I cannot recall," answered the android, "although I am certain I have seen him before."

"Me, too," agreed the Bolian. "Tough luck about your captain. I think they were kind of hard on him. I've talked to others who have been to Rashanar. Spooky place . . . and dangerous."

Data nodded. "It is not a region of space where one ever feels at ease." They talked for a few more minutes about the hazards and anomalies of the Rashanar Battle Site. The engineers were all attentive and curious. The consensus was that they wanted to see it, but wouldn't really put in for duty there. After all, if the *Enterprise* could get in trouble in the graveyard of lost ships, none of them wanted to brave it.

As the discussion was winding down, the door opened, and Admiral Nakamura raced back in, looking chagrined and angry. "I've been down to security," he began, "watching the logs of this lab, and I'm afraid we have an intruder. We saw the person who took Data's chip, but the image was so fuzzy that we have to presume it was a nonhumanoid, or perhaps someone with shielding technology. At any rate, Commander Data, you may be at risk."

Data wanted to agree that the potential hazard was mostly from the admiral and his engineers, but he merely cocked his head and said, "Permission to return to the *Enterprise,* where I will not be at risk."

Nakamura glowered, but he apparently couldn't think of a good reason to hold Data, not with so many technicians watching him. "Commander Moroz," he ordered, "take Data down to the transporter room and make sure he gets back safely to the *Enterprise.*" The admiral's eyes flashed, and he added, "When you get back here, we're going to have a little talk about security and procedures."

"Yes, sir," answered the Bolian with a gulp.

As he walked along a pedestrian bridge between Starfleet Engineering and Medical, the Traveler studied the replica of Data's emotion chip. He wasn't sure what programming they had intended to inflict upon Data, but he was suspicious of the source. Nakamura wasn't the only one in Starfleet who didn't understand or appreciate the android, but he was the highest-ranking one. The inquiry was over, and now it was time for the admiralty to do something constructive about Rashanar or back off.

Wes cringed. If he hadn't taken a few moments to check on Data, he never would have discovered their plan to install this new chip. He could go anywhere he chose, but he couldn't be two places at once; it felt as if he were neglecting Captain Picard. But the captain's situation was a lot more delicate than Data's, since he had been assigned to the custody of Medical Mental Health. Maybe it was time to visit the young counselor, Colleen Cabot.

The Traveler had seen her during the tribunal and his visits to Mental Health, but he had yet to decide how to approach her in a way that would help the captain. He had wandered through Picard's quarters pretending to be a holodeck character, but the captain wasn't in any mood for nonsense. In truth, Colleen Cabot was rather imposing—cold, calculating, and beautiful—and he wasn't sure how he could influence her thinking on the captain's behalf.

She needs to know that Data is telling the truth, thought Wes, *and that Picard is completely rational.* If she could just see the mysteries of Rashanar for herself, then she would know, and she'd lobby for his release. *Then again, is Counselor Cabot really in charge, or is she just a front for others?*

How could he know unless he talked to her? Unfortunately, Starfleet counselors weren't in the habit of chatting about their patients. Since he couldn't just stand in the corner and observe, he would need more than his usual tricks to confront her.

Before he entered the mental health facility, Wes stopped and flipped Data's ersatz emotion chip high into the air. As it spun in the sunshine, he made it disappear, sending it off to the Rashanar Battle Site to float with the other useless chunks of technology. The Traveler then willed himself to be standing in the corridor outside Picard's room, beyond the reach of security. His attuned senses picked up voices inside the room—the captain talking to an unidentified woman. Since the *Enterprise* was still making its way back from the warp trial, he knew it couldn't be anyone from the crew.

A moment later, the Traveler strode past the Vulcan cliff dwelling where Picard had chosen to take refuge. As before, the visitor was dressed as an elder, nondescript Vulcan, and neither the captain nor Counselor Cabot paid any attention to him as he lingered on the cliffside walkway.

"I'm sorry, Captain," insisted Cabot, placing her hands on her slim hips, "but you must take another round of tests. Either you switch to another room simulation with a computer, or I'll have a computer terminal brought in here."

"Didn't I take a dozen of your tests before the inquiry?" asked Picard. "Do you really expect my answers to have changed?"

"Frankly, I don't know unless I test you," insisted the counselor, appearing to lose a bit of her professional cool. "You're here to be evaluated under *my* supervision. I have to have some means to do that. If it's the impersonal nature of the computer that bothers you, I'll ask you the questions myself. Then you can pretend we're just having a conversation. But you will take these tests, Jean-Luc, or my evaluation will focus on your lack of cooperation and remorse."

"Remorse!" thundered Picard, jumping to his feet. "Do you think I'm not remorseful about what happened to the *Juno?* Or the *Vuxhal?* I've lain awake every night thinking about it, wondering what I could have done differently. Captain Leeden and I had reached a truce in our personal styles. We finally had mutual respect for each other. The fraternity of starship captains is competitive but very tightly knit, when it comes down to it. I feel the loss of the *Juno* much more acutely than you ever will."

Cabot smiled condescendingly at him. "Do you see, Jean-Luc? It's not so hard to talk about it. We just need to get your thoughts down in a form I can use in my report. Remorse is not only good for your personal healing; it's good for everyone's perception of what happened. Believe me, it's all about perception. You see it one way, the Ontailians another way, the tribunal a third way. I'm supposed to be neutral and explain my perception of *you.* That's why it's so hard to find truth in a case like this—it's like the theory of relativity. Space and time are different depending on where you're standing."

No, thought Wesley as he observed this dynamic and beautiful woman, *the regular approach isn't going to work with her.*

Looking defeated, Captain Picard sat back on the dusty floor of his cavelike dwelling. "I'll make a deal with you, Counselor," he said. "Let me try to get some sleep and approach your questionnaire with a fresh attitude. You can bring your computer back in a couple of hours, all right?"

Cabot mulled it over. "You rest, collect your thoughts, and I'll be back."

"Excuse me, Counselor Cabot," said the old Vulcan suddenly standing in the shadows. "You have an important visitor in your office."

The blond woman blinked in surprise at him. Picard seemed to notice him for the first time. "Since when do the holosuite characters give me messages?" she asked with annoyance.

He shrugged and said, "I do not know. Live long and prosper." With that, the elderly Vulcan disappeared into the illusory gloominess on the periphery of the hologram effect.

"I have to talk to the programmers," declared Colleen as she headed for the doorway. "The holograms shouldn't be interrupting me when I'm in here with a patient. How does this program know there's someone in my office?"

"Maybe they made an improvement," said Picard with a wan smile.

"That's really absurd," muttered the counselor as she swept imperiously out of the room.

Colleen Cabot had a strong sense of déjà vu as she walked down the corridor toward her office. It had been only yesterday that Admiral Nakamura had paid her a surprise visit. Had he come back? Could they have anything else left to discuss? She hoped not, because this arrangement was already making her queasy.

When her office door opened, she found herself facing a rather handsome man about her own age. He gave her a boyish smile, as if he already knew her, although she didn't recognize him. Or did she? As she looked at her visitor, he seemed more familiar; maybe they had met in passing. Oddly, he wasn't wearing a Starfleet uniform, just a sort of nondescript gray jumpsuit. Yet he had a Starfleet bearing about him, with a lot of wisdom in his intense, dark eyes. She guessed him to be a fellow counselor.

"I'm Colleen Cabot," she said curtly as she brushed past him on the way to her desk. "I'm very busy, so do you have something you wish to discuss?"

He gave her a pleasant smile and answered, "My name is Wesley. Did you ever read *A Christmas Carol* by Charles Dickens? Or have you seen one of the dramatic versions?"

She peered at him with annoyance. "If you don't leave right now, I'm going to call security and have you arrested."

"I'm afraid your com panel doesn't work anymore. Neither does the door."

Cabot promptly tapped the panel on her desk, but it produced no cheerful beep or attentive voices. She dashed to her door and plowed right into it when it didn't open automatically as expected. Desperately, she banged on the barrier and shouted in futility.

"I'm not going to hurt you," the young man assured her. "So, do you know *A Christmas Carol?*"

She stared at him, her voice finally croaking, "Yes."

"Good!" exclaimed Wesley. He took a step closer to her. His manner didn't seem threatening. Why should it, when he was in complete control of the situation? He continued, "Do you remember how Ebenezer Scrooge—that would be *you* in this case— is visited by the Ghosts of Christmas Past, Present, and Yet to Come?"

Colleen blinked frightened blue eyes at him. "Are you telling me you're a ghost?"

"No," he answered, "I'm as alive as you. Being Scrooge, you're only interested in work and filling out your forms properly. The bottom line, they used to call it."

"Are you another counselor?" she asked in confusion.

"No," he said with a warm laugh. "Look, Colleen—may I call you Colleen? You seem to like using first names. Remember, I'm Wesley."

"How did you lock this door?" she angrily demanded. "You are going to be in big trouble."

Wes nodded. "I'm afraid you're right about that, but it won't be from you. We're going to take a little trip, so you'll understand what happened better. Like

I said, just think of me as the Ghost of Christmas Present."

"I'm not going anywhere with you!" Colleen vowed, looking around for a paperweight, padd, or anything to use as a weapon.

The young man reached his hand for hers, and his dark eyes were serious but also playful. "You won't be hurt, Colleen, and you will be amazed. You'll be back before anyone knows you're gone."

We can't go anywhere unless he opens the door, she thought with confidence. *He's probably a patient who escaped from another floor. But how does he know so much about me?*

"A Christmas Carol is one of my favorite stories," Colleen whispered as she reached hesitantly for his hand. "By the way, I should warn you that I know martial arts."

"I didn't think you got that physique by just sitting around," he answered flirtatiously. Their fingers met. His hand was warm and oddly tingling. For the first time, she worried that he really was a ghost . . . or not as mundane as he appeared to be.

The counselor glanced at her frozen door only a step away, expecting it to open. Instead the man's grip tightened. The tingling increased until her whole body felt consumed—not unlike the sensation of a transporter but more intense. The floor went out from under her. She gasped as she dropped into total darkness—the floor, the walls, her office and furniture—everything in the physical world was gone.

Fortunately, Wesley was there to grasp her hand and keep her from falling. The blackness shimmered as strange shapes and lights coalesced all around them. Blurred vision seemed to be coming into sharp focus. Colleen realized she was floating in space—without an environmental suit! She trembled, but Wesley put a comforting arm around her shoulders. Shortly, it was clear that she wasn't going to suffocate or freeze to death. Cabot gazed at the man's face only a few centimeters away, felt the brawn of his arm, and marveled that he looked so normal. So human.

However, Wesley was clearly not human but the Ghost of Rashanar Present, for that's where the counselor realized they were. To one side was a depressing and awesome collection of scorched warships from a dozen different worlds, tumbling in confusion like a twisted mobile. On the other side were three extraordinary silver spacecraft shaped like shark's fins, keeping guard against the contents of the graveyard from escaping. Colleen couldn't blame them, because flashing energy beams rippled between the silent hulks, which were moving and twisting within the haziness of smaller debris. It looked like sheer chaos, yet was oddly compelling and beautiful—like the riotous dawn of the universe and the birth of worlds crammed with life and wonder.

Even more dazzling power spikes rippled deep within the battle site, near the center where the monsters supposedly lurked. Colleen got a chill, despite his arm around her. "How . . . how are we doing this?" she rasped. Her voice echoed more in her mind than her ears, where it was just a tinny hiss.

"Someday when I know you better, maybe I'll explain," answered Wesley, sounding humble about his godlike powers. "Those are the Ontailians' vessels—the narrow slivers."

"I see them," she answered. "What are they guarding?"

"You tell me."

"They can't see us, can they?" she asked with sudden fright.

"Technically we could be seen, but they would have to be looking for us. Besides, with all the space junk and flying energy beams, we're not going to get their attention."

"But something sure has their attention," she remarked. "Can we go farther in?"

"We can," he answered, "but there's no guarantee we'll see the mimic ship. I wish I could take you back to the past and show you what happened, but I can't."

He gazed off toward the glittering boneyard, where bright power spikes and giant arcs of energy lit up the eerie derelicts. Colleen could see vast swirls of trash moving. She remembered that the wrecks were supposed to be in orbit around a mysterious gravity sink at the center. Even from her safe perch, it was terrifying. She couldn't imagine piloting a huge starship like the *Enterprise* into such a maelstrom. Recovering bodies, chasing looters and anomalies—that had been reckless and impossible duty in this haunted battle zone.

"There's another Ontailian ship deeper inside," said Wes. "We'll find it, but we'll have to be careful."

He gripped her hand, and they were off again, moving so deep inside the Rashanar site that they seemed to be at the eye of a hurricane. Here charred hulks and glimmering curtains of debris swirled all around them, and a massive blackness seemed to suck at the core of her ethereal body. Even her gifted guide seemed wary, and he retreated to a point some distance away from the shimmering vortex. Colleen was beginning to feel nauseated, but she was too exhilarated to say anything.

When she was able to focus, she saw one of the unique Ontailian ships, with its lines like a three-bladed kitchen knife. It rippled strangely as it floated in front of an indeterminate blob of wreckage. Perhaps it was just a thick debris cloud, but it glittered gold and blue in the blackness of space.

"What's it doing?" she asked.

"Expelling antimatter," answered her guide.

"Why?"

"I don't know. The *Enterprise* reported a similar incident, but it was lost in all the testimony at the inquiry." He turned, scrutinizing her intently. "They're not the only ship in here," he said, removing his arm from her shivering shoulders and taking her hand once again. Before Colleen could take a breath, they were floating in another part of Rashanar. She could see sparks and lights glowing on the side of one abandoned hulk.

As they drew closer, it was clear that this wasn't an errant power spike but pinpoint phaser beams, welding or burning into the side of the crumpled relic. Attached to the greenish-hued wreck by umbilical cords was a smaller spacecraft that looked like a child's fanciful toy made of so many colorful, mismatched parts. She could see workers in extravehicular suits punching their way into the hull of the crippled starship. They took no care to preserve anything.

"Unauthorized salvagers," said Wesley. "Scavengers. Those are Androssi—the ones who started the chase on that fateful day. Doesn't look like the Ontailians have them under control."

Colleen nodded sheepishly, unable to speak; she could only grip his arm and hang on for dear life. Giving her a warm smile, the handsome guide seemed to sense that they should leave, and before she could blink, Colleen Cabot was sitting at her desk in her mundane office, her mind fuzzy and confused.

Wesley was standing at the door, looking at her with sweet concern. "Are you all right?"

The counselor nodded, still uncertain of her

speaking voice. She finally wheezed, "When will I see you again?"

He laughed and said, "Don't make me come back as the Ghost of Christmas Yet to Come." With that, the door opened, and the alluring man in the gray jumpsuit vanished.

Chapter Three

THE TRAVELER STOOD in the maelstrom at the center of the Rashanar Battle Site, watching the sleek Ontailian vessel surreptitiously expel antimatter and move on. The blasted hulks of dead starships circled him like sharks waiting for the right moment to attack. He moved from his perch every few seconds. Wes wasn't alone this time either, because in his hand was a blinking, high-tech, oblong container. After his journey here with Colleen Cabot, Wes had decided to offer Commodore Korgan a trip, minus the ill effects of warp travel. The Medusan had taken some time to respond, but in the end he had finally agreed to go, placing his faith and his life in the Traveler's hands.

Now Korgan's sublime thoughts were filled with

more happiness and pleasure than he could possibly express to Wesley. The human couldn't help but grin at his companion. It wasn't the danger that thrilled Korgan, as it had Colleen Cabot; it was the freedom. To move through space in the blink of an eye, without worrying about containers and logistics, the effect his appearance would have on humanoids, or the illness he usually suffered—these changes were like miracles to the Medusan. As Korgan radiated joy, Wes began to think that no one in the universe would enjoy being a Traveler more than the commodore.

When he turned to look at the Ontailian ship, he found it blasting into reverse as glittering tentacles of debris reached toward it. A moment later, the sparkling space dust began to turn black, as if seeping with ink from within. While the Ontailian ship barely managed to escape, the dark anomaly exploded like a billion fireflies set loose at once. The tranquil section of the boneyard rippled like the surface of a pool.

"Wild antimatter," warned Wesley. "We're getting out of here." Before his companion could comment, they were back in Korgan's elegant town house in the Russian Hill area of San Francisco. Streetlamps were the only objects glowing in the darkness.

"Thank you for going with me," said Wes as he set the Medusan's box on the dining table.

Thank you, *Traveler,* replied Korgan, speaking to him telepathically. *I normally dread travel, but this*

*experience was extraordinary. Yes, now I understand
how so many things could have gone wrong so
quickly. I am unsure what to do about it.*

Wes took a deep breath. "Someone from Starfleet
has to go back there," he replied. "The *Enterprise*
crew has experience at Rashanar and the most to
gain—they should be the ones to go."

The oblong box blinked a few times before the
young man heard the reply in his mind: *So do you
want me to intercede on Captain Picard's behalf?*

"Commander Riker can captain the *Enterprise*,"
said Wes, "but don't you think we owe it to Picard to
let him clear himself?"

I will do what I can, promised the Medusan.
*Thank you again, Traveler, for trusting me with this
knowledge of your existence. Just knowing there is
an advanced race watching us, remembering what
we do for posterity, gives increased meaning to
one's life.*

Wesley nodded thoughtfully as he walked toward
the door, and he stopped to add, "Your actions give
our lives meaning, not the other way around."

*But you are breaking your vows to help your
friends, are you not?*

"I am," agreed the young Traveler. "Even though
we make all kinds of vows and promises in our lives,
some are still more important than others. Good-bye,
Commodore."

Go in peace, Traveler.

Walking through walls and space and dimension

as if they were puddles on the sidewalk, the Traveler moved back onto the *Enterprise* just as it arrived in orbit over Earth. At this moment, it was the most painful place to be in the entire galaxy. Everyone was so gloomy and angry, even those who seldom got that way, such as Geordi La Forge and Deanna Troi. His mother would have been in that category if he hadn't revealed himself to her with a promise of help. He only hoped her expectations of him weren't unrealistic, because whatever demons lurked in the Rashanar graveyard were not going to be exorcised easily.

Wes arrived in transporter room two in time to see a happy reunion between Geordi and Data, who had also just returned to the *Enterprise*. The Traveler hovered in the background, blending in with a number of workers moving supplies onto the ship. He saw La Forge grasp his friend warmly by the shoulders.

"Are you okay? What did they do to you?" Geordi asked with concern.

"I am unchanged," answered Data. "Admiral Nakamura had plans to insert a prototype chip in the socket dedicated to my emotion chip."

"Damn him," grumbled La Forge under his breath. "You told him not to, right?"

The android cocked his head. "I am not in the habit of disobeying orders, even dubious ones, so I was relieved when they could not find the new chip. They had to let me go."

La Forge beamed. "Wow, somebody is looking out for you."

Data nodded thoughtfully. "It would appear so. I have sensed for several days now that somebody is indeed looking out for me. Today was the most dramatic instance."

The engineer grimaced as he moved toward the door. "We've been snakebitten until now, so maybe we deserve a break or two. We're going to be in dock another day at least."

"Why?" asked Data. "Were the warp trials unsuccessful?"

"Successful enough," admitted the engineer. "But we could stand to tweak the engines a bit. Say, several of us are going to see the captain tomorrow—do you want to go?"

"Give him my regards, but I should stay on the ship," answered Data.

The Traveler allowed the two senior officers to go on their way without him. He doubted if he was going to learn much more from them.

Maybe I should just rest, he thought, *and let the seeds I've sown take root.*

Then again, there were those who deserved more scrutiny than he had given them. He couldn't risk stealing *them* away to Rashanar to prove his point, but he could see how they were living with their decisions. A wink in time later, the Traveler strode down a nearly deserted corridor in Starfleet Command to the office of Admiral Ross. As he neared the door, his acute hearing picked up Counselor Cabot's voice, which was distinctly argumentative. Even facing an admiral, she gave as good as she got.

"I tell you, Admiral Ross," insisted Colleen's voice, "I have come to believe that Jean-Luc Picard is perfectly rational. I think he had enough justification to believe in this mimic ship to act as he did."

She lowered her voice to add, "I know there are also practical reasons why *we* acted as we did. I, for one, don't want to see the Federation weakened. But we ought to have some sympathy for Picard's position. Nobody's saying there weren't mistakes made, but look at the situation you put the *Enterprise* in! I have gone . . . and done some research on conditions in Rashanar—I know we've given our forces an impossible task."

The Traveler edged into the admiral's office and was glad to see that it was both large and dimly lit, befitting the late hour. He found a shadow behind a potted palm tree and melted into the collection of darkness. Admiral Ross looked properly dumbfounded by this uprising among one of his minions, who was no longer playing by the agreed-upon rules.

"Counselor, *you* were the one who suggested putting him in your care," insisted Ross. "Now are you saying you want to throw him back at us? Reopening this case would be like batting a hornets' nest with a stick!"

"I would rather see Picard on his own ship," answered Cabot. "You're not only trying to sweep Picard under the rug, but Rashanar too! The Ontailians are hiding something in that graveyard."

"What?" asked Ross skeptically. "Since when are *you* an expert on the Rashanar Battle Site? Or Ontailians?" He rose to his feet and tugged imperiously on his brocaded and bedecked tunic. "Counselor Cabot, what you are telling me is that you have fallen under Captain Picard's spell. I know he's a charming, erudite man, but he agreed to a settlement for the good of the situation. Even he agreed to keep a low profile. You want to push him back into the spotlight!"

The admiral heaved his brawny shoulders. His once proud visage looked worn and care-ridden, as if the weight of too many bad choices and too much death was taking its toll. Ross finally said, "Look, as soon as we work it out with the Ontailians, we'll send more ships to Rashanar, but we won't *risk* any more ships. You just follow our agreement and keep the captain safe and content."

"Content?" asked Cabot, shaking her head. "Yes, I know about the pact that you, me, and Admiral Nakamura made, but I'm saying that I'm beginning to believe him."

That remark made Ross wince, and he took on the pained expression of a sweet old granddad. "You can't show a little bit of patience, Counselor? And let's give the Ontailians a little respect before we either negotiate in good faith or invade them. Rasha-nar is in their space, and I don't want to fight a war over the right to retrieve our dead."

Colleen sighed loudly and collected herself. Wes marveled at how she could stand toe-to-toe with Starfleet Command and not break a sweat. He had taken on a lot of responsibility at a young age, so he knew how it felt.

"Couldn't we send a small craft disguised as a looter?" she asked. "We just need proof that this mimic ship exists."

"If it does exist, we'd be putting a ship in danger," answered Ross. "If it doesn't exist, we'd be driving the Ontailians out of the Federation for nothing. To go back in force, we need their blessing. Waiting is the prudent thing to do in this case."

"All right, I'll have some patience," muttered Cabot, backing toward the door. "Admiral, do you know officers who are still floating around in that miasma of scorched hulls and wild antimatter?"

Ross's face turned pale, and he looked as if he had aged a few more years. "Yes, I know a lot of them. They won't be the first Starfleet officers to be buried in space."

Feeling defeated, Colleen stepped into the corridor. *Well, that was a bust,* she finally decided. She wasn't sure how she could go over Ross's head, especially since her only other ally was Nakamura, who agreed with him. After several moments spent shuffling rather than walking, Colleen felt another presence at her side. She turned to see an average-looking ensign.

The officer smiled shyly at her and asked, "Counselor Cabot, do you remember me?"

"I know I should, and I'm usually good with names. You're, uh—"

"Ensign Brewster. Sometimes I help Admiral Nechayev."

"Ah, yes," answered Colleen, biting her tongue. She hadn't been impressed by Nechayev's defense of Picard, and she wasn't particularly impressed by the admiral's aide either.

"Nechayev's office is just on the floor below," said Brewster. "I think she could use a visit from you, if you have something to tell her. She has another visitor at the moment—Commodore Korgan."

Colleen stopped in her tracks to look at him. "Why should that interest me?"

"Because the Medusan wants to help Captain Picard, and you want to help, too."

"How do you know that?" she asked suspiciously.

Brewster shrugged. "I saw you coming out of Admiral Ross's office, and you don't look very happy. It was just a hunch. But don't give up, Counselor, because Nechayev will listen to you. Come, I'll show you the way."

She peered curiously at Brewster. It seemed for a moment that he wasn't quite the cipher he appeared to be. In fact, she felt she knew him from somewhere else . . . someplace more exciting than the drab corridors of Starfleet.

He opened the turbolift door and motioned for her to step inside. When she did, he followed her and said, "Computer, level three, northeast wing."

As they moved down and across, Cabot studied her escort with interest, and she said, "You know, I would be happy if we just gave Picard a vacation and released him on his own recognizance."

"No, we have to do better than that," countered the ensign. "That would be like putting him out to pasture. He needs his ship back—at least to find the thing which put him here."

Now Cabot peered curiously at her escort. "Do you happen to know a fellow who gets around . . . name of Wesley?"

He smiled slightly and replied, "It doesn't sound familiar."

The door whooshed open, and they stepped out of the turbolift. Colleen felt oddly detached as Ensign Brewster led her to Admiral Nechayev's office. It was late at night; few people were around Starfleet Command except for the ubiquitous security officers.

When Brewster barged into the admiral's private lair, the sandy-haired woman jumped to her feet as if to demand to know who they were, but her expression softened when she saw it was her trusted assistant. Also present were Commander Emery and, as Brewster had promised, the floating antigrav container that housed Commodore Korgan.

"Admiral, I'm sorry to interrupt," announced the ensign, "but I believe Counselor Cabot has had a similar change of heart over Captain Picard." The humans looked at one another as if they didn't know who should start the round of explanations.

"It's not a change of heart," explained Commander Emery, wringing his hands with anxiety. "Oh, heck, I don't know *what* it is. I only know that Commodore Korgan is now convinced that Picard is telling the truth."

"He *is* innocent," declared Cabot. She wanted to ask the Medusan whether he had also met the mysterious stranger, Wesley. But she hated to bring up bizarre evidence that couldn't be proven.

"Well," said Nechayev, somewhat astounded, "I didn't expect Picard's prosecutor and custodian to step forward and say they want to reopen the case they won. This is highly unusual . . . but welcome. You realize, there is going to be *no* support for reopening Picard's case. We don't want to drag the Ontailians back here just to impugn their testimony, not when we're involved in delicate negotiations with them to reopen Rashanar."

The lights on Korgan's container blinked. Emery straightened and said, "There is a matter of justice."

"Justice?" said Nechayev with sarcasm. "You weren't too concerned about that at the inquiry. Basically, we all agreed to placate the Ontailians and let Picard take one for the team. I've been convinced since day one that the captain was innocent, but you played hardball and forced us to settle."

Cabot stepped forward, taking on her third admiral of the long day. "Well, we were wrong. You're wrong to hold us to a deal that isn't in anyone's best interest. I don't know exactly what Commodore Korgan discovered that changed his mind, but I suspect he learned more about the Rashanar Battle Site than he knew before. Anyone who has been there can tell you that we left a nasty job unfinished."

"You've been to Rashanar?" asked Nechayev skeptically.

Cabot gave the admiral a wistful smile. "In a way, I have. Please, Admiral, we've got to get back there, and we've got to reunite Captain Picard with his ship."

Nechayev stepped away from her chair and paced thoughtfully. "Counselor, you are Captain Picard's sole master. Right now nobody can give him an order but you. You can set him to picking up trash in Golden Gate Park, if you wish. You could send him back to the *Enterprise,* but you can't let him out of your custody. Until he's officially absolved, you're his ball and chain. Any place he goes, *you* have to go."

The young woman gulped but firmed up her resolve. "I will accompany Picard to the *Enterprise.* I'll go back to Rashanar with him, too."

"Nobody's going to Rashanar until we conclude our negotiations with the Ontailians," said the admiral. "You have to promise me that much. We should know in twenty-four hours if they're going to give us access again."

Nechayev chuckled. "Ross and Nakamura aren't going to like this one bit."

"So be it," replied Cabot forcefully.

Commander Emery looked squeamish about the repercussions, but Korgan's container twinkled brightly. With a sigh, the gaunt human said, "Commodore Korgan is willing to take the chance."

"Of course, if Picard is right," the admiral ventured, "the guilty party is a lethal shapeshifting anomaly that has destroyed hundreds of ships. Are you ready to take that on?"

Cabot wasn't so quick with her reply. Even the Medusan and his assistant were strangely quiet. It was a voice from the doorway that finally ended the silence, when all-but-forgotten Ensign Brewster said, "We have no choice. The Ontailians are not going to do it."

"Then it's decided. I'll go tell my patient," said Colleen, heading for the door. "In case it doesn't work out as planned, I'll tell him it's just a visit to the *Enterprise*. When negotiations with the Ontailians are concluded—"

"You'll be the first to know," answered Nechayev. "Thank you for coming, Counselor. I know it took a lot of courage."

"Don't thank me," said Cabot. "Thank your assistant, Ensign . . . um—" She turned to find him, but the unprepossessing officer had already left.

* * *

Maybe I'll just take the medical discharge, thought Jean-Luc Picard as he sat on the floor of his cell, studying the reddish clouds that drifted past his dark window, simulating Vulcan at night. *Other captains have retired at a younger age than I am, and I could consult in training and planning. Or I could finally do some writing . . . or tend the grapevines.*

Somehow that latter option seemed more attractive than it ever had before. The weather and the soil were tricky but worthy adversaries; also, they played by natural rules. The physical labor would be cathartic for him and would probably prolong his life more than continuing in Starfleet. *Let the Ontailians and the admirals worry about Rashanar,* he decided. *One man with a ship can't fight that thing, anyway.*

A Vulcan walked past his doorway, blocking the starscape from his view for a moment. Picard sat up, because this was a holosuite character he had never seen before; this one wore the silver and white robes of a diplomat. The Vulcan stopped in the shadows and turned to face Picard, his features remaining blurred and indistinct.

"No one can do a mind-meld on himself," said the stranger, his voice surprisingly youthful.

"What does that mean?" breathed the captain, his voice hoarse from disuse.

"Only that you cannot analyze what is inside you, what is happening *to* you," answered the Vulcan official. "You have to leave that to others. After you have made a logical decision, your task is finished.

Let fate, history, and the natural order make the final determination."

"So accept what's happened to me?" asked Picard, growing bitter. "I'm sorry, I've never been very good at just sitting still and waiting."

"To every thing there is a season," said the Vulcan, "and a time for every purpose under the heavens."

The captain frowned. "That's the Bible—Ecclesiastes, not anything Vulcan. The programmers will have to do better than that."

"I think you'll feel better after Counselor Cabot's next visit," he acknowledged, stepping back into deeper shadows.

"I doubt that." Picard sighed. He stared after the departing figure, because such characters weren't supposed to break the theater's fourth wall and refer to the audience. They were supposed to pretend he was a monk in a Vulcan cliff dwelling, not under a doctor's care and custody.

Picard even rose to his feet to look for the old Vulcan, but he was gone. From the other side of the walkway, Colleen Cabot stepped into view, carrying a bundle of clothes in her arms. Upon entering the hovel, she looked around disgustedly at the dusty floor and ragged stone walls.

"Hello, Jean-Luc," she began. "You may want to return to more modern quarters to get cleaned up and shaved, because we're moving out of here. Here's your uniform—we're going to the *Enterprise*."

Picard jumped to his feet. "What is the catch?"

"You notice I said *we* were going," she answered. "You're still in my custody and my care. Commander Riker is still the acting captain of the *Enterprise*. You've done well enough here to warrant outpatient status, and for you, living at home is the *Enterprise*."

"Interesting," said Picard, taking a few steps and mulling it over. "What if I don't want to go back to my ship as a tourist or a patient? What if I'm ready for the medical discharge?"

"Then you'd be letting a lot of people down," answered Cabot. "You'd bring relief to a few people, I suppose, but not to yourself. Don't you want to fight that thing that destroyed all those ships at Rashanar and tarnished your career?"

The captain whirled upon his jailer. "I thought you didn't believe me?"

"A visitor showed me the error of my ways," answered Colleen enigmatically. She stepped toward Picard and handed him the bundle. "Here's your uniform. Your crew doesn't know we're coming, but I figure you would just like to show up as if nothing's happened, rather than have a big homecoming."

"You have gotten to know me fairly well," agreed the captain as he took his clothes. "So my fate is still in your hands?"

"For now." She gave him a brief but sympathetic smile. "I'm willing to be on your side, but you can't forget that I can keep you under my care as long as I deem necessary."

Picard's lips thinned. "I'm well aware of your power over me, Counselor. This week has taught me that if nothing else."

"You stuck to your story," said Cabot with admiration, "and you have allies I don't think you even know about. I'll be back in half an hour, because I have to pack. Is that enough time?"

"Plenty," answered the captain. "Thank you, Counselor."

"You're never going to call me 'Colleen,' are you?"

"No," he admitted.

"I like your honesty, Jean-Luc. See you in a bit." She turned on her heel and walked briskly down the walkway that ran along the illusory Vulcan cliff.

Captain Picard let out his breath, relieved that his laborious cooperation had finally accomplished something. *But I'm still a prisoner,* he told himself, *no longer master of my fate. How will they accept me back on the* Enterprise?

Chapter Four

DEANNA TROI PACED the bridge of the *Enterprise*, alone except for Lieutenant Kell Perim, who watched a combination of readouts at her conn station. In spacedock over Earth, with most of the workers gone for the day and most of the crew on leave, it was rather lonely and dull duty. When she wasn't pacing, Troi went over personnel files to give Will Riker a hand. More crew members than usual had requested a transfer off the *Enterprise*. She couldn't blame them. There were always others willing to take their places on the famed vessel, although several prime candidates had suddenly withdrawn their names owing to the recent trouble. Perhaps this was not the best time to join the *Enterprise*, thought the counselor.

Because the ship was technically repaired and fit for duty, the bridge had to be manned, and Troi had drawn this shift. Will, Beverly, Geordi, and Data were indulging in a poker game in Riker's quarters. She hoped that it afforded them some distraction, but she doubted if it was the usual jovial gathering, full of reckless bluffing and good-natured ribbing. These days, the only one who seemed to be in a good mood was Dr. Crusher, although maybe that was just a brave front.

Troi didn't feel like taking shore leave and doing recreational activities since Will was tied up as acting skipper of the *Enterprise.* They had expected him to get his own command someday, but this wasn't how any of them had wanted it to happen. Will certainly didn't want to take command away from Captain Picard, and it felt disloyal to be running the ship while the captain languished in Medical Mental Health.

"There's been some activity in transporter room two," reported Perim from the conn, where she was monitoring the ship's main systems. "Two people have beamed up from Starfleet Command."

"From Starfleet Command?" asked Troi, scratching her head. "Are they admirals or just a couple of technicians reporting early to work?"

"We should know in a minute," answered the Trill, "because they seem to be on their way to the bridge."

Troi cringed. "I hope we're not talking admirals— we don't need any more bad news."

"Do you want me to alert the captain?" asked Perim.

"No. Let's see who it is first." It was still strange, thought Troi, for everyone to refer to "the captain" and mean her Will, instead of Captain Picard. If the real captain had died in the line of duty or had retired with full honors, none of this would seem strange, but it felt as if Picard had been captured by an implacable enemy.

She was still fretting over his fate when the turbolift door opened. Kell Perim blinked in amazement, whirled in her seat, and gazed attentively at her board. "Captain on the bridge," she announced.

"Done with the poker game already?" asked Troi, turning to meet her beloved. She nearly swallowed her tongue when she came face-to-face with Jean-Luc Picard, accompanied by her colleague, Colleen Cabot.

"Hello, Counselor," he said cheerfully. "Don't let me interrupt you—I just wanted to tell you I was on board."

"Good to see you, sir!" With difficulty, Troi resisted rushing forward to hug her superior, who had miraculously returned from exile. She looked instead at his escort for an explanation.

Cabot hefted the duffel bag in her hand and said, "He's on outpatient status. Since this is his home, I'm going to have to stay here with him, so if you could find me a bunk somewhere, I'd appreciate it."

"We have spare quarters," replied Troi. "Lieutenant Perim, assign Counselor Cabot to a nice state-room near the captain."

"Yes, sir," answered the Trill, working her console.

Cabot looked impressed and said, "Deanna, I didn't realize you had qualified for command duty."

Troi shrugged humbly, but Picard cut in, "Commander Troi can run this ship as well as anyone. She's saved us on more than one occasion. I'm sure they've been doing fine without me."

"The senior staff would love to see you, Captain," said Troi with a grin. "They're in Will's quarters, playing poker."

Picard smiled wistfully, turned to Counselor Cabot and asked, "With your permission?"

Troi bristled at the sight of her proud captain having to ask the much younger woman for her consent, but she knew Picard's legal status. He had obviously won Cabot over to some degree, or he wouldn't be here.

"Go ahead, Captain. I'll just visit with Counselor Troi for a bit, then see my room. I packed lightly."

"We've got everything you need," Troi assured her.

With a grateful nod, the captain hurried toward the turbolift and was gone.

"He's rather remarkable, your captain," said Cabot with admiration. "And he has remarkable friends."

"Is this permanent?" asked Troi hopefully.

Colleen Cabot shook her head. "Who can say

what's permanent in this life? I may be in big trouble tomorrow, but for tonight I feel pretty good."

"Oh," said Troi with dawning realization, "you didn't really get approval for this?"

"I discussed it with Admiral Nechayev, and technically this is *my* decision." Colleen circled around the empty bridge, gazing with awe at the blinking instruments and expansive screens. "Of course, they could assign him to you or some other counselor, if they felt like it. I can't believe I'm on the *Enterprise!* What's it like, being a ship's counselor?"

"It can get rather exciting sometimes," admitted Troi. "Stick with me, and you'll get a good idea whether you'd like it."

Cabot stretched her arms over her head. "It already feels good to get out of those offices . . . and the politics."

"Make yourself at home, Colleen," said Deanna Troi with a warm smile. "Would you like something from the food slot?"

"I've assigned you a really nice room, Counselor," added Kell Perim. "Maybe you'd like an appointment in the spa?"

"The spa?" Colleen almost purred. "I think I might like it here."

"Dealer takes two," said Data, adjusting his green eyeshade. He deftly dealt himself two cards, slowing his normal hand speed so that everyone could see he was dealing fairly. "Geordi, it is still your bet."

"Huh? What?" The engineer had been marooned in his thoughts, and he blinked at his friend. "My call?"

"Your bet," replied Data. "You took one card, and you opened the betting with kings or better."

"Oh, yeah," said La Forge, giving his cards a desultory inspection. "I'm sorry, my mind isn't really into this tonight."

"It's okay," Riker assured him. "Nobody's is."

Data cocked his head and said, "My mind is quite active and engaged."

"And that's why you have all the chips," added Beverly Crusher. "Here, I've got kings or better. I'll bet three."

"I'll see your three," said Riker, and the betting went around the table until it came back to La Forge.

"I fold," he muttered, tossing down his cards. "In more ways than one. I think I'll get to bed early and get an early start on the matter reactant injector." He rose to his feet.

"Don't fix it too fast," warned Riker. "We want to put in a full day tomorrow before we have to go out again."

"Do you really think this is going to do any good?" asked La Forge, frustration creeping into his voice. "We don't know if it will do Captain Picard any good, and they may come after Data again. I'm putting in for early retirement, so wherever we go . . . it'll be my last cruise."

That brought a gloomy pall to the game. No one

knew what to say next. Since Data was the dealer, he felt obliged to keep the game going. "I will fold if it will increase your chances, Geordi."

La Forge gave a chuckle, which lightened the sour mood. Data was gratified to have made a joke, under the circumstances.

"Sit down and play poker," ordered Beverly Crusher. "Doctor's orders."

The engineer shook his head with amazement as he sank into his seat. "You seem unfazed by all this, Doc. How do you keep from worrying?"

"Don't you feel the tide turning?" asked Crusher, brimming with optimism and hope. "I do."

"Well, I'm still going to win this hand," said Riker. "La Forge, are you in or out?"

Geordi shrugged and reached for his meager chips. "My last three. My luck had better start changing, or this is it." He tossed his markers into the pile just as the door whooshed open.

"Do you have another seat?" asked a familiar voice, forcing everyone to whirl around.

"Captain Picard!" "Jean-Luc!" There was a babble of voices as everyone leaped up to greet their leader.

When they all tried to question him at once, Picard held up his hand and hushed them. "I'm just visiting—as an outpatient. Counselor Cabot surprised me with this, so I don't really know what to make of it. My status hasn't changed, and neither has yours, Number One. It's your ship. I'm here by the counselor's good graces, and she's here with me. Treat her as you would a visiting dignitary."

"I think we can do that," said Riker. "Even if I didn't like her much before."

"Well, like her now," ordered Picard, moving to grab a chair from another table. "And, remember, she's basically my commanding officer. She has spent a week learning everything there is to know about me. The Cardassians weren't nearly as thorough. That's all I want to discuss about this for now. Who's winning the game?"

"Data, as usual," said La Forge a big grin on his face. "They took his emotion chip, so now he's ruthless." The others laughed.

While Data pondered whether ruthlessness was an emotion, Crusher grabbed her glass and hoisted it skyward. "Welcome home, Captain Picard."

"Hear, hear!" exclaimed Riker.

Picard lowered his head and nodded, and Data wasn't sure that the captain was able to speak.

"This is outrageous!" bellowed Admiral Nakamura as he stomped around Admiral Nechayev's office. The Traveler considered himself very lucky that he could blend into the wall paneling as Ensign Brewster; he didn't want this unbridled fury directed at him. Nechayev appeared oddly calm and more than willing to let Nakamura blow off steam without interruption.

"You spirited him away in the middle of the

night—back to his ship!" he continued to roar. "Without telling any of the members of the tribunal! That's unethical, Alynna."

"I agree. You have every right to be angry. However, Picard wasn't in *my* custody. Counselor Cabot has all the authority she needs to take him anywhere she wants, without consulting either one of us. Ensign Brewster, do you have the pertinent regulations?"

"Yes, I do," answered the ensign as he fumbled with a padd.

"Never mind," growled Nakamura. "We'll just transfer Picard to someone with more sense . . . and experience."

"Actually, you won't," said Nechayev. "All three members of the tribunal would have to approve the transfer of Picard. Admirals Paris and Ross have been speaking with Commodore Korgan. They all believe that Picard's story should be checked out. Also, they agree he should stay in Cabot's care. I have a statement from Paris. Care to hear it?"

"No!" Nakamura slashed his hand through the air in blind anger, then took a deep breath to calm himself. "You've thought ahead, Alynna, as you always do. I don't care where Picard is, but keep him under wraps until we conclude our negotiations with the Ontailians. That's all I ask."

"That was the intention," answered Nechayev. "The *Enterprise* is still testing her repairs. After that, she has a survey mission. Riker is acting captain. Are we on our final offer to the Ontailians?"

"We're going to let them run things at Rashanar. Starfleet will have very specific missions and zones of responsibility," Nakamura predicted with confidence.

"They'll turn it down," she said.

He bristled at the suggestion. "They can't do better than this, unless they want to keep us out permanently."

"Right," said Nechayev. "Just remember, when it falls apart, we can still do black ops inside Rashanar. It might even be safer."

"Black ops? Safer?" scoffed Nakamura. "Alynna, I know you always want to rely on espionage, but in this case it won't be necessary."

"Brewster here had a good idea," she said, taking a moment to find the ensign leaning against the wall. "We could send small craft into Rashanar disguised as illegal salvagers."

The Traveler cleared his throat. "Actually it was Counselor Cabot's idea."

"I see." Nakamura slapped his palms on his thick thighs and began to pace. "So now you would *invite* the Ontailians to fire on us! You would also compete with the real looters, who might not take too kindly to this idea, and you'd be operating without a safety net."

Nechayev shook her head and replied, "The idea of any safety net inside that graveyard is a delusion. I've been reading the reports. It looks to me that a larger ship could slip in, find a place to hide, play dead, and act as a base for our fake looters. I'm just telling you that we have an alternative other than war, if negotiations fail."

"Don't do anything else until you talk to me," warned Nakamura as he strode toward the door and exited.

As soon as the admiral was gone, Nechayev tapped her chin thoughtfully. "Brewster, tell the *Enterprise* to take off for their survey mission as soon as possible."

"I'm on my way. Good-bye, Admiral." By the time the door slid shut behind him, the Traveler was in a corridor aboard the *Enterprise*.

"We can't get all of our crew back that quickly," complained Commander Riker, leaning over Data's shoulder at the ops console. Looking on were Dr. Crusher and Captain Picard. "We'd have to go on the survey at about one-fourth crew strength, with the reactant injector untested. Doctor, it would help if I knew where this advice was coming from."

"It came from Ensign Brewster, the aide to Admiral Nechayev, after her meeting with Admiral Nakamura. I think she sent him to me because she didn't want this to be an official order. Just good advice," Beverly replied.

"We could even go at impulse power," said Picard, "while La Forge finishes work on the warp engines. If need be, there are lots of repair bases around the asteroid belt. I wouldn't ignore advice from Ensign Brewster."

"What about Counselor Cabot," asked Riker. "Is she willing to ship out with us?"

"She's here, isn't she?" replied Crusher. "She knows we're not a colony or a space station, but a starship. With warp drive, we could have her home in half an hour if she whines too much. Listen, we've got all our senior staff. Data can do the survey."

"The doctor has a point there," remarked the android. "The demands are relatively simple."

"Should we call back as many of the crew as we can find on short notice?" asked Riker. "Or should we just go?"

"If we've got enough crew for the tests, we've got enough crew for the mission," answered Picard. "If we put out the word we're leaving, the wrong people may find out."

"All right," answered the acting captain, making his decision. "Data, find out from La Forge how soon we can depart."

"Ensign Brewster is going too," added Beverly Crusher. "Sort of a liaison with Admiral Nechayev."

Riker waved his arms, giving up. "Okay, we're going on a mission with three-fourths of our crew missing, but several unofficial passengers, including our captain. This doesn't look to be our typical journey."

"When do we ever have a typical journey?" asked Crusher with a wry smile.

We're moving, thought the Traveler as he stood in the newly assigned guest quarters of Ensign

Brewster. The place where he really wanted to be was only two doors away, the stateroom of one Colleen Cabot, but he was frozen in indecision. *How am I going to approach her? What am I going to say?* Out of all the rules of being a Traveler he had already broken, becoming intimately involved in the lives of those he observed was the most egregious.

I may not be a Traveler much longer, he told himself. He thought he could feel it becoming harder to pull off his miraculous feats, although in subtle ways he couldn't explain, like walking in heavier gravity. He didn't know if it was his own failings, a lack of focus, or his fellow Travelers drawing away from him—but it felt that resistance was increasing. He wondered, *Does observation strengthen the lens, while intervention weakens it?* For certain he knew one thing: When the last of his fellowship stopped experiencing this vigil, he would be cut off from their combined focus. He would again be just Wesley Crusher, mustered out of Starfleet and unemployed.

So the sooner I embrace that unfamiliar persona, the better.

Wes thought he heard a nearby door open and shut, and he fought the temptation to surprise Colleen in her room. He didn't know who might be with her. It was the Traveler who intrigued the counselor, not Wesley Crusher or Ensign Brewster. *For the moment, I am the Traveler and I am*

Wesley Crusher. Why should I behave any differently around her?

Walking out of his quarters and down the corridor, the young man looked like his true self in the gray, unadorned garb of the Traveler. Of course, he knew there were few crew members on board, and could mentally befuddle one or two if he passed them. The real question remained: *Why don't I want to tell my shipmates that I've returned? I told my mother and two complete strangers, but I can't tell my old comrades that Wesley is back. Why not?*

He didn't like any of the possible answers: *Maybe I don't want to be that nebbish kid who kept saving the* Enterprise, *when that's why I'm here. Maybe I just don't want to explain what I've been doing or where I've been. Every time I come back to the* Enterprise, *it's because I've failed somewhere else.*

Before he had time to choose an answer, Wes found himself standing before Colleen Cabot's quarters. He knew she was inside, and pressed the chime rather than stepping through the bulkhead.

"Who is it?" came her voice.

He looked around to make sure he was alone in the corridor. "It's Wesley," he answered.

At once, the door opened. Colleen rushed to greet him, brushing her glowing blond hair out of her face and tugging on her tight-fitting blue tunic. He decided that she must have been napping, since she had been up all night arranging the return of Captain Picard. She smiled at him girlishly, then seemed to recover long enough to pull him into the room and close the door.

"You're here? On this ship?" she asked excitedly. "I should have known. Who else would have a . . . whatever you are."

"I'm not stationed on this ship," he answered, "although I once was. Do you know that we've left Earth?"

"Really?" Cabot rushed to her small porthole and gazed at a disc of blackness with vague glints of light. "Yes, we've left. Nobody mentioned this to me. Where are we going?"

"Just making a survey of the asteroid belt near Jupiter."

As Colleen gazed out into space, she bounced on the balls of her feet. Then she turned and looked sheepishly at him. "Excuse me for being excited, but I've just taken off on the *Enterprise*."

He took a step closer to her.

Colleen gazed at him with big blue eyes. "Is this the way you really look?" she asked.

"Yes," he answered hoarsely.

Colleen moved in close, and he leaned down for an exploratory kiss. She responded passionately. They were very much alike—two gifted people giving up everything for a monastic existence that focused solely on work, study, and advancement. Alone together in the strange stateroom, the young man and young woman sought out human contact and love.

Hours later, Wesley Crusher slipped out of her warm bed and pulled on his gray jumpsuit. "I've got to go."

Colleen stirred and rubbed her eyes. "You'll be back?" she asked.

"Yes," he answered with a smile. "My quarters are only two doors down."

Cabot sat up. "I thought you said you weren't stationed on the *Enterprise?*"

"Not as you see me," he answered. "You also know me as Ensign Brewster. I'd appreciate it if you kept my secret."

She frowned, puzzled. "But you don't look anything like Ensign Brewster." Her frown deepened. "Or do you? I don't remember *what* he looks like."

"That's the point." He bent down and kissed Colleen, and she nearly succeeded in pulling him back into bed. Reluctantly, he drew away from her urgent kisses.

"I'll be back as soon as I can," he promised.

"I'll probably be busy," said the woman, stretching luxuriantly in her bed. "In an attempt to keep me happy, Counselor Troi is taking me to a spa, a tour of the ship, lunch, holodeck racquetball, and whatever else you have. If they only knew that I've got eveything I need to be happy right here." Her hand grazed his thigh, and he laughed.

"Yes, if they knew about us, they would certainly be surprised," agreed the Traveler. "Let's keep it our secret a while longer, okay?"

"How much longer?" she asked with a pout. "I'm happy for the first time since . . . I can remember. I feel great I've returned Captain Picard to his ship, I'm away from those admirals, and I have you."

She gave him a come-hither look and smiled at his obvious discomfort. "How can you not love a guy who can travel through space in a wink, and doesn't think there's anything special about him?"

"You'll see, when you get to know me better," answered Wesley. "I'll be back soon. If I'm Brewster, don't let on."

"Take care, Wesley."

He focused himself back to Rashanar, only this time aboard the new Ontailian flagship, the *Yoxced,* which had replaced the fallen *Vuxhal.* In a reception room intended to entertain humanoids, a stern Tellarite and a proud Vulcan stood face-to-face with a teeming collection of Ontailians, who twisted and squirmed around their trellises like large hairy worms. Every few seconds, a slothlike individual descended upon the smoothly sculpted computer terminal, where it looked like a furry octopus squirming around the large levers and knobs.

The Traveler lurked in the background with the Starfleet security personnel, watching the Ontailians' frantic activity. He forced his persona into near obscurity in order to observe this historic event. Although the Ontailians would eventually produce an answer, they were going to take plenty of time to quarrel among themselves.

In due time, a gray-haired Ontailian with a span of three meters to his hairy tentacles descended from the rafters and plucked a parchment from their computer's printing mechanism. As the senior diplomat, the Vulcan took the document and read it first. His face showed a glimpse of disappointment, as he handed it to his colleague. When the Tellarite was done reading, the two of them shook their heads in consternation.

"This decision is most regrettable," said Ambassador Telek of Vulcan. "You blame the humans for essentially being human. You have not been in the Federation long enough to know what you are giving up, but I can tell you it's a great deal. The Federation was here for you during the Dominion War; now you deny us access to our hallowed dead from that conflict. Are you sure this is what you want to tell the Federation?"

The chittering and squeaking grew very loud. Evol, the Tellarite ambassador balled his hands into fists as if he would bash a few of the recalcitrant Ontailians. "You are unworthy allies" he cursed them.

Amid heckling and squawking from their hosts, the diplomatic delegation from the Federation took their leave and beamed out of the *Yoxced* and back to the runabout *Ohio*. The Traveler left with them, but he didn't go to the runabout. Instead he slid through space and dimension, feeling the power of his fellow Travelers returning to guide him. *Yes, they know I've broken rules, but they still know how important this is.*

There was no doubt now—the *Enterprise* would have to return to Rashanar.

Chapter Five

IN THE CAPTAIN'S READY ROOM, Will Riker gritted his teeth as he listened to the grim assessment from Admiral Nechayev. The first officer felt somewhat awkward sitting at the captain's desk and taking the admiral's orders from his viewscreen, but there was some consolation from the fact that Captain Picard stood by his fish tank, listening intently.

"And so," concluded Nechayev, "we're left with rotten choices. We can declare war against the Ontailians, but that will alienate other nonhumanoid races and make it harder to recover bodies and manage the Rashanar. We can do nothing, which leaves us in the dark and allows the possibility of a lot of advanced technology falling into the wrong hands. Or we can operate on the sly, as the looters are doing."

The admiral narrowed her eyes and said, "We need to find out how long the Rashanar Battle Site will last before the gravity sink and other elements destroy it. We need to know what the Ontailians are doing to make it safer. I don't mind backing off, if the Ontailians can make improvements and get control of the situation. If they aren't doing the job, we can't let the site deteriorate. We need to find out exactly what the *Enterprise* encountered there."

"We want to return, but are you saying we'll be alone?" said Riker carefully.

"Yes. If you go back, it has to be a volunteer crew and unofficial. There will be no help or backup. Starfleet will deny that you're there. Officially, the *Enterprise* is on light duty while testing repairs, *not* on a mission to Rashanar. No matter what you find out, no matter if you perish or return victorious, no one will *ever* know about this. There will be no honors or memorial services. Those are the conditions."

"You make it sound awfully inviting." Riker glanced at Captain Picard, who nodded in agreement. "All right. Count us in. What do you think we'll find?"

"Our diplomats report that the Ontailians have the battle zone surrounded and aren't letting anyone in or out," answered Nechayev. "But the Ontailians don't seem to be operating *inside* the graveyard anymore. We're sure the looters are still getting in, which is why you should think about disguising some of your shuttlecraft as salvagers. The *Enter-*

prise could hide in there, too, if you played dead among the wrecks."

"And if they catch us?" asked Riker.

Nechayev gave him a smirk. "You're operating alone to seek revenge. That's not far off, is it?"

"No," admitted Riker. "What about our passengers?"

"I know Ensign Brewster and Counselor Cabot are there, and I think both will agree to go with you. I have faith in the *Enterprise* to find some answers, especially when you can make your own rules. There are small salvage ships around the asteroid belt. I'll see if I can assign one or two to you, so don't leave right away. I'll also send you *all* the information we have on the Ontailians, and you might find some clues in there. Good luck, Captain. Nechayev out."

The screen on the captain's desk went blank, and Riker leaned back in his chair. "Are we going to get revenge?" he asked Picard. "Because I don't want to dance around this thing . . . not if it's as lethal as we think."

"If we find the mimic ship, we'll deal with it," vowed the captain, his lips becoming a thin, straight line.

"And this is sickbay," said Deanna Troi, conducting her visitor into Beverly Crusher's domain. Colleen Cabot strolled into the spacious and mostly empty suite of examination rooms, surgeries, and laboratories. They could see Dr. Crusher in her back office, going over her work. An orderly was checking supplies in the infirmary.

"With most of the crew gone, it's fairly quiet here now," said Troi just as her combadge beeped. "Excuse me, please."

"Go ahead," said Cabot with a wave of her hand.

"Troi here."

"Deanna," came Will's familiar voice, "is Counselor Cabot with you?"

"Yes, she is," answered Troi, sensing his anxiety. "We're just taking a tour of the ship. What is it, Will?"

"We're going to leave the asteroid belt and return to Rashanar. It will be dangerous, and Counselor Cabot has to be given the opportunity to leave."

"Captain Picard, too?" asked Troi with concern.

Cabot was standing only a few steps away, and she gave her colleague a smile. "I overheard. It's okay, Deanna, I'm with you all the way. And Picard goes with me."

"She's on for the new mission," reported Troi.

"Good. We're having a staff meeting in an hour in the observation lounge. Both of you should be there. Riker out."

Cabot pointed toward Crusher's private office and asked, "Can we just say hello to the good doctor? I feel like I ought to make an effort to mend fences."

"I'm sure Dr. Crusher doesn't hold anything against you," said Deanna.

Colleen looked doubtful. "I'll just say hello."

Troi hovered nearby as their guest ducked her head in and said, "Good afternoon, Doctor. Beautiful sickbay you have here. Makes me almost wish I were a medical doctor."

Crusher looked up and gave the visitor a cordial smile. "Thank you, Counselor. Are you having a good tour of the ship?"

"Why, yes! The *Enterprise* is like a floating city, only with better services." Suddenly Cabot's eyes lit up and her mouth dropped open. She was drawn into Beverly's office as if pulled by an invisible force. Her eyes and her hand went straight toward an old-fashioned photograph on the doctor's bookshelf.

Troi followed and noticed that the object of her attention was a photograph of Wesley Crusher. It was an image that Beverly hadn't displayed for some time, but the doctor was making more of an effort to acknowledge her son these days. Beverly and Deanna stared curiously at the younger woman as she almost reverently touched Wesley's photo.

"This was taken . . . when?" asked Cabot.

"About nine years ago. You know my son, Wesley?" asked Crusher with surprise.

A broad grin spread over Colleen's face. "Yes, I know him. *He's your son?*"

"Yes, but he's been away for several years," said Troi, trying to spare Beverly any more pain.

"He's alive and well," Colleen blurted out. "But you must know that already."

Now Beverly dropped her padd and jumped to her feet. Troi felt like strangling Colleen. "I think we should be going," insisted the counselor. "We've bothered the doctor enough."

"No . . . no, that's all right," breathed Crusher, waving off her friend's concerns. "I don't mind if our guest talks about Wesley. When did you meet him?"

"I have said too much," replied the young woman. "Your son is very handsome."

"Thank you." Crusher looked confused but oddly exhilarated too.

"It was a pleasure talking to you." Cabot moved toward the door. "However, the spa and lunch and all that wiped me out, Deanna, and I think I'll get a little nap before our staff meeting. Perhaps you'd be so kind as to come for me and show me the way to the observation lounge?"

"Certainly," answered Troi. "Can you find your way back to your quarters?"

"Yes. Thanks again, and good-bye." With that, Cabot sauntered out of sickbay.

Troi turned to her friend and shrugged her shoulders apologetically. "I'm sorry, Beverly, I don't know what that was all about."

The doctor frowned deeply in thought, but she didn't look angry. "It's okay. She looks about Wesley's age—she could've gone to the Academy with him."

"But she seemed so certain that he was . . . alive and well. Like she had just seen him."

"I see him too . . . sometimes," said Crusher with an enigmatic smile. "That's a most unusual young woman. I think we were wrong about her."

"Well, something changed her attitude a hundred and eighty degrees," muttered Troi.

"Yes, *someone* got to her and showed her the truth."

In the *Enterprise* shuttlebay, Geordi La Forge and Data studied an awkward vessel that looked better suited for a carnival ride than collecting junk left among the asteroids. The lumpen craft was covered with so many harpoon guns, winches, antennas, saws, and valves that it looked like a puffer fish left out in the sun for a few days. La Forge inspected the gears on a winch and got black grease all over his hands.

"This isn't the only one," he said, as Data handed him a towel. "The admiral is sending us another tug, which should be here in half an hour. I don't know about this . . . I think we'll be sitting ducks in a ship like this."

"Not necessarily," replied Data. "Speed and fire-power are not prerequisites for success at Rashanar. A maneuverable craft that can extricate itself from difficulty is more desirable. This vessel reminds me of the one that extracted me from the wreckage just before I entered the vortex. Those salvagers saved my life."

"I guess this ship will be authentic," said Geordi.

"We had to off-load four shuttlecraft to make room for these two clunkers."

"The sacrifice may be worth it," predicted Data, "in order to fool the Ontailians."

"I'm not worried about Ontailians," muttered La Forge. "What if we see two duplicate ships again? What are we going to do? So far, nobody has a plan for handling that thing."

"Perhaps we destroyed it when it appeared to be the *Vuxhal*," remarked Data.

"Nobody buys that," said the engineer, turning back to the newest addition to their shuttlecraft fleet. "So are you going to help me modify this bucket of bolts?"

"I have other matters to attend to," said the android. "Admiral Nechayev sent us several volumes of information about the Ontailians, which I must study before the briefing."

La Forge nodded thoughtfully as he circled the salvage ship, and his footsteps echoed in the cavernous shuttlebay. "We'll make room for the other scow and whatever else we can steal. You know, Data, if we're going to be looters, maybe we should really grab a Jem'Hadar polytransporter. We could use one of those. This could open up a whole new career for us."

"You are no longer planning to leave Starfleet, are you?" asked the android.

His friend laughed and said, "It was just a joke, Data. I have low expectations for us as looters. And, no, I'm not leaving Starfleet as long as Captain Picard is still here."

"Nor am I," replied the android sincerely.

The Traveler stood in mud so thick that it oozed over his ankles, which was an odd feeling considering how light his body felt in the low gravity of the Ontailians' homeworld, Ona. The icy wind and sleeting snow had no effect upon him, but the sight of the mammoth purple fir trees was awe-inspiring. The Ontailian conifers grew at least twice as high as the greatest sequoias on Earth, and they were dotted with spherical nests about a meter in diameter hanging from almost every branch, like Christmas ornaments. Each immense tree was a village, although those under a hundred meters tall were devoid of Ontailian nests. The firs were too young and fragile, he recalled.

A slight hum greeted Wesley's ears, and he realized that the trunks and branches of the trees were alive with the flow of energy. Although the Ontailians appeared to be primitive beings, their communal ways had evolved over millions of years into an advanced civilization with nonpolluting thermal power, fanciful art, and space travel. They lived peacefully with a wide variety of native flora and fauna, although all of them had to be hardy to survive the cold temperatures on all the landmasses except the islands near the equator. A specialized breed of hunter Ontailians lived on those remote islands. He knew this from the wealth of experiences of his fellow Travelers, who had taken an interest in Ona some millennia ago.

He couldn't shake the feeling that the Ontailians knew what was out there in Rashanar, or at least they were hiding vital information. Or could it all be a hoax? *Could they be trying to scare the Federation away, so as to keep the salvage rights to themselves?* Considering how poorly they were policing the graveyard from various and sundry looters, Wes didn't think greed was their motive. It definitely seemed more like fear—something inside Rashanar was more terrifying than Starfleet.

Perhaps he wasn't skilled enough as a Traveler, but observing a nonhumanoid species was difficult for him. Without the familiar organization of a humanoid society, he didn't know where to spy or where to watch. As he mulled over his next move, the majestic forest was shaken by a small explosion that felt deep underground, and a meteor streaked outward over the treetops and vanished among the glittering stars.

The Ontailians' spaceports were underground affairs where small, spherical craft were blasted into orbit like escape pods. Orbital space stations and starships gathered the pods, and all repairs and ship building took place in orbit. Because of their aptitude for low gravity, the Ontailians didn't need the elaborate synthetic gravity of Starfleet vessels. They were as comfortable in space as on the ground, as long as they had their trellises.

So the Traveler had come down to study the Ontailians in their native habitat, seeking clues to their behavior. At night in the twinkling, snowy grove, it was hard to even remember the Rashanar Battle Site, which seemed light-years away rather than at the edge of this solar system. On such a cold, peaceful evening, it was difficult to ponder angry tempers, vengeful urges, war, and killing.

That is, until he heard an anguished roar from somewhere deep in the towering forest. Wes covered the distance in half a second and stood in a glade that was more primitive and overgrown than the civilized woods he had left. Tree branches rustled loudly over his head, even though the wind was barely a whisper. The snowflakes were so large that they looked like albino spiders dropping through the night.

Wes, hearing crashing in the woods, managed to move out of the way a moment before a beast on six legs plowed through the underbrush. The creature was the size of a buffalo and as fearsome as a wild boar, with curved tusks, a bloody snout, and bony plates and spines along its back. Tall at the withers, the animal had a narrow torso and spindly legs, but it had the weapons to inflict considerable damage. Plus it looked and sounded angry, as if it had been rousted from some sleepy lair. In the trees above him, the Ontailians whooped and chittered, causing the brute to slash through the underbrush like an enraged bull.

Wes looked for intelligence similar to the Ontailians', but the spiny boar didn't register as anything other than a common animal. From the excited noises in the trees, he assumed the Ontailians were hunting the beast; they were certainly taunting it. The rustling was from braver individuals descending along the trunks and tree limbs, and he wondered if they would leap upon their prey. He marveled that the Ontailians could see so well without artificial light.

Without warning, the giant plated creature roared again, shaking the trees, and this time its cry sounded plaintive, desperate . . . hungry. As if in answer, a few shrieking Ontailians dove from the trees to land near the wild animal, and the battle commenced. It was a short melee, as the handful of Ontailians were torn apart, trampled, and eaten by the enraged monster. The pristine snow turned red from the carnage. High above, the Ontailians screeched loudly, and it sounded like full-throated approval— cheering!

If it was an execution, it was a voluntary one, thought the Traveler. Despite the loud acclamation, a rain of seedpods, rocks, and twigs greeted the beast, and it dashed off on its six legs, roaring with satisfaction. This brought more chittering from the Ontailians in the trees, followed by high-pitched wails that blended together in eerie harmonies. Wes had heard this singing aboard their ships, and he wondered if there was a connection. Unfortunately, he could discern only a general feeling of relief and duty, as if this strange event had been essential to the community, not some mere blood sport.

After that, most of the Ontailians crawled silently into the boughs, dispersing in all directions. Some gathered in hollowed-out trunks and cavities to sleep in a communal knot of furry appendages. Silence seemed to have been restored to the forest of Ona, just when Wesley heard the animal, or another like it, roar in a different part of the wilderness.

He had a feeling that the same strange ritual would be repeated in that new location, and didn't feel the need to observe it again. However, the Traveler resolved to watch the Ontailians for a few minutes each day, until he felt he knew them better.

When he finally returned to the *Enterprise,* it was time for the briefing in the observation lounge. He knew his way there, but joined his mother in sickbay in order to arrive with her as his apparent guide. In his Ensign Brewster persona, he preferred to avoid Colleen Cabot, even though she knew who he really was, as he didn't quite trust her to keep his secret.

Colleen gave him barely a glance when she entered the observation lounge with Deanna Troi. Ensign Brewster claimed a chair against the bulkhead, allowing Colleen and the senior staff to have the seats at the conference table. One by one they all arrived. The last one was Captain Picard, who also grabbed a seat along the bulkhead, away from the table. He acknowledged the person he knew as

Brewster and crossed his arms, waiting to be briefed. Even though Wesley hadn't been on the *Enterprise* in years, he could tell that the crew was distracted by the notion of Captain Picard as passenger.

Riker finally stood up. Data sat attentively, obviously waiting to speak, and Riker let the low drone of conversation die down by itself.

"Before we start this meeting," said the acting captain, "I want to make one thing clear. Our trip to the Rashanar Battle Site is voluntary. I want to make sure you have all agreed to go. Counselor Cabot, Ensign Brewster, Captain Picard, if any of you want off, say so now—we have a shuttlecraft waiting."

"I'm staying," said Cabot. She looked at Picard and added, "My patient will remain with me."

"I'll stay, too," said Brewster, melting into the background.

Data cocked his head and remarked, "That gives us a crew and passenger count of one hundred fifty-three volunteers. No one has requested to leave. The crew size is acceptable with longer shifts."

"Thank you, Data. Riker to bridge."

"Vale here."

"Tell our shuttlecraft to stand down. Nobody is leaving the ship. Have the conn set course for Rashanar and depart when ready, maximum warp."

"Yes, sir."

The acting captain turned to his chief engineer. "La Forge, good job on the matter reactant injector. Did we get both those salvage vessels on board?"

"Yes, sir, we have two well-used salvage ships, Ekosian design. They need a lot of work just to be spaceworthy at Rashanar. One has no shields, the other has a bad tractor beam; neither one has any weapons. Both are very slow, meant for asteroid work."

"Will they be ready by the time we reach Rashanar?" asked Riker.

"We'll try," promised La Forge, "although we're shorthanded, too. I think we can get *one* of them ready in time, which brings up the question: How are we getting into the boneyard?"

Riker tapped the table with his fingertips and said, "We'll talk about that right now. The Ontailians are going to dictate a lot of our actions. Essentially, we have to observe them and get past them into the boneyard, without being caught. It's okay if they think we're scavengers, since they've given up trying to control the looters."

Dr. Crusher turned and looked at Ensign Brewster, as if to say, *Now would be a good time to tell the truth.*

Wes wanted to yell *Mom!* If he let go of his guise and became Wesley Crusher full-time, that would bring him one step closer to ending his existence as a Traveler.

If only I hadn't looked into the Pool of Prophecy and seen the Enterprise *autodestruct,* he thought, *I wouldn't be here at all.* He fervently hoped that the crew would be able to exorcise the ghosts of Rashanar without his help being crucial, allowing him to keep his choices open.

"Data," said Riker, "what about the Ontailians' mind-set?"

"Admiral Nechayev was very thorough," Data began. "I have studied all available literature on the subject, including some of the Ontailians' own popular theater. They are nonhumanoid but very dramatic, in the way that they love overt demonstrations and meaningful gestures. The Ontailians seem to enjoy a certain amount of chaos. They communicate vocally and through body language, which requires animated discourse. In their politics, they are isolationist, therefore have not formed close ties with other Federation members, even nonhumanoid species. Since they joined the Federation during the Dominion War, they did not undergo the usual scrutiny. The Battle of Rashanar saved their homeworld, Ona, from destruction, but they have served notice on the Federation that our presence in their space is no longer welcome. Although not officially, for all practical purposes, they have withdrawn from the Federation.

"As for specifics which might help us in the current situation, I uncovered very little. Since their dealings with other cultures have been limited, there is no history of war or diplomacy to study, and their own society has changed very little in the last nine hundred years, except for technical advances. But the Ontailians do have a few traditions which may influence their thinking.

"Monsters figure prominently in their mythology," Data continued, "and they allow predatory animals to run free on their planet, despite the danger. From their earliest days of space travel, five hundred years ago, the Ontailians have been on guard against something which roughly translates as the 'demon flyer.' This may be similar to the *Flying Dutchman* and other ghost ships in Terran seagoing mythology. The legends state that the demon flyer has no soul, which might indicate an automated or robotic space-craft, although I am uncertain of that interpretation. Since this is a figment from their own mythology, they might have decided to deal with it alone, with-out our interference. They denied that the mimic ship we encountered is real, but their recent actions indicate that they view *something* in Rashanar as a genuine threat."

"Any clue how this demon ship works?" asked Riker.

"That is uncertain. How does the legend of the *Flying Dutchman* work? It is something frightening, beyond the norm, which may cause destruction to the unwary. Even if the demon ship does not exist, it explains some of their behavior."

"Excuse me, Mr. Data," said Colleen Cabot, "does this have anything to do with Ontailians expelling antimatter inside the graveyard?"

Riker looked at the counselor with new respect. "You must have read our reports."

"Yes," she lied, stealing a glance at Ensign Brew-ster as she surveyed the room. "That's strange be-havior, isn't it?"

"Very strange," answered Data, "especially inside Rashanar. We have no idea how that may be connected. We wish to observe them doing it again. There is also the mystery of the Ontailian distress signal, which they denied even though we saw the ship in distress. They have withheld information from us and have been less than truthful. I have nothing else to report, except that the Ontailians have improved their weaponry since the war, and the ships at Rashanar are the best in their fleet, experienced in battle. The *Yoxced* has replaced the *Vuxhal.*"

"They're in charge of the boneyard, but they're afraid," said Riker. "From the latest reports, their forces are spread thinly around the entire battle zone. They have the gateways and major gaps covered. *They're* not going in and out, but the looters sure are—however, the Ontailians aren't pursuing. They seem to be in defensive mode. The question is, how do we get the *Enterprise* past them?"

Nobody replied, until Captain Picard shifted impatiently in his chair. "With a diversion," he answered. "If the Ontailians are poised to keep something from getting *out,* then give them what they fear most. They'll congregate to stop it."

"Okay, La Forge, get one of those salvagers working," said Riker. "We'll check cartography to find the best place to stop and launch it. Once we have our looters inside the graveyard, we can plan the diversion. Does anybody have anything to add?" Several officers glanced at Captain Picard, who was quiet and attentive.

Riker rose to his feet and added, "Let's all remember to get some sleep, too, whenever we can. We'll soon be pulling double shifts under stressful conditions, but I don't expect this mission to be as bad as our last visit. This time we'll be a free agent—no chasing looters around, no guard duty, no trying to please everybody, just a simple mission to find out what's going on. Thank you, you're dismissed."

There was a bit of small talk as the officers filed out of the observation lounge. Most of them were going back to the bridge. But the Traveler could go anywhere he wanted, and right now where he preferred to be was at Colleen Cabot's side. He lingered by his chair to watch the lovely woman pass by. When he saw his mother gazing at him with overt curiosity, he was close to waving her off and telling her to mind her own business. She was going to give him away or at least call unwanted attention to him. Reluctantly, he left the group and wandered by himself down the corridor.

"Ensign Brewster!" called a voice behind him. He tried to control his emotions as he turned around, because he knew it was Colleen. She was quite deadpan as she said, "It's not urgent, but I need Admiral Nechayev's authorization. Can we meet after dinner to send her a message?"

"Yes. Twenty-one hundred hours, my quarters."

"That will be fine," she answered brusquely, turning back to Captain Picard.

Wes hurried away, glad to end the conversation before his mother emerged into the corridor. Somehow his sudden infatuation with Colleen had heightened his senses of being a human being. He felt bombarded by fears and pangs that he hadn't experienced since he was a teenager. This was the *Enterprise,* so reminiscent of the ship where he had grown up and felt all the crushes, loves, and defeats of youth. He felt like the prodigal son who'd come home after being gone for years to find that nothing had changed. The raw emotions were more painful than he remembered—yet more wonderful! This existence was so intense that he almost longed for the detached simplicity of a Traveler's life, and so fled into the peace of space.

Colleen watched the man-shaped blur walk down the corridor, fading from her perceptions like an early-morning dream. *What is Wesley Crusher? My lover, a superbeing, the humble son, an interstellar drifter? All those things, none of them?* Had she completely lost her senses—shipping out on the *Enterprise* for a secret, dangerous mission, then falling in love with a specter of a man? She had chewed out two admirals before stealing the most controversial patient in Starfleet Medical. It seemed her career was on life-support. Yet the *Enterprise* crew was risking just as much to clear their names and Picard's, and they exhibited no hesitation. *I have to be brave like them, do what's right, and trust for it to work out,* she told herself.

Yet there is something I can do to redeem myself in Admiral Nakamura's eyes, thought Cabot. *If this technology can be captured and studied, rather than destroyed, I have to lobby for that outcome.* She owed that much to her benefactor, and it could even make the difference in salvaging her career.

"Counselor Cabot," said a clipped voice, breaking her out of her reverie. "Will you have dinner with Dr. Crusher and me?"

She turned to see Captain Picard, smiling pleasantly, and Beverly Crusher even looked enthused at the prospect of her company.

"I suppose I should keep tabs on my patient," answered Cabot. "How have you been feeling, Captain?"

"Anxious," he admitted. "And impatient. It's a little difficult to be a passenger on this ship, especially when she's shorthanded. I feel like pitching in, but I can't."

"I think you're doing well," answered the counselor, her blue eyes sparkling. "Your presence alone is good for morale. It helps that Riker is so capable. Also, the amenities are excellent. Strangely, I'm looking forward to some excitement."

"Don't forget the famous corollary by Robert Louis Stevenson," warned Picard. "When you're sitting in your armchair, you long to be on an adventure. When you're on an adventure, you long to be sitting in your armchair."

Colleen smiled. "Are you saying that I might regret my thrill-seeking?"

"Probably not," said the doctor. "You don't seem like you shy away from a challenge."

"Not lately," admitted Colleen, sharing a knowing look with Crusher. She took Picard's arm, allowing Beverly the other arm, and the three of them strolled down the corridor as a trio. "Are we going to your excellent commissary?"

"It's only replicator fare," answered Picard. "When we have a full crew, there's fresh food, too."

"I'll suffer," the counselor answered with a wink.

Colleen did suffer during dinner—not from poor food or boring company, but from separation pangs. She wanted to be with Wes. Oddly, the topic of conversation turned often to Beverly's long-missing son, and Captain Picard seemed delighted to tell Wesley stories—about how precocious he was, often irritating, but then again every bit as important as any member of the crew. He had always been an extraordinary person, it seemed, saving the ship when he was but a youth. They were all shocked when he got into trouble at the Academy, then nearly bailed from Starfleet; however, no one had been particularly stunned when he opted to go with the Traveler. The path least taken seemed to be Wesley Crusher's destiny.

From the captain's joy in talking about the prodigal son, it was clear that Wesley Crusher was usually an uncomfortable subject. But no more. To the captain, Colleen gave the erroneous impression that she and Wes had been acquaintances in the misty past. Beverly often peered at her and asked loaded questions, trying to fathom how much she knew about her son or how involved they were. But playing mind games was the counselor's stock in trade, so she carefully gave the good doctor no useful information.

The smitten young woman wanted to rush through dinner. She knew she had hours to go before she could meet him. To her, Brewster was the spectral Wesley, the strangest manifestation of his powers, because no one could see him as he really was. As a psychologist, she found that fascinating. He impersonated a nonentity, which had to be some aspect of Wesley's own personality. On the other hand, she might be reading too much into his behavior. Wes had been trained to behave as he did. Most people spent their lives trying to be noticed; a Traveler was expected to do just the opposite.

After-dinner tea and coffee concluded on a civil note, and Colleen was able to excuse herself. She felt as if she had scored some points—at least she wasn't the enemy anymore. That distinction belonged to the Ontailians and the deadly anomalies that ruled Rashanar. She left Jean-Luc and Beverly talking about their options like two academics.

She dashed down the empty corridors and

stamped her foot impatiently in the turbolift. Finally Cabot arrived back at her room, then realized that he had told her to wait in *his* stateroom. But what if he wasn't there?

She needn't have worried, because the door slid open at her approach. Wes was standing only an arm's length away. He grabbed her and pulled her close, as the the door snapped shut, sealing out the rest of the world. They held each other tightly; even surrounded by this immense ship, it felt as if they were the only two people in the universe. No one and nothing else was as important as the two of them.

"I thought you'd never come back," rasped Wes, stroking and nuzzling her hair. "I can't think about anything . . . when you're gone."

"Then we'll just have to be together," she agreed, resting her head on his chest. "That's possible, isn't it?"

He didn't answer immediately, as if he couldn't trust himself to speak. So she spoke for him. "This thing you're looking for in the graveyard, you'll be able to understand it and learn how to control it. I have confidence in you, Wesley."

"Control it?" he asked.

Colleen squeezed him, then gazed into his startled eyes. "Yes! You don't have to destroy it. I don't know why, but I think the Ontailians are trying to do just that when they expel antimatter."

"Or feed it," he answered. "Or appease it. I saw

something on their planet last night, when they threw themselves at a wild animal . . . as if they were sacrificing to it. Maybe they have a belief system to appease things they consider dangerous."

"We're all making sacrifices and taking risks," she whispered. "Why should I be here, risking my neck? Or you? We're a lot like the Ontailians."

"*You* don't need to be here," he said hoarsely. "You could be safe somewhere else."

"I *need* to be here," she disagreed. Colleen's lips found his, ending further discussion.

Chapter Six

"HERE IT IS, COMMANDER," said La Forge, motioning to the lumpen scow, which took up a good chunk of deck space in the shuttlebay. "She's not much to look at, not very fast either, but now she has shields. I also borrowed an idea from the Androssi and put two photon-torpedo launchers on her, like they did with the *Calypso*. The tractor beam might actually work now, but it needs a good test under load."

"We have renamed it the *Skegge*," said Data. "After an Ekosian bird."

Riker nodded sagely as he inspected the ungainly craft, trying not to either laugh or cry. Physically he tried to avoid the jutting antennas, robotic arms, hoists, and winches that threatened his clean uniform with grease and corrosion. "Yes, good job."

"We could have cleaned it up," said La Forge, "but this is more authentic."

"How big a crew does it take?"

"A minimum of two," answered Data, "one to operate machinery while another pilots. Four is probably optimum, with room for a few passengers."

The acting captain frowned in thought and muttered, "Who can we spare from the crew when we're already shorthanded? And don't suggest yourselves."

"I suggest Captain Picard," answered Data. "He is not being fully utilized."

"But then Counselor Cabot would have to go with him," said a doubtful La Forge. "She's really a noncombatant."

"She volunteered the same as the rest of us, and Nechayev said this was *her* idea. All the Starfleet counselors I know are hard as nails. Besides, if you're posing as a scoundrel, it never hurts to have a pretty face around," Riker opined.

"There is also Ensign Brewster," said Data. "He is underutilized as well."

"In fact, I volunteer," said a voice behind them. Riker turned to see the ubiquitous ensign, who often appeared just when you were thinking about him. "For the fourth crew member, may I suggest Christine Vale."

"Vale is a good idea," allowed Riker, "but let's talk about *you* first. We need someone who can pilot this thing and hold their own under battle stress."

"I'm a little rusty," answered the ensign, "but I logged plenty of conn work—on a much bigger ship than this salvager. Captain Picard is a good pilot, too, and so is Vale."

Data cocked his head. "It is gratifying that you know so much about our personnel, but piloting is not the only criterion—this is a dangerous, covert mission."

"He works for Nechayev," said Geordi. "That might be enough credentials for a covert mission."

Not only that, there is something about this inconspicuous lump of a man that is reassuring. Riker was determined to keep Data and La Forge on the *Enterprise*. The rest of the skeleton crew were essential as well. Brewster must have been sent along for a purpose, and maybe this was it.

"Data, put Mr. Brewster on the conn simulator and see if he's as good as his word," ordered Riker. "I'll talk personally to our other 'looters.'"

"Yes, sir," answered the android. "On which class of vessel should we test him?"

"Let him choose." Riker crossed his arms and gave Brewster a piercing look.

"A *Galaxy*-class starship would be fine," the ensign responded after a moment.

Riker exchanged a surprised look with La Forge. "Did you know the last *Enterprise* was *Galaxy*-class?"

"What a small universe," said Brewster.

"Test him well," ordered Riker, striding across the

shuttlebay. "And hurry. We have to get this crew together in four hours."

Five minutes later, Will Riker located Captain Picard in sickbay, assisting Dr. Crusher and her few staff members in setting up a triage for possible injuries. None of them were more shorthanded than Crusher, but she was determined to be ready if they saw action.

"I see you pressed one of our passengers into service," observed Riker with a good-natured smile.

"It was this or more reading," replied Picard, "and I've been doing plenty of reading lately."

"I'd like to give you a job," said the acting captain. Beverly immediately stopped what she was doing to join the two men.

"He's not allowed to do anything on the *Enterprise*," she pointed out.

"This wouldn't be on the *Enterprise*," answered Riker. "I don't believe there's anything in the reglations against the captain running a small salvage ship."

Crusher looked aghast, but Picard nodded with comprehension. "Yes, I could do that."

"Think what you're saying, Jean-Luc," said the doctor. "You're in enough trouble already."

"Precisely why I'm a good choice," he replied. "We don't want to get anyone else in trouble, plus I'm not doing anything. But what about Counselor Cabot?"

Riker shrugged. "She would have to agree to go with you, but I think she would. She seems game for anything. That's two, and you need a crew of four on the *Skegge*. I'm going to ask Lieutenant Vale, too, and Ensign Brewster has already volunteered to go."

"Brewster?" asked Picard and Crusher in unison.

"He claims to be a pilot. Data is testing him on the simulator."

"He's a pilot all right," said Crusher with a wistful smile. "If he's going, I feel better about it."

Both Riker and Picard looked curiously at the doctor, but neither one questioned her unusual confidence in Nechayev's assistant.

"Captain, you'll be in command," said Riker. "You and your crew should be disguised and operating as much like looters as you can. We don't think the Ontailians will pay any attention to you after you get past their lines and into the graveyard."

"The first order of business will be to mount a diversion that will get the *Enterprise* into the boneyard," Picard observed. "I've been thinking about that, but this seems like an instance where the best-laid plans will go awry."

"Be ready to go in four hours," said Riker.

"Let's schedule a briefing for the crew of the *Skegge* as soon as possible."

"Yes, sir," answered Riker. He smiled at his slipup, but the captain was still the captain.

Next stop was the bridge, where Deanna was in charge for this leg of their journey. She and Kell Perim were going over navigation charts when he approached, and his beloved looked at him proudly.

"I think we've found a place where we can drop off the salvage ship without them spotting us," she claimed. "If we use their sun and put it directly behind us, the solar radiation should mask our presence for a few seconds. If we're fast, we can get in and out without their sensors picking us up."

"Good work," said Riker. "When we come out of warp, we might want to cut all power and coast into position."

"I'll get on those calculations," said Perim, turning back to her console.

Riker glanced at the tactical station and Christine Vale, who was already scanning for Ontailians and salvagers, even though they were hours away from their destination. "Deanna," he said, "I'm going to take Vale off the bridge and put her on the ship with Picard, Cabot, and Brewster."

She blinked at him. "All of our passengers? Isn't that tug a little small to have a ship's counselor?"

"That's who we can spare. But I'm not convinced about Brewster. I have to talk to Vale. The bridge is still yours."

"Yes, sir," she replied. Then she lowered her voice to add, "Will, you know how dangerous this is."

His combadge beeped. "I understand. Riker here."

"This is Data. We are at the simulator, and Ensign Brewster checks out on the conn of a *Galaxy*-class vessel. In fact, I would not hesitate to give him the *Enterprise* conn."

"Hmmm," said Riker, "then I guess he's going to join a gang of looters. As soon as I have Vale lined up, we'll call a meeting. Riker out."

"Lined up for what, sir?" asked Vale as he approached her station.

"I'd like you to go on the *Skegge*, the salvage ship we're sending into Rashanar. You'll be disguised as scavengers, and Captain Picard will command."

Vale smiled. "Do I have to practice saying 'avast me mateys' and 'shiver me timbers'?"

"It might help," said Riker. "But first you have to volunteer."

"Of course I will."

"You'll be the only official crew member of the *Enterprise* going on the *Skegge*," he added, "because our three passengers make up the rest. Lieutenant, you should understand how dangerous this is."

"I consider going in there as a looter safer than going on the *Enterprise*."

"I can't argue with that," admitted Riker with a shrug. "Stay here until you're relieved for the meeting."

"Yes, sir. Where will that take place?"

"Aboard your new ship. Now I've got one more able body to shanghai." He turned to Deanna and asked, "Do you know where Counselor Cabot is?"

"I think she's in the spa." Troi chuckled. "Do you want me to contact her?"

"Yes, please," said Riker. "I'll be in the ready room."

Fifteen minutes passed quickly as the acting captain went over duty rosters for the shorthanded crew, assigning them to longer and split shifts. His door chimed. "Come in."

Counselor Cabot entered the ready room with her blond hair still wet and dripping on her snug blue dress. "You wanted to see me, Captain?"

"Yes." Riker rose from his desk and offered her the guest chair. "I hope I didn't disturb you."

"Well, I was trying to have fun before things got serious. When we get to Rashanar, it will get serious, won't it?"

"Definitely," he answered, trying a bit of charm on the counselor. "Everyone says that you came up with the idea to break into the graveyard in small craft, disguised as looters."

Colleen laughed. "I was desperate—trying to win an argument with Admiral Ross. I'm not usually big on military strategy. Is that what this is about?"

"Yes, we'd like Captain Picard to command our scavenger ship."

"Hmmm," she mused with a slight frown. "He's not supposed to be in command."

"We would send you, too," Riker assured her, "along with one of our best officers, Lieutenant Vale. To round out the crew, Ensign Brewster has volunteered."

"Oh. But how is it going to look if Picard screws up?"

"You know what Admiral Nechayev said," stated Riker, his jaw tightening. "It's going to look the same whether we succeed or fail, live or die. This mission never happened."

She crossed her arms and looked sternly at the acting captain. He suddenly realized this was not going to be so easy. "He may be captain of your looter ship, but I'm still *his* captain," she explained. "If I judge that his behavior is out of line, I can relieve him of command. I want you both to agree to that, or he can sit in his stateroom and rot. Those are my conditions."

Riker didn't say anything as he paced behind his desk, considering his options. If he had anybody else to spare, he would tell this pretty counselor to go stuff herself, but Picard was his best and only choice to head this crucial stage of their mission.

Finally he answered, "In that case, Lieutenant Vale would take over the *Skegge*."

"That's fine," she answered magnanimously. "Or Ensign Brewster. Just remember, Picard is my responsibility . . . whether he's saving the galaxy or brushing his teeth."

"All right, I'll talk privately to him."

Rising to her feet, she asked. "Now, how should I prepare for this assignment?"

"Dress like a scavenger, think like a scavenger. We're counting on you to set the tone here, because the rest of your crew aren't exactly undercover agents."

She smiled enigmatically and said, "I think one of them can pull off a disguise."

* * *

"The controls are much like a Starfleet shuttlecraft," said Data, who was seated at the pilot's chair in the nose of the *Skegge*. The android was surrounded by the vessel's new crew, Picard, Cabot, Vale, and Brewster—and had no way to keep his distance from the others in the small cabin. Wesley wondered if he could maintain his alternative persona in such close quarters. He didn't have much choice. Unfortunately, having any more privacy with Colleen was out the door. Thanks to the spherical hull, there was a large viewport, which cut down on the feeling of claustrophobia somewhat.

"The ship can also be piloted from both of the auxiliary stations," continued Data, "but not the rear console, which is only for the machinery control. There is no transporter."

It was cramped inside the old ship, which had a distinct odor of sweat, solvents, and grease. So many chipped coats of blue paint were laid on so thick that it looked like the interior was covered in icing. The sleeping quarters were sparse, just a bunkbed for two behind a curtain, plus a rudimentary head. The only source of nourishment was a food slot that looked as if it had been salvaged from another ship. The *Skegge* was an old, working tug, not a vessel meant to race, go great distances, or fight anyone. The shields were fine to ward off debris, but one good blast of an energy spike would fry them. The Traveler was beginning to think that Colleen was right—they were all crazy.

He listened as Data explained the propulsion system, while Picard asked pertinent questions, making sure they understood the trimpots and sliding levers on the controls. It actually took longer to explain how the winches, saws, and hoists worked, and they couldn't really test anything until they got into space. Wes could see Colleen bouncing on her toes excitedly, and felt a pang of guilt for bringing her on this dangerous mission. That added to the self-reproach he already felt for ignoring the disciplines of a Traveler.

"Has this craft got subspace communications?" asked Lieutenant Vale. "Regular frequencies don't work very well in the boneyard. Subspace has a delay, but it gets through."

"That is a valid point," answered Data. "The *Skegge* does have subspace communications, but none of Starfleet's encryption devices. The warning buoys in Rashanar were functioning as subspace relays; however, we have no way of knowing if the Ontailians have left them with that capability. Communications between our two ships may be a problem."

"Plus the *Enterprise* will have to stay in warp until it's time to sneak her in," said Picard. "We know from our last visit here that anything that *can* go wrong *will* go wrong. So we need some kind of signal, or a meeting place."

Wes took a deep breath, and Colleen gave him a glance. Only she knew that the Traveler could ferry messages instantly between the two ships, if he was willing to reveal his identity to everyone. The man they knew as Brewster cleared his throat to get their attention.

"If we don't check in on schedule," he began, "the *Enterprise* will know we're either having com problems . . . or something more serious. At that point, they'll start looking for a signal. We have our two photon torpedoes, which we could shoot out the main gateway."

"Gateway three," offered Data, pointing at the chart on the navigation console, "where we entered the first time."

"Fine," said Brewster. "If we shoot one torpedo, that means we're okay, just suffering poor communications and on standby. If we shoot both torpedoes, that means either we're in serious trouble, or it's time for the diversion that is going to distract the Ontailians and get the *Enterprise* inside. Either way, the *Enterprise* has to come running."

Data lifted an eyebrow as he considered the suggestion. "It is not a perfect solution, but it is workable."

"However," said Picard, "we might have to use those torpedoes in defense."

"You could take an extra two torpedoes," said Data. "It would require a spacewalk to load them into the launchers, but you will have EVA suits and enough equipment. I can arrange for them, although that will cut down on the storage space in the hold."

"That's okay. We'd rather have photon torpedoes than lots of luggage," said Colleen with a smile.

The android turned back to his control panel and said, "Allow me to go over the targeting and launching procedures. Lieutenant Vale, you might want to pay particular attention."

Fifteen minutes later, they all had a good idea how to fire the weapons, although no one was thrilled about going into battle in this little tug. They would mainly be hiding among the wrecks and rubble. Wes realized that it would be difficult for him to sneak off while a member of this cramped crew. He might have been better off staying on the *Enterprise,* but it was too late now to make that decision.

"Do we have suitable clothing?" asked Picard. "All of us need to be in plain but worn clothes with no Starfleet markings. Use the replicator if you have to. Don't bring anything on this ship that might identify you as Starfleet. Grab whatever you need, and return here quickly. I believe our launch is less than an hour away."

"Forty-eight minutes and thirty-seven seconds," replied Data. "The launch must be precise—we cannot remain out of warp for more than a few seconds, even with the sun's radiation masking our presence."

"So get your gear, then meet back here," said Picard, clearly relishing being in command again, even if it was an old salvage tug with a crew of four.

The Traveler ducked out first, followed by

Colleen Cabot. She poked him in the ribs and grinned slyly. "We have a little time."

He gave her a wan smile and shook his head as they walked across the shuttlebay. "I don't think so. I've got to say good-bye to my mom. You have a lot to do, too."

"I do?" she asked, puzzled. "Maybe make out my last will and testament."

He frowned sourly. "This isn't fun and games."

"I beg to differ," answered Colleen. "Trying to dig into Captain Picard's psyche wasn't fun and games. This *is* fun to me. I'm looking forward to being part of a bunch of space pirates."

"Being Brewster in that little box is going to make it impossible for me to go anywhere else."

"Then level with them," said Cabot, "like you have with me and your mother."

"I can't. Not yet. When I become Wesley Crusher full-time, I cease to be the Traveler. I'm not ready to give that up." He looked pointedly at her. "Are you?"

"Good question," she answered. "Whenever a patient tells me they've fallen in love with somebody on a vacation or an exciting mission, I say, 'Whoa!' Get to know this person in cold reality, the mundane world, then tell me you're madly in love."

He stopped to gaze at the stunning beauty. He had to focus hard to keep the guise of Ensign Brewster as he talked to her. "Then what are we doing? This isn't even *me* you're looking at!"

"Which proves my point . . . that *I'm* on vacation," answered Colleen, giving him a wink as she sauntered away. Wesley had to laugh and shake his head.

From his seat at the controls of the *Skegge,* Captain Picard glanced back at his motley crew, thinking that he had no idea how Brewster and Cabot would react under fire. True, they had the trust of admirals, but this wasn't an office building on San Francisco Bay. He wore dirty pants and a tunic, while Vale and Brewster were dressed in well-worn jumpsuits without any external markings.

Of more concern to Picard was Cabot's insistence that she still had control over him and could relieve him of duty at her pleasure. She had made that clear to Riker, who coveyed the message to him. He trusted the young lady. This was no different from going on a mission with an admiral in tow—but it was still disconcerting to think that he wasn't his own master.

Once again, he took a look around the small cabin. Vale manned the copilot's seat behind him to the left, Brewster was on navigation at the other console, and Cabot sat in the rear at the machinery controls. There were two photon torpedoes strapped to their underbelly, two extra torpedoes in the hold, and enough fuel and supplies for their mission, even if it ran a little long. However, Picard didn't think this would be a leisurely cruise through the Rashanar graveyard; it would mostly be dodging and hiding.

He hoped they were all prepared to be knocked around a bit.

"Remember," he said, "we're breaking through the Ontailian fleet, then heading straight into the boneyard. No hesitation. Ignore any hails or potshots they take at us, and let's hope our shields hold long enough to get past them."

"The gap we're entering is free of Ontailian ships," remarked Vale, studying the *Enterprise*'s scans.

"For now," replied the captain. "They'll have time to catch us on their sensors. It just depends how badly they want to keep us out."

His combadge chirped, and a voice said, "Bridge to Picard."

"Picard here."

"We're coming out of warp in thirty seconds," said Riker. "We'll drift into position at low power. Is there any reason why we should abort this mission or try later?"

"We're ready," answered Picard. He noticed that his hands were clenched on the old-fashioned controls. He let go and stretched his fingers.

"Nervous?" asked Lieutenant Vale. "I could pilot."

"I'm sure you could, but I haven't had much fun lately. Due to my age, I've had more experience on these type of controls than you."

Riker's voice broke in, "Good luck, Captain. We won't talk again until check-in. Riker out."

Picard could see shuttlebay personnel evacuating

the area. None of them were exactly sure how the ungainly craft was going to fly. Picard double-checked all of his instruments in the waning seconds.

"We're stopping," said Brewster. "Any second." Picard had no idea how he could tell.

The outer shuttlebay doors drew open, revealing a sprinkling of stars with an ominous swirl of wreckage in the distance. Seeing the graveyard again sent a chill down Picard's spine. He realized he wasn't going to stop until he destroyed whatever was haunting Rashanar.

"Hold on," he said, plying his controls. With a jerk and a thump, the little tug shot through the opening into space with her afterburners sparking. Picard marveled that the craft was so responsive—like an old Type-6 orbital shuttle. He felt growing confidence in his piloting, and didn't need to look at the readouts on his console. Their destination shimmered in the darkness about a thousand kilometers away—an ominous cloud of scorched starships and glittering rubble. He pushed the lever forward, sending the propulsion system into maximum, shooting the craft through the darkness. So far, he couldn't see any Ontailian vessel with the naked eye. He knew they were out there.

"The *Enterprise* is gone," reported Vale. "We're on our own."

They were already halfway to their goal. Behind him, Brewster said, "Ontailian light cruiser off starboard, six hundred kilometers and closing fast."

"Only one?" asked Picard.

Vale worked her board and reported. "They're hailing us. They demand that we stop immediately, or they'll open fire."

"I know I said not to respond," answered Picard, "but let's buy ourselves a few seconds. Tell them . . . one of our ships put out a distress signal from Rashanar. We're responding."

Vale relayed the message without hesitation as the giant globe of junk loomed ever closer. Now they could see raw spikes of energy deep within the wasteland of scuttled ships. The dark hulls were illuminated like windmills in a lightning storm.

"Prepare for impact!" announced Vale. They barely had time to catch their breaths before a brilliant beam struck the ship, shaking it violently. Sparks spewed from Brewster's overloaded console. The *Skegge* was knocked off course, but Picard kept his hands on the controls and his eyes on the objective. Cabot responded quickly to the console fire, grabbing an extinguisher and spraying the affected area with a stream of retardant. Then she jumped back into her seat and buckled in.

"One more!" shouted Vale over the rattling and shaking.

Picard dipped the tug. The next beam just grazed her. He felt a weightless sensation, but he was strapped in his seat and was able to keep on course.

From the corner of his eye, he caught sight of the Ontailian ship through the viewport; it looked like a shark's fin slicing through the waves in the dead of night. Although they had lost artificial gravity and were under fire, his biggest concern was not the Ontailians but the twisted derelicts that drifted in front of him. Most of them whirled slowly in stately orbits; however, some went crashing about the junk-yard like maddened bulls, sending other hulks reeling into new chaotic orbits.

"Losing gravity is normal!" shouted Vale. "The power goes to the shields when they start to fail."

The Ontailians gave a parting shot, which clipped a charred hulk, sending it spinning. The tiny tug just slipped past it, missing the spinning hull by centimeters. Abruptly, the Ontailian cruiser veered away, allowing them to enter the graveyard through a cloud of shimmering debris that flashed against their shields. Picard at last let out his breath and loosened his grip on the controls. Although more at ease, he was still flying like a madman, weaving his way between ghost ships and ominous wreckage. Picard felt the strange confluence of beauty, horror, and grief that was Rashanar, and he began to look for their real foe in the scattered ruins.

The gravity came back as Brewster crawled into his scorched seat. "I think we lost them, but we're out one console."

"That was about the maximum these shields can take," said Vale, studying her board. "Another direct hit, and we would have been part of the decorations."

Picard was listening, but he had to keep his attention on the chunks of wreckage that rolled through the void. He could see pastel plasma clouds glowing in the distance and wild energy spikes rippling between the dead vessels. Both of those anomalies were lethal. The gravity sink, antimatter asteroid, and mimic ship were equally deadly. Inside the boneyard, there was no respite from danger, especially in a small craft like this. He wasn't sure where to seek shelter.

"Any idea where we should hole up?" asked the captain. He slowed the craft down, but continued to maneuver carefully.

"Yes," answered Brewster hesitantly. "There's a fairly intact *Ambassador*-class ship, the *Hickock,* near buoy seven. I think we're close to it. If we could dock, we could take refuge inside."

Picard could only glance at the guileless ensign, but he asked, "How do you know so much about Rashanar, Mr. Brewster?"

"Study," he answered. "I learned a great deal going over all your reports and logs. In fact, one of the *Enterprise* shuttlecraft logged the new position of the *Hickock.*"

"He's right, sir," Vale added. "I recall that."

Brewster rose and looked over his shoulder. Picard could feel his presence a bit stronger now that he was close. Otherwise, the man was such a blank that it was hard to figure him out, although he supposed that such an unprepossessing person might be useful in Nechayev's favorite line of work.

"Bearing one hundred twenty, mark sixty-five," suggested Brewster.

Picard made the course correction. He was glad to have a destination in this vast maelstrom of destruction. In short order, they saw the *Hickock* drifting along, looking more stable and more intact than most of its neighbors.

"You seem to have the navigation sense of a Medusan," said Vale, sounding impressed.

"He's good friends with one," said Colleen Cabot with a smile. "Maybe some of that has rubbed off on him."

"I just do my homework," replied the ensign humbly.

An unknown force suddenly rocked the *Skegge*, and Brewster and Cabot were knocked into each other's arms. The feeling of weightlessness returned as the lights flickered. Picard and Vale stayed in their seats, while the captain tried to get command of the little ship. The controls were absolutely dead.

"Shields are out," reported Vale. "Is it—" She didn't have to finish her sentence.

Yes, thought Picard, *this is the way every encounter with the mimic ship begins.* "Quick! Get your suits on!"

Pandemonium erupted as everyone in the cramped

cabin tried to obey his order in a weightless state. Picard remained in his seat. His heart pounding and the ship's systems failing one by one, he peered out the viewport, searching for the Ontailians' demon flyer.

Chapter Seven

INSTEAD OF a shapeshifting apparition that was poised to paralyze and duplicate them, what Captain Picard saw out his viewport was a greenish-black scow that looked in worse shape than the *Skegge*. The oblong craft was only distinguishable from the derelicts by the thrusters firing to keep it in a stationary position. Slowly the *Skegge*'s systems began to come online, even while the craft was jerked roughly. Gravity abruptly returned, landing Brewster, Cabot, and Vale in a pile on the deck, tangled in their spacesuits. Picard tried to accelerate his way out, but the engines were ineffective.

"That feels like a tractor beam," said the captain. He studied his readouts and had his hunch confirmed as his shipmates crawled back to their posts. "Definitely a tractor beam. We don't have enough power to get away from it."

"I'll try to hail them," said Vale, picking up an old-fashioned headset. "Should we ready a torpedo?"

"No, we're too close . . . and getting closer . . . less than fifty meters."

A circular saw on the bow of their captor began to whir, and what looked like robotic arms snapped at them.

"They're going to board us!" said Cabot with alarm.

"That's exactly right," answered Vale, working her board. "The quality isn't good, but listen to their hail."

Amid the crackling and pops of static came a gruff voice. "Ekosian ship, prepare to be boarded. Open your hatch, or we will force our way in."

"Put me through to them," ordered Picard angrily. Although he was painfully aware that he didn't have the might of a *Sovereign*-class starship behind him, he still greeted the attackers sternly. "Salvage ship, back off! We have photon torpedoes. Release us from your tractor beam immediately."

He motioned to Vale to cut off communications. "Ready torpedo one. Put all power to shields."

"Yes, sir," she answered. "At this range, we might be destroyed in the explosion."

"I know." The greenish vessel hesitated for a moment, but they were still only twenty-five meters away. Suddenly a mounted harpoon gun on the intruder shot at them. A missile exploded directly in front of the *Skegge,* shrouding the tug in a giant energized net. Once again, the lights flickered, and all the onboard systems began to fail.

"Now we can't fire," muttered Vale, listening to her earpiece. "And a new hail is coming in . . . exactly the same demand as before."

"They're not Ontailians," said Brewster, peering over Picard's shoulder. "Who are they?"

Picard responded slowly. "I don't know who they are, but we're about to find out. Vale, tell them to dock at the cargo bay. Then open it to show them . . . that we give in."

"Captain!" shouted Cabot in alarm. "Do you know what you're doing?"

"Would you like to relieve me of command, Counselor? Now would be a good time."

Brewster stared at Colleen for a second, and she seemed to relent under his gaze. "Like Mother always said, put your best foot forward."

"They could have destroyed us," said Vale; however, she didn't sound convinced that they would be spared much longer.

"They want the tug, not us," replied Cabot. "We'll have to *make* them want us."

"Sir, do we distribute weapons?" asked Lieutenant Vale.

Picard turned to his board. "No, the counselor is

right. This is our competition—a welcoming party from the local looters. We'll have to get along with them or be destroyed. Just in case, I'm locking out the controls with a security code."

"Captain," said Vale worriedly, "they might torture you for that code."

He glanced at the counselor and said, "Wouldn't be the first time. Don't flash any weapons around, but if I were you women, I'd see if I could conceal something on my person. These looters aren't always interested in salvage."

They heard a metallic clang and felt a jolt, and both Vale and Cabot rummaged through the weapons cabinet to find knives and small phasers. The net surrounding the tug suddenly stopped glowing, and artificial gravity returned. For an instant, Picard thought about firing the engines to get away, but with another ship attached to them, they would probably careen into one of the derelicts and be destroyed in seconds. Ensign Brewster was oddly calm through the entire scenario. Picard decided that he was the coolest customer he had ever met, a perfect complement to Admiral Nechayev.

When the ensign noticed Picard looking at him, he said, "As long as we're alive, there's always a chance."

"I know," agreed the captain.

The hatch in the center of the deck flew open with a crash, and a shaggy mane of green hair appeared in the opening, followed by massive green shoulders and a muscular torso that was naked except for a studded, purple sash. A large Klingon disruptor was pointed directly at Picard, only the wielder wasn't Klingon—he was Orion, one of the most barbaric races in the Alpha Quadrant.

As the Orion climbed up the ladder, he turned his attention to the women, especially the lovely Colleen. She gave him an insouciant smile and shifted her weight. The intruder grinned and hurried up to the deck. Picard thought momentarily about attacking him, but the Orions were physically much stronger than any humanoid race in the quadrant save Vulcans. Plus that disruptor pistol looked menacing.

The brute gave Colleen and Vale an appreciative look. "When we didn't see anything in the hold but torpedoes, we thought this was a worthless haul. Not so." He shouted down into the hold. "Vengus! Tell them we're bringing the ship and prisoners!"

"We're not supposed to bring prisoners," grumbled a voice, and a second green head with sloping forehead, beady eyes, and pug nose poked out of the hatch. When he looked around, he said, "These aren't Ekosians. They're *humans!*"

"We're ex-Maquis," said Picard. "We've been doing this for years."

"Well, you tried to do it in the wrong place," growled the Orion with the disruptor. "Follow us, all three of you."

Three of us? thought Picard. He looked around and saw that Ensign Brewster was gone. Still being friendly, Colleen Cabot looked unconcerned about the missing crew member, and Picard's glance at Vale told her to keep quiet. *How could Brewster have escaped without anybody seeing him? As far as these thugs are concerned, he doesn't even exist.*

There was no time to ponder this mystery with a disruptor waving at him. "Move it!" growled the Orion.

Without hesitation, Picard stepped toward the hatch. Since he wasn't a comely young woman, he would be the first to die if the Orions got trigger-happy.

Brewster, he thought to himself, *wherever you are, I hope you can do some good.*

Will Riker tried not to pace across the *Enterprise* bridge. It was difficult to just sit still when he didn't know the fate of Captain Picard and the *Skegge* crew, and he wouldn't find out until they checked in twenty minutes from now, which should have given them enough time to find a hiding spot and settle in. Their sensors had picked up an Ontailian ship firing at something near the gap where the tug had entered the battle site. Only a few meters into Rashanar, sensor readings became worthless, so the *Skegge* could have been destroyed without anyone knowing.

If the *Skegge* didn't report in, he would have to crash Rashanar like a cadet at the admiral's banquet. Not only would they draw every Ontailian ship in the system, but the covert part of their mission would be over. It would be no picnic to pilot the mighty starship safely into Rashanar at full speed, even without anyone shooting at them. They would have to come out of warp almost on top of the grave-yard. That in itself was dangerous.

At the ops console, Data had taken over Vale's tactical duties as well as his own. "Captain," said the android, "there is a strange message for you."

"Strange, why?" asked Riker. "Who's it from?"

"Unknown, but the sender of the message is in your ready room."

"In my ready room?" Riker chuckled, until he realized that Data was not likely to make a joke without his emotion chip. The only way into the ready room was through the bridge. Nobody had passed through, and with only him, Data, and Kell Perim on duty, a newcomer wouldn't have escaped their attention.

"We're traveling at warp speed and have our shields up," said Perim. "How could somebody just materialize in the ready room?"

"Should I call security?" asked the android.

"No," said Riker, walking toward the door to the captain's private office. "There must be a logical explanation for this."

As soon as the door slid open, he stopped and almost changed his mind about calling security. The person who stood before him couldn't possibly be there.

"Come in," whispered Ensign Brewster, motioning him inside. "I'm not a ghost."

Riker entered, and the door whooshed shut behind him. "How can you be *here?* Didn't you go with the captain?"

"Yes, I did. Listen, I haven't got time to explain everything to you, but Captain Picard is not going to check in when he's supposed to. The *Skegge* and her crew have been taken prisoner by some Orion scavengers."

"And you escaped . . . but how?"

The mild-mannered Brewster looked animated for the first time since Riker had known him. "The next time I see you, I promise I'll explain. For now, just don't charge into Rashanar when the *Skegge* doesn't report in. You can't help them. Let me see if I can free them."

"You? By *yourself?*"

"I'll return with word as soon as I can," promised Brewster.

Riker had questions, but he swallowed them whole the moment that Ensign Brewster disappeared. He gawked, then rubbed his eyes. Yes, the ensign had vanished without a trace, not even the sparkle of a transporter beam. Not that anyone could transport out of a starship going at warp speed with shields up—that was impossible.

He reminded himself that he had seen strange things before in this job. Riker looked at the chronometer on the desk and thought, *I only have ten minutes to see if his news is confirmed.*

Trying not to appear too shaken, the acting captain strode out of the ready room and stood before his bridge crew. He must have looked troubled, because Data instantly inquired, "Are you unwell, sir?"

"I'm okay. Data, was there any evidence of an intruder coming or going from the *Enterprise* in the last few minutes?"

"No, sir. Was there someone in the ready room?"

"I'm not sure," answered Riker, looking back at the closed door. "Maybe it was a projection of some sort. There's no one there now."

"That is true," agreed Data, running a scan of the room. "However, *someone* activated the com panel in the ready room."

Deciding not to worry them with possibly false information, Riker crossed to the command chair and sat down. "We'll know in ten minutes," he said. "Steady as she goes."

As two hulking, green-skinned Orion males admired her, Colleen Cabot thought, *This is more adventure than I expected.* A third Orion was flying the filthy, corroded salvage ship, with the *Skegge* in tow.

She glanced at her shipmates, Captain Picard and Lieutenant Vale, both of whom looked stunned by this turn of events. Although they wisely had said nothing, they were probably wondering about Ensign Brewster's sudden disappearance more than the hijacking of their little tug. They weren't going to win many fights in the *Skegge,* and if they were going to fit into the scavenger community of Rashanar, they would have to find some other way to get along.

"What are you going to do with us?" Colleen asked their captors.

"Sell you," growled the one named Vengus. His black eyes traveled lasciviously from Cabot to Vale, but his brutish face wrinkled when he saw Picard. "I don't know what we'll do with *him.* Old human males are not worth much."

Colleen appealed to the other one, Hidek, who had spared them in the first place. "Why don't you let us join your fleet? We'll split everything we salvage with you."

"Your ship *will* join our fleet," replied Vengus. "We don't need you. We keep everything for ourselves."

"Well, that's not much fun," said the attractive blonde, gazing at Hidek, who had yet to contradict his partner. "We could have so much fun if we stuck together. You know, loot isn't everything."

Hidek gave her a wry smile. "We might keep you with us . . . for a while."

Colleen gave him an encouraging smile, all the time wondering when Wesley Crusher would intervene to get them out of this mess. Although the Traveler had amazing powers, she didn't think he could subdue three huge Orions in the confines of this small craft. Nor would it work for him to disable the vessel in the middle of the graveyard, where they could be destroyed by an errant energy spike or a crumpled relic. No, Wes would have to wait for a better opportunity than this.

Picard shifted uncomfortably in his seat on top of a spool of metal cable. "Have any of you seen it?" he asked. "The demon ship?"

That wiped the smile from Hidek's face, and his partner looked as if he'd been punched in the stomach. "You talk too much, human," barked Vengus.

"You know what I'm talking about," said Picard. "The demon ship takes on the appearance of other vessels . . . after it destroys them."

"Old woman's tales," Vengus retored. He didn't sound convincing in his denial.

Picard nodded sagely. "You've lost ships to that monster, too. So have we. That's what annihilated half the vessels in this graveyard."

"But we're going to capture it!" Colleen blurted out. Now everyone turned their attention to the young lady. Even the Orions looked impressed. "Think of it," she said, her eyes wide and glistening, "that would be the ultimate salvage. If you had command over a shapeshifting spacecraft, no vessel would be too great for you to conquer. All the important powers of the Alpha Quadrant would lie at your feet and have to pay tribute, lest you unleash the ship on them. Plus you could duplicate any craft you wanted, even the newest starships."

Vengus snorted a laugh. "And how do you propose to capture this thing, if it even exists?"

"It has a forced-energy weapon," she answered, "which paralyzes other ships. We've determined that this weapon uses gamma rays. We plan to reverse the stream and paralyze the demon ship before it can paralyze us."

"That's enough, woman!" snapped Picard angrily. "Keep quiet."

Good job, Jean-Luc, thought Colleen, *help me play these creeps.*

"Enough fairy tales!" called the pilot from the cockpit. "We're at the base. Prepare to dock."

Vengus and Hidek glanced at one another, as if sharing the same forbidden thought. Colleen tried to appear contrite under Picard's stern glare, hoping to sell the idea that they were too valuable to sell into slavery or kill. Cabot turned to a grimy viewport at what looked like a corral full of small ships and salvage vessels, floating under the scorched nacelle of a mammoth Jem'Hadar battle cruiser. A gunner in a spacesuit was mounted in a hollowed-out part of the nacelle. He waved them in with their prize, and there was sparkle as a forcefield deactivated in order to allow the Orions to enter the corral with the *Skegge* in tow. They knocked against one of the other scows while docking, but nobody seemed concerned. All the ships were banging around, like a clump of balloons floating on a string.

"Stand by to transport," said the pilot. "Are we taking everybody in?"

Hidek waved his disruptor pistol at Picard. "Yes, . . . for now."

The muscular pilot turned around and tossed necklaces with green medallions to each of the three prisoners. "Put those on. They're transporter locaters." He grinned at their uneasy expressions. "Don't worry, we can transport inside our forcefield. Who goes first?"

While the Orions discussed the transporter order, Cabot saw Vale lean over to Picard and ask, "What if there are Androssi in there? They may recognize us."

Before the captain could reply, Vengus grunted, "We'll each take one of the prisoners. You, Fair Hair, come with me." He pointed directly at Colleen.

"No, she goes with *me*," said Hidek gruffly. "You take the skinny one."

The two Orions faced off, growling and snuffling until the third one pushed them apart. "I'll take the skinny one—I like them lean." He grabbed Vale roughly and hauled her to the cockpit. Cabot saw the feisty lieutenant tense as if she would resist, but Picard shook his head not to, so meekly she went with the strapping Orion. The two of them disappeared in the shimmering residue of a transporter beam.

Picard stepped toward Vengus, effectively volunteering to go with the more unfriendly Orion, while Colleen tried to look demure. Grumbling, Vengus rudely pushed Picard into the cockpit, then joined him there, beaming off the salvage vessel a moment later.

Hidek jerked Colleen toward his rippling green chest and said, "Now we're alone. I want a kiss."

She disarmed him with a platonic peck on the cheek as she tickled his ribs. When Hidek started laughing and squirming under her probing fingertips, it was easy to pull away from him and dash to the cockpit. "Come on, I want to see your hideout!" she called playfully.

Totally smitten, the hulking Orion peacefully held her hand as they were transported inside the Jem'Hadar derelict.

Captain Picard tried not to stare at their new surroundings, but it was difficult not to gawk when a Jem'Hadar transporter room had been turned into what appeared to be the rowdiest bar in the sector. Scantily clad emerald-skinned females danced on almost every table, but the number of Orions in the place was relatively few when compared with the plump Pakleds, weaselish Androssi, boisterous

Hok'Tar, and ape-shaped, scaly Kreel. Two slovenly Pakleds in stained aprons were manning a makeshift bar and dispensing what looked like Romulan ale, while raucous music roared from dented speakers in every corner. The door to the outer corridor had been blown open and was now just a jagged hole large enough for two Orions to enter at once . . . and here two now staggered in, arm in arm, singing off-key to the wild music. Smoke hung as thickly as on a Klingon bridge.

Picard was shoved by Vengus onto the dance floor, but he managed to keep his feet. "Human!" someone cried out, and at once he was bombarded with flying mugs and sloshing ale. Picard dove under a table to protect himself—an action that was greeted by uproarious laughs and jeers, hollering that he was a coward and several other things that were not as kind. *Nobody is going to recognize me here,* he thought, *because they probably won't let me live long enough for that.*

The captain heard thuds above him, and he realized that the Orion slave girl was still dancing on top of the table. He looked around for Christine Vale but didn't see her; he did, however, see Colleen Cabot step off the transporter platform, and she looked as if she had her escort, Hidek, well under control. The way he glared at the other males made it clear that he would fight for the right to traipse behind the counselor as she sauntered into the room.

"Hey, Jean!" she called cheerfully, crouching down to wave to him. "Is this a blast or what?"

"I need a drink!" Picard shouted back. That wasn't far from wrong.

Just then, he heard a howl and a mammoth Pakled dropped to the deck at the end of the bar, a black sword sticking out of his back. Standing over him was an Orion who was trying unsuccessfuly to look innocent. Since he also was holding a struggling Christine Vale in his arms, it was clear what had initiated the deadly brawl. One of the Pakled bartenders drew a pistol, and the Orion responded by holding Vale in front of him as a shield.

Picard crawled out from under the table and jumped to his feet. "Stop!" he shouted, pointing to the Pakled. "Don't fire!"

Slowly the Pakled turned the weapon on Picard. Hidek had to step between them. "Hold it, Morgo! You want revenge, you know what to do. Drop that weapon before we tear this place apart. Our new ship has photon torpedoes, and we left our weapons officer on board." He tapped the medallion as if to summon aid.

"Ah, forget it!" shouted the Pakled jovially. "One less greedy mouth to split profits with." He went back to pouring drinks, as Picard breathed a loud sigh of relief.

Incredibly, only a few customers in the riotous tavern even paid any attention to this exchange. Nobody bothered to pick up the dead Pakled, who continued to bleed profusely onto the deck. The captain went up to Hidek and said, "Thank you."

"You want to thank me, drag that body out of here," ordered the Orion.

Picard looked forlornly at the beached whale of a Pakled and nodded. He didn't have a lot of choice if he wanted to make himself useful.

Tugging on the corpse didn't move it much, so he asked the pilot, "Can my shipmate help?"

The Orion was just served a frothing mug of ale, and he didn't have enough hands to grab it. He released Vale, who glared at him with abject hatred. "Come on," Picard said, "help me move him."

"Yeah, make yourself useful," snapped the Orion just before he filled his mouth with ale that spilled all over his verdant chest. "There's an airlock just down the corridor. Don't go past the forcefield if you value your lives."

"We'll try not to," answered Picard. "Hey, this is some headquarters you've got here."

"The clubhouse, we call it," he grumbled, "for the syndicate. Move it, you puny humans!"

He tried to kick Picard, but the captain sidestepped out of the way. With Vale pulling for all she was worth, they managed to drag the dead Pakled a few meters. Hardly anyone even got out of their way as they maneuvered around tables, chairs, and dancers.

"I think the artificial gravity is set higher here than we would have it." Vale groaned. "Compared to this bunch, we *are* puny humans."

"You'll get no argument out of me," said Picard through heavy panting. As they struggled with the body, he looked up to see what Cabot was up to. Sure enough, she seemed to have a whole table full of customers entranced. He looked closer and saw that she was performimg card tricks for Hidek and his friends. Colleen pulled a card out of his tight britches to much laughter. Her sleight of hand was very impressive, and that was good, because Picard felt they could use a trick or two. Colleen glanced his way but kept a buoyant grin on her face as she enchanted their captors.

Leaving a trail of purplish blood on the deck, Picard and Vale finally dragged the deceased Pakled out into a blasted corridor, following a path of spills and similar smears to an airlock hatch at the end. Just beyond, two portable forcefield emitters kept the oxygen atmosphere intact, as well as the prisoners in. Drunken customers were loitering toward the other end of the corridor, where a foul-smelling room had been turned into a makeshift latrine. No one paid much attention to them.

With backs straining and sweat dripping, Picard and Vale finally dropped the dead weight near the hatch. The captain barely had enough energy left to punch the wall panel and open the door, rolling the monstrous body into a horrible garbage dump. The two looked up at an outer door that led to space, where a potpourri of debris was drifting past. Making sure their burden was entirely inside the compartment, they backed out and shut the hatch to the corridor.

"That could be our way out of here," whispered Vale, still panting. "What do you think, Captain?"

"Call me Jean, like Cabot does. We would need EVA suits with propulsion systems. The transporter would be a better choice, because we've got to get to our ship."

"You there!" growled a Kreel, waving his long arms at them. "Hurry back here! We've got more for you to do."

Picard nodded and hit a second wall button, which had warning signs all around it. That opened the outer hatch, and the Pakled corpse was blown out into space.

"We've missed our check-in time," muttered Vale as she walked back down the hall.

"I know." Picard realized that the *Enterprise* was probably crashing through the Ontailians' line of defense and into the graveyard right now, and that frightened him more than their own predicament.

"No word from the *Skegge*," reported Data at the combined ops and tactical station. "They are five minutes and nineteen seconds late."

"I know," snapped Riker, jumping to his feet. "Data, if Ensign Brewster had shown up in my ready room twenty-five minutes ago—even though that's impossible—and he told me that the away team wouldn't check in because they'd been captured by

Orion scavengers, would you be inclined to believe him?"

"If what you say occurred, Ensign Brewster cannot be a normal human being. If the first part of his information is true, it stands to reason that the second part may also be true."

Riker slammed a fist into a beefy palm. "Brewster told me not to do anything . . . that *he* would rescue them."

"This is a great deal to take on faith," said the android. "Then again, Captain, we have no idea where they are. Merely getting into Rashanar is problematic."

"I've been thinking about that too," mused Riker. "When we were here before, everyone was worried about impostors posing as Federation ships to get into the boneyard, and with good reason. What if we could doctor the *Enterprise* to make it seem as if we were actually impostors doing a bad imitation of a Starfleet ship? That way, it won't get back to Starfleet if we're spotted."

"La Forge could try to alter the warp signature," suggested Data, "a subterfuge that is never fully successful. I could do an EVA and alter some of the markings on the ship."

"Let's do it," said Riker, making an immediate decision. "That will give Brewster, or whoever he is, extra time to rescue the away team and contact us by subspace. Conn, we're out of Ontailian space, aren't we?"

"Yes, sir," answered Kell Perim.

"Prepare to come out of warp."

His top-heavy torso lurching and his knuckles almost grazing the deck, the Kreel scavenger led Picard and Vale down the corridor of the crippled Jem'Hadar battle cruiser. Hok'Tar, Pakled, and Orion looters laughed at them as they passed, and Picard soon guessed why. Judging from the foul smell, they were about to clean the latrines. As they neared the door, where a mass of flies were inexplicably buzzing, the captain had to breathe through his mouth and cover his eyes. That forced him to stop, but the muscular Kreel grabbed the butt of a pistol weapon and pointed inside with a grunt.

Cristine Vale appeared as if she would throw up.

The captain looked at his taskmaster, who could only vaguely be called humanoid. "What do we clean it with?"

"Your clothes!" blared the Kreel, causing the bystanders to erupt in hysterics. He roughly shoved them inside and loped in after, shutting the door behind him.

The stench and the sight of all this intergalactic bodily waste was almost enough to make Picard faint, as he gave some serious thought to attacking the Kreel bare-handed. They outnumbered the alien two-to-one, although it became fifty-to-one in the transporter room beyond. Vale swooned from the odor, and Picard had to catch her, effectively ending that desperate plan.

"Captain," whispered the Kreel, "it's me, Brewster. Give Vale to me."

Wide-eyed with surprise, Picard didn't know how he knew that this savage was Ensign Brewster, but he somehow placed the unconscious lieutenant in his rangy arms. She was already starting to come to, and the Kreel glanced nervously at the door. "Listen," he continued, "both of you. I'm taking you back to our ship one by one. Captain, take off your shirt and start cleaning."

Fully regaining consciousness, Christine Vale tried to pull away from the scaly brute. Before Picard could reassure her, the two of them disappeared. It wasn't even like a transporter beam—it was as if they were never there. A pounding fell on the door, and he instantly stripped off some clothing and got to his knees to clean the muck.

"I'm cleaning!" he shouted. "Wait a minute!"

There was low grumbling, but the door didn't open. Only a few seconds passed before the big Kreel appeared again, materializing out of foul air.

"Colleen is so charming, I can't get her away from them," it snorted, "and that big Orion won't let her out of his sight. I'm going to get you to the *Skegge*, Captain; then we need a major diversion. Get ready to launch, fire a torpedo right at the guardpost. Wait for us. With any luck, it will only be a few seconds."

"How are you doing this?" The captain waved off his own question. "Never mind . . . later."

The Kreel grabbed his arm. In an instant they were crouched on the deck of the *Skegge*. Through the viewport, the captain could see a dozen other scavenger ships nestled in the forcefield corral under the battle cruiser's mammoth nacelle. He turned to thank his savior, but no sooner did the alien let go of his arm than he was no longer there.

Vale gawked. "I didn't believe it, but now I do."

"Ensign Brewster is a man of many talents," said Picard, rushing to the pilot's seat. "They took that tractor beam off us, didn't they?"

"Yes, sir." Vale dropped into a seat at the other working console. "But we've still got the guard and the forcefield to deal with."

"I hope we can take care of both of them with one torpedo." He continued to work his board, going through the prelaunch checklist, arming and aiming weapons, and finally raising shields. He gazed out the viewport, but the guard in the hollowed-out gunnery position under the nacelle didn't seem to notice their activity.

"We still have full power in the engines, such as it is," reported Vale.

"Don't turn anything on until we fire."

She pointed to the crumpled Jem'Hadar battle cruiser. "Our friend . . . is he going to get the counselor?"

"I certainly hope so," said Picard grimly. "I'm ready. This should be interesting."

A TIME TO DIE

The lieutenant braced herself in her seat. His jaw clenched, the captain fired a photon torpedo at a dead ship full of merrymakers less than sixty meters away.

Chapter Eight

IN A FORCEFIELD CORRAL shimmering under the nacelle of a blackened Jem'Hadar battle cruiser, a dozen little tugs and salvage scows drifted peacefully. A vast maelstrom of destruction whirled around this island of calm. Laughter echoed in the transporter room inside the forlorn derelict. This unearthly peace was violently ruptured when a grimy tug suddenly launched an avenging torpedo, which streaked from its underbelly like a comet and slammed into a hollow section of the nacelle. The guard in the gunnery had no chance. The explosion ignited a riotous rippling of energy spikes that spread outward across the Rashanar Battle Site. Within seconds, the dazzling arcs had turned this section of the graveyard into a new war zone.

"Hang on!" shouted Picard, trying to maintain control of the *Skegge* while other vessels detonated all around them. Sparks flew as the tug slammed into another scow.

Vale sat grim-faced at the other console. "The force-field is down! Let's get out of here!"

"Not yet." Picard looked worriedly at the Jem'Hadar ship, which was suddenly lit up like the grand opening of a used-spaceship lot. "Where are Brewster and Cabot?"

Large chunks of wreckage went crashing around the corral. "Shields are weakening!" warned Vale.

"One more second," replied the captain through gritted teeth. One of the other salvage ships managed to escape, its thrusters scorching a third vessel as it roared into the darkness.

Suddenly a brilliant white beam blasted off the remains of their shields, and Vale yelled, "They're firing phasers at us!"

"From where?" The captain peered through the smoke, flames, and debris into the heart of chaos. He could see that they had missed a second gunnery position in the hull. A cloud of rubble drifted between them, and that was their only protection.

"Let's go!" said another male voice, and Picard looked back gratefully to see Ensign Brewster holding an unconscious and bloody Colleen Cabot in his arms. He leaned on the trimpots, and they zoomed away just as another phaser blast grazed their stern and sheared off a winch.

"That was more diversion than we needed," muttered Brewster, laying the wounded counselor on the lower bunk at the rear of the cabin. He grabbed the first-aid kit and took out a bandage, using it to dab the blood from Cabot's forehead.

"Give her ten cc's of lectrazine," said Picard. "It's in the kit." He spared no time glancing over his shoulder or at his incoherent scanner readouts—all he knew was that the *Skegge* had to flee at top speed.

"We need to get word to the *Enterprise* as soon as possible," remarked Vale.

"I've taken care of that," answered Brewster as he prepared the hypospray. Deftly he administered the medicine, but he still fretted as he looked down at Colleen's unconscious form. "Her pulse is strong, but I wish my mother were here."

"Your mother?" asked Picard suspiciously. "Who are you really, Ensign Brewster?"

"He's a shapeshifter," said Vale.

"No, I'm not." The ensign shook his head, and his plain, dumpy features began to morph into a more handsome, youthful visage attached to a tall, slender body.

Picard gasped and forced himself to pay attention to his controls. Hoarsely he said, "Wesley—"

"Hello, Captain. I'm sorry for the subterfuge," said the young man, still gazing worriedly at Cabot. "I only set out to help you a little during your inquiry . . . but I guess I got carried away."

"Wesley?" asked Vale with a dawning realization. "Not *the* Wesley? But you aren't human."

"I'm all too human," he admitted. "But I've spent the last eight years training to be a Traveler, and I was finally born into the fellowship. Do you know what a Traveler is, Lieutenant?"

"I know it's something pretty darn special with what you did back there."

"Beverly must know," said Picard with a smile. "That's why she's been so damned cheerful."

"Yes. Colleen knows, too, and so does the Commodore Korgan."

"I'd like to know," said Vale. "My education must have been limited."

Not wasting words, Wesley described the remarkable existence of a Traveler as simply as he could, ending with the confession: "But I'm not sure how much longer I'll be a Traveler."

"Can you look like *anyone?*" asked Vale, entranced by this exotic young man.

Wes brushed a strand of blond hair from Colleen's forehead. "Yes, I suppose I could look like someone specific, but I would have to practice their mannerisms and voice. It would be difficult. We're taught to blend into the background. You know, someone you can't remember five minutes after you met them. We're only supposed to observe and record for posterity . . . which is not what I'm doing now."

"And you got word to the *Enterprise?*" asked Picard. "What are they doing?"

"I don't know for sure," admitted Wesley. "But I told them not to invade the boneyard just because we missed our check-in."

The counselor groaned and shifted on the bunk. Wesley anxiously gripped her hand. "Colleen? Don't try to move—just lie still."

"Wesley," she breathed with a grateful smile. "I knew you'd come to rescue us. Did you finally tell the others who you are?"

"Yes, but there hasn't been much time for a reunion," he answered, gently holding her hand and swabbing the grime off her face. "You had that whole bar entertained—we had to destroy the place to get you out."

"Just biding my time until you got there, love," she answered weakly.

Picard looked away, realizing that these two were much more than accidental shipmates. He had a million questions for young Crusher, but this was hardly the time or place to catch up. It was enough just to see him and know he was safe, even if he was possessed of remarkable abilities which he wasn't using as intended. That much was clear from everything Picard knew about the remarkable beings called Travelers. It was also apparent from the anguished expression on Wes's face—he was risking everything for his old comrades and the young woman lying before him.

"Wesley," said the captain, "do you know someplace safe we can go to rest and get our bearings?"

The Traveler nodded. "Yes, let me take over the controls. Here, Captain, will you check Colleen with the tricorder?"

"I'm okay," insisted the counselor. "Something just hit me on the head."

"Yeah, like the butt of a Klingon disruptor," muttered Wes angrily. "I don't much like your Orion friends."

"I had them right where I wanted them. You're just jealous."

"Maybe," he admitted. "Captain?"

"I'm stopping to let you take over," said Picard. "Be careful."

"Yes, I know."

A few moments later, they had switched seats, and the captain was tending the wounded counselor. He maintained his best poker face as he checked her with the medical tricorder. She seemed to have a serious hematoma under her bruises.

"She should see your mother," suggested Picard, "although the lectrazine has stabilized the injury."

Wes nodded with determination. "That's the next step—getting the *Enterprise* in."

The captain cleared his throat, wondering if his next question was overstepping the Traveler's boundaries, but he had to ask. "Did you see it, Wes? Is the mimic ship real?"

"I haven't actually seen it, Captain, but I've seen enough to make me think it's real. The Ontailians are very afraid of *something* out there."

John Vornholt

"So are the looters," added Vale. "That big Orion turned chartreuse when we asked him about the demon ship."

"The demon *flyer*," corrected Cabot. "Let's be accurate in translation—I'm sure Data was."

"You should rest," insisted Wesley.

Cabot gave him that smile he had gotten to know—the one that said *you have no control over me*. "To me," she said, "a flyer means a bird or something alive. How could it be a mechanical vessel or a mammoth replicator? Christine, you thought Wes was a shapeshifter. What if what we're looking for is just another shapeshifter ... only larger?"

"A living being?" asked Picard, disliking that prospect more than the other theories.

"Which means that we shouldn't kill it," added Cabot.

She was only a few centimeters away from him, and the captain narrowed his eyes at her. "If we get a chance, we're destroying that thing."

"Jean-Luc," she said in the tone of voice a mother uses with a toddler, "you aren't letting your personal feelings get in the way, are you?"

"There's nothing personal about an entity that paralyzes your ship without provocation, pretends to be your ship, destroys you, and then uses this new disguise to stalk another vessel. That's predatory behavior, which I have no compunction about ending."

156

"Whatever you say." Cabot lay back on her pillow and closed her eyes.

"You know," said Wesley at the controls, "it almost sounds like a computer virus. They attack looking like something familiar and innocuous, paralyze the system, take it over, then replicate themselves to attack another prey. It almost *is* mechanical, although it could well be alive. In fact, that's not much different from how an actual virus works."

Picard sighed and rose from the edge of Colleen's bunk. "So far I've heard about ten theories, which all sound plausible. Starfleet even seems to think it's a giant hologram. Where are we, Mr. Crusher?"

"We're almost at our destination, the *Ambassador*-class *Hickock*. It has the advantage of a stable orbit, and it was cleaned out before the looters got to it, so they've left it basically intact. There it is."

The classic lines of a massive Federation starship shimmered just ahead. Wes killed the impulse engines and applied thrusters to slow their speed, while Picard glanced out the viewport just to make sure no one was following them. He couldn't see any salvagers, but then again, the shadows were deep and dark in Rashanar. The ripplings of errant energy beams made it look as if a bloody battle were still being waged over the bones of the dead.

Wes skillfully piloted them under the cover of

the *Hickock*'s heavily damaged but still discernible saucer section. The ventral plane seemed to have rectangular holes all over it where panel sections had blown outward. The captain didn't want to imagine what kind of death throes they had suffered. For now, he was reminded of old Westerns he had read, where the wounded cavalrymen sought refuge in a crumbling old mission in the middle of Apache country. They had only just arrived, with a difficult time ahead of them, and already it seemed as if they had been beaten to a pulp.

Wes timed their drift with the speed of the shredded saucer section and deactivated the thrusters. After sitting in silence for several moments with no evident danger about to pounce, everyone let out a sigh of relief.

"I'm putting her on low power," said Vale. "I can't believe this crate held together through all of that."

"Thank the Ekosians," said Crusher, "although I helped make these two tugs available to Nechayev."

Picard cleared his throat, assembling his words very carefully. "Wes, now that we know about your secret—and I don't judge you for anything you've done—what else are you able to do for us?"

"I can go back to the *Enterprise* right now and lead them here."

"What about finding the mimic ship?"

"I know instinctively where to find anyone I'm familiar with, or anything in the Travelers' experience, but I'm drawing a blank on the thing that haunts Rashanar."

A low chuckle came from the bunk, and they all turned to look at Colleen, whom Picard had thought was asleep. "Find the Ontailians," she offered. "They know. And there's something about the antimatter—the way they expel it. You know that too, Wes."

Crusher nodded and rose to his feet. Picard marveled that the lad had gotten taller since he had last seen him. Of course, that was six or seven years ago, and he was still in his teens back then. "First things first," said the Traveler. "Let me get the *Enterprise.*"

The captain grinned, grasped his long-lost comrade by his shoulders, and said, "I don't care how you came to be here, Wes, or if you can do anything to help us. I'm just glad to see you're safe and well."

His former officer smiled back, and neither one of them seemed to trust their voices to speak without cracking. Wes gripped the captain's forearms in return. They gradually lowered their hands to gaze at one another in admiration.

Crusher looked past Picard's shoulder to the young woman lying in the lower bunk. "Colleen," he said, "I could take you back to sickbay right now."

Weakly she waved him off. "I'm not going anywhere. They need me here. Who will do card tricks if we get captured?"

Crusher gave her a brave smile, although he still looked gravely concerned. Then in front of Picard's startled eyes, the former Ensign Brewster disappeared as if he were no more than a fond memory on a summer's afternoon.

"Captain Riker," came a voice, which startled the acting skipper as he looked over Kell Perim's shoulder on the conn. Deanna Troi was also on the *Enterprise* bridge, working the ops console in Data's absence, and she turned to look as well.

"Brewster, you sure give a guy a start," muttered Riker. "What about the *Skegge* and her crew? Are they all right?"

"They've been rescued," answered the ensign. "But Counselor Cabot is injured. We should get the *Enterprise* into Rashanar as soon as possible."

Riker pointed out the viewport and said, "Data is out there on an EVA, changing our markings to make us look like a Starfleet impostor. La Forge has already altered our warp signature just enough to make it look suspicious. What do you have in mind?"

"Captain," said Kell Perim urgently. "I've detected a ship at five thousand kilometers—they've just come out of warp and are closing fast."

Forgetting all about Brewster, Riker turned to his conn officer. "Who is it?"

"Ontailian," she answered grimly. "The *Yoxced*.

They must have picked us up on their scanners."

Riker hit his combadge and barked, "Bridge to Data! Get inside now. We've got Ontailians headed this way."

"Yes, Captain," responded the android. "It will take me two minutes and twenty-two seconds to reach the hatch."

"We'll transport you. Stand by." Riker scowled at his sparse bridge crew. "We can't put up shields until Data gets inside."

"But we're outside Ontailian space," Troi pointed out. "They haven't got any business bothering us."

"I don't think they see it that way," grumbled Riker. "Bridge to transporter room one."

"Erwin here."

"Lock on to Data and get him inside right now."

"Yes, sir. Locking on signal."

"Who's on tactical?" Riker turned to see that Ensign Brewster had manned the crucial weapons console. At the moment, there were no extra personnel on the bridge to take the station. "Do you know what you're doing back there?" he asked.

Brewster nodded. "Yes, sir."

"Transporter room one to bridge," broke in a voice.

"Go ahead," snapped Riker.

"I can't get a lock on Data, sir. Something is jamming the transporter signal."

"That's confirmed," replied Troi, checking her ops

board. "The Ontailians are jamming all of our frequencies with their own transporters."

"Their transporters?" Riker's worst fears were realized a moment later as swarms of Ontailians materialized on the bridge of the *Enterprise.* Three of the long-limbed, furry creatures descended upon him, wrapping their boa-like appendages around his neck and trying to strangle him. More of them attacked his legs and brought him crashing to the deck, struggling for air. It took both hands and all his strength just to keep the hairy appendages from crushing his windpipe.

Riker heard screams, and saw Deanna and Perim fighting for their lives with a seething morass of the chittering slothlike beasts.

"Computer!" he rasped. "Increase gravity fifty percent shipwide!"

"Increasing gravity," replied the calm mechanical voice.

Now it was as if he were swimming in quicksand while fighting a dozen furry boa constrictors. But his desperate manuever worked, and he was able to peel off the Ontailians. They stuck to the deck where he slammed them, squirming around like immense, multilimbed caterpillars. Data appeared from nowhere with Brewster clasping his arm. The android turned into a blur as he pried Ontailians off Troi and Perim and flung them into a corner. Data and Brewster were like avenging exterminators, ridding the bridge of a horrible infestation. As the wounded foe writhed around, they screeched in a manner that made his teeth hurt.

Riker lumbered to his feet in the heavy gravity and pointed to the conn, abandoned by Perim during the attack. "Data, take the conn, put up shields, and get us out of here!"

"Yes, sir," replied the android, jumping into the seat as if the gravity were at normal.

While Data worked his board, Riker helped Troi and Perim to their feet, keeping an eye on the subdued intruders.

"We are under way," said Data. "The Ontailian ship is not pursuing."

"Good." Riker went to his command chair and hit the com panel. "Bridge to engineering."

"La Forge here," came a breathless reply.

"Were you attacked down there?"

"Yes, sir, but that gravity trick worked. They tried to sabotage the engines. A few attacked the computer."

"We're shorthanded on security," said Riker. "Do you think you can manage down there?"

"A phaser set to stun calms them down pretty well," answered La Forge. "We'll round them up and take them to the brig. So are we headed into Rashanar?"

Wondering what his supernatural scout would say, Riker turned to look at Ensign Brewster, who stood behind Data at the conn. He nodded to Riker and said, "Captain, there's no reason for subterfuge now."

"We're headed in," declared Riker. "Geordi, I'll keep you posted. Riker out."

"Why did the Ontailians board us?" asked Troi, glancing at the wriggling mass of fur and spidery appendages cowering in a corner of the bridge. There had to be a least twenty of the slender creatures, who now seemed pathetic and harmless.

"They didn't want to destroy the ship," answered Brewster, "They could have with our shields down. They wanted the *Enterprise* for some reason."

"Brewster, I need some answers from you," Riker snapped. "Like how are you transporting on and off the *Enterprise?*"

The turbolift door opened, and Beverly Crusher walked out slowly under the increased gravity. "Wesley!" she blurted. "Are you all right?"

"Wesley?" echoed Riker. He felt as if he'd been hit in the head by a conduit pipe, but that one word was the only answer he needed. "Ah, Wesley," he said with a big grin. "Welcome home."

Begrudgingly, Wesley Crusher showed the *Enterprise* bridge crew his true appearance. He now felt as if he had lost another piece of his identity—the uniqueness that made him a Traveler. His mother eagerly filled in some of the blanks since he had disappeared eight years ago. While they talked, Wesley helped Data navigate to the entry point closest to the *Skegge*'s position. Whether it was from embarrassment after their unsuccessful attack, concern about the prisoners, or plain fear, the Ontailians allowed them to enter the graveyard of ships without incident. The *Enterprise*'s sensors spotted the *Yoxced* and three other Ontailian ships in the vicinity, but they kept their distance.

A security team showed up and threw a big net around the captured Ontailians, who also didn't put up any resistance now that the fight was knocked out of them following their foiled surprise attack. Four Ontailians were dead; Riker had personally killed two of them in the melee. The remaining forty-three were secured in the brig, where they lay despondent on the deck, barely moving.

Counselor Troi tried to question them via the universal translator, but the Ontailians refused to answer even the most rudimentary queries, such as "Do you want food?" Apparently, they were content to die in ignominy after their failure. It was impossible to say for certain what they had hoped to accomplish. Riker ordered Dr. Crusher to watch them and force-feed them, if necessary. No prisoners were going to die on his watch.

Carefully, the mighty starship picked its way through dazzling energy arcs, shimmering clouds of debris, and somber wrecks. As before, the shields took a considerable beating but held up. Data's skill on the conn was crucial to getting anywhere inside the eerie boneyard. Even before they reached the shipwreck of the *Hickock*, Wes had a feeling of dread. As usual, sensors were unreliable inside Rashanar, but he didn't need them to know that something was wrong. By the time they reached the *Hickock,* he could see the awful truth for himself.

The *Skegge* was gone.

Chapter Nine

"WHERE ARE THEY?" demanded Captain Riker impatiently. "Wes, I thought you said they were here?"

"They were . . . I mean, this is where I left them." The young man stared at the *Enterprise* viewscreen, where the blackened *Ambassador*-class hulk was clearly visible.

To Riker, the *Hickock* seemed to be enmeshed in confetti from a ghostly parade. Cold ripples of light turned it into a haunted specter every few seconds.

The captain turned to Data at ops, who was concentrating intently on his readouts. "I do not detect the *Skegge*," said Data, "but I believe there is an Androssi ship on the other side of the *Hickock*."

Riker turned his attention to tactical, and transporter chief Erwin, a slim Bolian who'd been drafted into bridge duty.

"Ready phasers. Yellow alert."

"Yes, sir," answered Erwin.

"Send subspace to the *Skegge*," ordered Riker. "No encryption—just send message one on your list."

"Wait a second, Captain," said Wes Crusher, stepping toward the viewscreen and peering closely at the wreck. In due time, a relieved smile slid across the young man's face. "They're in there . . . somewhere."

"There is no indication," began Data, but he never got a chance to finish.

"They're cloaked . . . or something," Wes cut in. "Let's back out of here before we send that subspace message."

Riker shook his head. "Wes, we're glad to see you, but you're not in charge of the ship."

"I'll check on them," promised the young man, who was more mature and serious than Riker remembered him. "Come on, sir, you've trusted me this far."

Beverly looked beseechingly at him. Even Deanna nodded to show that they had to use the Traveler if they had one in their midst.

"Be careful," warned his mother, wringing her hands.

"Please back off a distance . . . until I find out what's going on. I can go to the Androssi vessel too." With that, he was gone. Riker glanced at Beverly, who didn't seem to know whether to be proud or terrified of her son's extraordinary abilities. Deanna put her arm around the doctor and said, "Good job of keeping a secret."

"I thought I gave it away a million times."

"Now that I know," muttered Riker, "you did."

Colleen nearly hit her head on the top of the bunk when Wes appeared inside the *Skegge's* tiny cabin. Vale clapped her hands, and Captain Picard jumped to his feet from the pilot's seat. But Wesley didn't see either one of them as he knelt at the counselor's side.

"Colleen, are you all right?" The young man's brown eyes glowed with concern.

"Wesley, I am awfully glad to see you," said Captain Picard, stepping up behind the Traveler.

"I'm fine," said Colleen, gently patting his hand. "Now listen to your captain."

Reluctantly, he turned away from her. "What's going on, Captain? Do you know the *Enterprise* is out there?"

"We do now," whispered Picard. "Right after you left, we were visited by an Androssi salvage vessel, which is still around here somewhere. We made a deal with them for a Romulan cloaking device, which we were just testing. Naturally, we're trying to be good looters, so we can't acknowledge that the *Enterprise* is out there. So you see the difficulty we're in."

"Are these the same Androssi who offered you a cloaking device when you were here before?" asked Wes. "I saw that in the log."

"No, because they're dead," answered Picard gravely. "But these are definitely their associates."

Colleen chuckled hoarsely, then coughed. "They were impressed by the way we tore up the Orions' den of iniquity . . . and escaped. They want to be partners."

"You don't sound so good," said Wes.

"You should take her back to the *Enterprise,*" said Picard.

"Captain, you don't have any control over me," countered Cabot feistily. "I'm staying here."

Picard shook his head, obviously not going to waste his energy. He gripped Wes's shoulder and said, "Go back and tell Riker we're fine. We'll contact them when the Androssi are gone, and they should keep their distance with no contact until then."

"They've already pulled back," replied Wes. "I'll return when I can." He knelt awkwardly at Colleen's side, not used to showing his emotions in front of others. Being a Traveler must make a human a bit repressed, the counselor decided.

"It's okay," she said calmly. "See you soon, Wesley." They embraced, and he seemed to melt in her fingers until he was gone.

If the truth were known, she still felt a little

woozy, but she didn't feel badly injured. Then again, she was drugged. That was certainly masking some pain and discomfort. If she were smart, she'd get some sleep, which was probably the thing she needed most; but Counselor Cabot didn't want to miss any part of this adventure.

"The Androssi are hailing us by subspace," reported Vale. "They say it's safe to come out of cloak."

"How did the device affect our ship's systems?" asked the captain, returning to his seat in the cockpit.

"Well, everything we do seems to be a major power drain," answered Vale, frowning at her readouts. "The cloak is no worse than the others, especially if we're drifting and playing possum. I wouldn't want to try to cloak while the engines were on."

"Very well, bring us out," ordered Picard.

"I'll get it," said Colleen, rising from her bunk. It had proven difficult to route the cloaking device to the *Skegge*'s main consoles, so the Androssi had patched it into the mechanical controls at the rear of the cabin. Colleen was only about a meter away, and she tried to ignore her dizziness when she moved across the deck.

"Rest up," said Vale, "I'll get it."

"No, I'm not an invalid," Cabot retorted. "I've got to pull my weight if I'm going to stay with you." She grabbed the central lever and asked, "It just engages forward, right?"

"Right," answered Vale. "The starboard winch is disconnected because of it."

"Cloaking is off," announced Cabot as the lights in the cabin seemed to brighten a notch.

"Confirmed." Vale looked at her board. "We should also think about replacing the torpedo we fired. We need an EVA for that."

"Let's deal with our Androssi friends first," said Picard.

"They're coming around to dock," replied Vale just as the Androssi salvage ship shot into view and slipped under their hull. Seconds later came the clank and thud of docking mechanisms taking hold on the cargo hatch.

"Do we have a story to keep straight?" Colleen asked.

"You know what we're looking for," said Picard grimly. "This cloaking device might be a great advantage."

There soon came a knock on the hatch. Showing that she was no invalid, Colleen jumped to her feet and pulled it open. A slender Androssi male with short-cropped auburn hair on top, long ponytail in back, and a full red beard rose slowly from the hold and took Cabot's proffered hand.

The visitor's yellowish eyes glimmered in his pale sepia face, and he gave them a ferret smile. "As promised, the Starfleet vessel did not detect you with your cloak engaged."

"Indeed, Overseer Jacer," allowed Picard. "However, you haven't told us what you want for it."

"True," said the Androssi scavenger. He glanced at their food slot and asked, "Could I trouble you for a drink of ale?"

Acting more spry than she felt, Colleen again leapt up. "I'll get it. Won't you take my seat, Overseer?"

Cabot wasn't even sure the food slot could produce any ale until she requested it, and was rewarded with a frosty mug of amber liquid.

Jacer took the beverage. "I was preparing to get a drink at the Orions' headquarters . . . when you blew it up. That's when we grew impressed with the abilities of your crew, Captain Jean."

Picard shrugged with humility. "That was more improvisation than planning."

"It showed efficiency under stress." The Androssi took a long sip of his drink and wiped his beard with the back of his slender forearm, while his audience waited for him to go on.

"As you must know," continued Overseer Jacer, "there are few humans in Rashanar who do not work for the Federation. We need you to impersonate Starfleet officers in a negotiation. To explain further, I must speak of a salvager named Fristan."

The elegant Androssi took another sip and went on. "Fristan was engaged in the dangerous but lucrative endeavor of salvaging antimatter."

"From the wrecks or wild antimatter?" asked Picard.

"Both," answered Jacer. "He was virtually the

only one who was able to harvest the wild antimatter here, although several others have died trying. Fristan ran afoul of the Pakleds, and they are holding him here in Rashanar until he repays his debts."

Picard exchanged a glance with Cabot, then smiled. "Why do you need fake Federation officers?"

Jacer shrugged. "Because we cannot appear to be the ones paying his ransom. The Pakleds have dealt with the Federation before. They would prefer to ransom Fristan to some neutral power like it, not a competitor. The latinum will come from us."

"And we show up in this old tug?" asked Vale.

"No," he replied. "We have a Starfleet shuttlecraft. We had a Starfleet yacht at one time, but lost it. You arrive, pay the ransom, take the prisoner, and leave. We have already been communicating with them by subspace to arrange the deal. You will help to facilitate it. If you succeed, the cloaking device is yours."

"What species is this Fristan?" asked Colleen.

"Androssi," replied their guest. "I'm not sorry to say that, because he is a genius. He knows many things about Rashanar—" His voice trailed off, and a look of concern graced his hairy face for a moment. "I must be going." Overseer Jacer chugged his drink and rose to his feet.

"Does he know about the demon flyer, the shapeshifter?" asked Cabot.

The Androssi whirled to face her. He looked startled, although he recovered quickly. "You've heard those tales, I see."

Cabot smiled and sat back on her bunk at the rear of the cabin. "We know it's got something to do with the antimatter."

Overseer Jacer's red eyebrows merged together, and he looked menacing for a moment. "That is not your concern. You've been well paid for this small acting job—in advance. Fristan and his knowledge will belong to *us*. We'll be back here in twenty-nine hours, and I advise you to stay out of sight until then. The Orions are not pleased with you."

He descended into the hatch, and they heard the docking clamps releasing a few seconds later. All three of the crew members of the *Skegge* watched the cobbled-together Androssi ship as it slipped away into twinkling golden clouds floating in the abject darkness of Rashanar.

"It could be a trap," said Vale. "We're just going to walk into another den of thieves?"

"They did pay us in advance," said Cabot, suddenly feeling very tired. She lay back on her bunk and added, "This Fristan sounds like a good person to know, plus we've got Wesley to protect us."

Picard frowned. "Yes, however, I'm worried about depending too much on him. You know, Counselor, this is not how a Traveler is supposed to conduct himself."

"I've got no complaints," she murmured, closing her eyes. "Good night."

Colleen woke up with Beverly Crusher staring down at her. The young woman was startled, but the doctor put a comforting hand on her shoulder and gave her a welcoming smile. "Just lie quietly," she cautioned. "My son brought you to the *Enterprise* while you were asleep. It was a good thing, too, because you had some fluid on the brain."

"But I—" Colleen looked around and saw that she was clearly in sickbay. It was too late to protest, because it had already happened—so she lay back and tried to relax.

Crusher chatted pleasantly as she took a reading on Colleen with her tricorder. "You know, you would think that someone couldn't crush your skull with the butt of a disruptor pistol, but you'd be wrong. Especially when it's an Orion swinging it."

"How long do I have to be here?" asked the counselor, keeping her eyes closed.

"At least twenty-four hours, plus light duty for a few days after that," answered the doctor solemnly.

"But the *Skegge* has a job we've agreed to do," Colleen protested, "and I need to help."

"They're discussing that now," said Crusher soothingly. "Remember, the same power you have over Jean-Luc, I have over you. If you want to go back to the *Skegge* any time soon, I suggest you be a good patient."

"Right, Doctor. So Wesley disobeyed my orders?"

Crusher laughed and folded up her tricorder. "He has disobeyed my orders too, more than a few times. But he's a good boy. I wouldn't want to see him get hurt."

"Do you think I'll hurt him?" asked Cabot in astonishment.

"I really don't know what you'll do to him," replied the concerned mother with a sigh. "But you're certainly in a position to bring him great joy or misery."

"The same power I have over him, he has over me," replied the counselor, paraphrasing the doctor's words. "However, I don't know what to do about him staying a Traveler."

Beverly shook her head and rose to her feet. "He doesn't think he can keep both lives. Really, you should start worrying more about yourself, Colleen. Go back to sleep. I'll tell Wes and the others that you've been stabilized."

Cabot gave a hoarse chuckle. "Funny, I don't feel stabilized."

Wesley Crusher trod lightly through sickbay, well aware of his mother's eyes upon him as he passed her in the triage. Nevertheless, the doctor made no effort to intercept him as he made his way to Colleen's bed in the private nooks at the rear. He didn't want to disturb her either, and he wondered what he would do if she were asleep. But Colleen must have been partly psychic, because she said "Hello, Wes!" even before he spotted her.

When he finally saw her, she was sitting up, practicing more card tricks. Even in her loose-fitting gown, she could make them appear out of thin air, although the third time she tried the sleight of hand, she dropped a card into her lap.

"Oh, rats," she pouted. "I never drop them like that. By the way, *you* abducted me against my will."

"My mom's a doctor, remember. I know she doesn't like to see other medical people about a problem. You're not invincible, you know."

Wes sat beside her on the bed. She pulled him closer for a kiss. He was gentle with her, although she wasn't nearly so gentle with him; he had to pull away and straighten his collar.

"My mom's just out there," he whispered, pointing a thumb over his shoulder.

She gave him a husky laugh. "There's something appealing about that. Oh, Wes, let's find this thing and deal with it . . . then get on with our lives, whatever they are."

"Or will be," he answered, cupping her hand. "Captain Picard made a good case for going ahead with this favor for the Androssi as long as I'm available to help you. They want to question this Fristan character, although I'm afraid it may be a trap."

"The cloaking device doesn't hurt," said Colleen. "So when am I going back to the *Skegge?*"

"When my mother says so. You still have twenty-five hours before you meet the Androssi, so there's time to heal. Did they say at all where the Pakleds are holding this master salvager, Fristan?"

"No, but you want to scout ahead."

"I would. The sooner, the better." Reluctantly he rose to his feet, and she immediately grabbed his arm.

"Can't you stay a little while longer?" she pleaded.

"Not right now. I don't know how much longer I have to be a Traveler. As soon as I return to the ship, I'll come right here."

"Be careful," she murmured, her delicate brow creased with worry. "And bring back proof."

"Proof," he replied thoughtfully. "Yes. Good-bye, Colleen." He kissed her again, but made it a mere peck.

On his way out of sickbay, Wesley stopped to talk to his mother. "Do you have a standard tricorder I could borrow?" he asked.

She pointed to a utility cabinet. "Right in there. White and blue are medical tricorders."

"Thanks, Mom." He crossed to the cabinet and grabbed a tricorder, which seemed more compact and colorful than he remembered. He checked the portable scanner/recorder and made sure it was functional.

"Where are you going?"

He decided not to say he was going to search for demon ships and Pakled scavengers. "I'm going back to the *Skegge*," he answered, glancing over his shoulder. "Take good care of her, Mom."

The doctor looked down at her work. "She means a lot to you, huh?"

"Yeah. Believe me, I didn't expect *this* to happen."

"You never know when love will bloom," replied Beverly with a knowing smile. "Just when you think you've got the universe all figured out, it pulls the rug out from under you."

"If you see Captain Riker, tell him I'll be back," said the Traveler a moment before he disappeared from sickbay and the *Starship Enterprise.*

Moving through space and dimension as if they were open doors, he arrived at the blasted hulk of the *Hickock* and made sure that the *Skegge* was safe under its saucer, or as safe as any ship could be in Rashanar. He didn't disturb Picard and Vale, because he sensed that both were using this lull to catch up on their sleep. The irony of Starfleet officers pretending to be looters who were asked to pretend to be Starfleet officers was not lost on him. Still, he hoped this was a wise decision to cooperate with the Androssi and their ransom scheme.

Moving past his comrades on the *Skegge,* the Traveler searched aimlessly through the vast graveyard, avoiding the brilliant bolts of wild energy and the more unstable wrecks. In his mind, he envisioned the Pakled scavengers he had seen at the Orions' hideout, hoping that maybe some of them were involved with the prisoner named Fristan. In due course, he came close to the center of the boneyard, where the strange gravity sink kept all the rubble swirling. The orbits of the blasted hulks tightened around the unseen power, turning the area into an eerie merry-go-round of careening derelicts. In the center, a vortex of wreckage had formed around the gravity dump; this shimmering pinwheel looked inviting and beautiful, but Wesley knew to keep far away from it.

La Forge had offered the theory that the anomaly was a remnant of the artificial gravity systems blasted to bits during the war. The released gravitons had attracted a mass before they could disperse. Now, like so many things in Rashanar, the sink had taken on a life of its own. It was the glue that kept the entire graveyard somewhat together. Unfortunately, the gravity dump also imposed a finite life span on the Rashanar remains, all of which would eventually join the spectacular maelstrom in the center of the boneyard.

As he soared through the void, the Traveler thought of the dead Pakled lying on the deck in the Orions' hideout. He had watched Picard and Vale drag the alien body down the corridor. That gruesome image conducted him to a sleek cruiser hidden under the tail of a battered Cardassian warship. He looked at this vessel—not a salvager but a warship—and he knew he had found the prison of the Androssi named Fristan.

Down in the bowels of the cruiser, the Traveler found a gathering of scurvy-looking Pakleds in a cramped torpedo room. Two dead Pakleds had been crammed into an empty photon torpedo casing. Wes realized with a start that one of them was the unlucky customer of the Orions, the one blown out the airlock. The other he didn't recognize, but it was a somber group of Pakleds who were gathered to see their comrades into the afterlife.

Amid guttural chanting, two of them loaded the corpse-laden torpedo into the tube. The eldest of the mourners contacted the bridge. As the scavengers sobbed and screamed words of revenge against unnamed enemies, the Traveler decided that he had better try to find Fristan while most of the crew was occupied. Materializing inside a dingy corridor that didn't seem wide enough to accommodate Pakleds, he hurried along, trying to avoid meeting anybody. Wes pushed on each door he passed until he found one that tingled with the energy of a forcefield, then passed through it as if they were rays of sunlight.

"No! No!" screeched a dirty, disheveled Androssi male who cowered in a corner and held up his hands at the sudden appearance of this apparition. It was a featureless cell, save for the badly stained deck and bulkheads. Wes tried to ignore the stench. "Don't beat me!" shrieked the Androssi. "Leave me alone!"

Wes realized that he still had the bulk and vague

appearance of a Pakled. He slimmed down into his own appearance as he walked forward. The Androssi peered suspiciously at him, then began waving his frail arms as if he were swatting away flies. "I don't know you! Leave me alone . . . go away!"

"Fristan, I'm here to help you," said the Traveler, holding out his hands to show they were empty. "I've been sent by Overseer Jacer."

Fristan stared suspiciously at his visitor, and he bared his teeth in a feral snarl. "I know all your tricks! You won't get me to tell you *anything*. Not anything!"

"I only want to see you freed," said Wesley, who was worried that this traumatized prisoner would never trust anyone, even those who came to pay his ransom. Wes sat cross-legged on the floor to be at Fristan's level. This seemed to calm the Androssi. At least he stopped hissing and snarling, although he stared wild-eyed at the visitor as if seeing a ghost.

"Some humans, like me, are coming to pay your ransom," explained Wesley. "Don't fight them—go with them. They will be coming to free you and take you back to Jacer."

"Jacer," echoed Fristan with a high-pitched laugh. "That *turgut* sold me to them, you know. Jacer betrayed me! He used me to squirm out of his debts, but I didn't give in. Fristan keeps his secrets. Fristan never tells. Drugs, beating—I don't care! Fristan never tells his secrets." He began to hum to himself as he picked at the six filthy toes on his right foot.

The Traveler sat a few more minutes, but the disturbed Androssi never seemed to notice him again. Or maybe he did, but his mindless humming was his coping mechanism. By the looks of his condition, Fristan had been pressured into doing a lot of coping by the Pakleds. Wes wondered what he had suffered at the hands of Overseer Jacer, because it seemed that Fristan didn't trust his fellow Androssi any more than he trusted the Pakleds.

"Do you know how to find the monster of Rashanar?" he asked. "The demon flyer?"

Fristan blinked curiously as if he had heard the buzzing of an insect around his head. Then he laughed and said, "It finds you."

"But how? How does it find you?"

The Androssi wheezed a laugh and scratched the soft fur on his concave stomach. "Fristan keeps his secrets. I know the avenger will come for these *turguts* . . . you'll see!"

"How?" insisted Wesley. "If you tell me, I'll save you from the Pakleds and Jacer—I'll take you to the Federation for safety."

"For safety?" cackled Fristan. "Safety in *here*? No one is safe, you will all die." His laughter degenerated into a coughing fit, and he lay down on the filthy deck.

Wes couldn't allow himself to give up when he didn't know how long this madman would stay alive.

"What does the antimatter have to do with it? Why do the Ontailians expel antimatter?"

The Androssi pouted, groaned, and poked at his stomach. *"They* don't know anything. All guessing . . . all fools. All pathetic fools." He went back to humming contentedly.

Wes got up and stood over Fristan. "If I save you from all your enemies, will you tell me your secrets?"

"Die first," answered Fristan with a snicker. "All of you will die first."

Figuring this was getting him nowhere, the Traveler assumed the form of a Pakled and stepped back into the narrow corridor. The crew members were coming back from their memorial service in the cramped torpedo room. One squeezed past him without paying him any attention. The Traveler decided to make a stop at the bridge of the cruiser before he went back to the *Enterprise.*

The Pakleds seemed to have enough crew for a starship six times bigger, so Wes was able to easily blend in with the onlookers on the bridge. Spotting the elder he had seen below, he assumed he was the captain of this vessel. The white-haired eminence scratched the bushy eyebrows that consumed most of his forehead and peered thoughtfully at the readouts on a console.

"Buoy number two reports no contact," he said. "What about the distress signal?"

"We've modified it again to duplicate the Ontailians' frequency," answered a younger officer, "but maybe we're still off."

The Pakled elder scowled. "Is there anything else we can get out of him before we sell him?"

A female officer snapped her fingers. "His brain is gone. He speaks only gibberish now."

Wesley edged closer to the captain and the station that was of so much interest to him. He got a glimpse of some coordinates a moment before a brutish officer pushed him back with a grunt. Immediately the Traveler began to fade into the background and was gone before anyone else noticed that he was there.

He found the Pakled's buoy in a fairly expansive part of Rashanar, with few dusty hulks to attract the errant energy bolts. Wispy clouds of silver debris drifted by, making it look like a Terran sky seen in a photographic negative. There was so much open space, he decided, that even the *Enterprise* could get in here to service this device, which was disguised to look like the Rashanar's Federation buoys.

To him, the buoy appeared inactive. He couldn't sense any signal or power output—just another chunk of dead metal floating in the graveyard. Detached from everything, floating in space, it seemed important to connect with something, so Wes touched the protruding antenna tips and ran his hand down the shielding onto a disc that illuminated at his touch. At once, the buoy began to vibrate and emit both signal and radiation. The Traveler didn't have to guess at this, because he turned on his tricorder and began to take readings. He felt a pang of guilt, because he was supposed to be recording events for the Travelers, not for Starfleet with this inferior mechanical device.

What if I lose their trust and the ability to do this? Is anything—Colleen, my mother, Starfleet—worth giving up these gifts and becoming mortal again? The only answer he could think of was the *Enterprise.* A need to protect his ship had brought him to Rashanar in the first place and was drawing him deeper and deeper, like the gravity sink at the center of the vortex.

Wesley hadn't realized his mind had been wandering until an actual shadow passed over him, and the buoy went silent once again. His tricorder stopped working. Silvery debris began to pop and explode like magical popcorn—like matter annihilated by antimatter.

With sheer dread, already feeling faint, the Traveler looked up to see an amorphous black shape, rippling and shimmering on the edges where it obliterated the space dust. Wes watched awestruck, barely breathing, while the entity writhed and seethed like a neon amoeba as big as a house. It gradually took on an outline that was familiar to him—a compact hull with twin warp nacelles below her sleek underbelly. *What ship is that?* he thought in panic.

With horror, Wes whirled around to see the Pakled cruiser approaching their position at a good rate of speed. "No!" Wesley cried, although no one could possibly hear him in the twilight universe between matter and antimatter.

Chapter Ten

WITH EFFORT, Wesley tried to focus on escape while annihilation danced before his eyes. Remaining dark except for its glittering edges, the massive shapeshifter assembled itself like a giant origami paper structure, molded by unseen hands. Wesley could feel the lens of every Traveler focusing on him and his plight. It took all of them to rip him away from the ominous presence. It seemed to want his soul . . . to possess him . . . become him. Before Wesley fully gained his senses, he stumbled onto the bridge of the Pakled ship. In his true form, he grabbed the thick lapels of the Pakled elder, who stared in horror at this mad human who had suddenly appeared.

"What?! Who are you?!" yelped the captain.

"You've got to get out of here . . . right now!" He pointed out the viewport, but there was nothing to see. Their sensors were probably fooled. By the time they got close enough to see it, they'd be dead. "The demon flyer is out there! You're almost on top of it!"

"Security!" called the captain. Wes barely had time to squirm away as two beefy Pakleds dove for him.

The Traveler was shoved hard from behind and landed on the deck, where his captors could easily pummel him. As one grabbed him by the scruff of the neck, the lights on the bridge began to flicker. The weightless sensation came only seconds later, and every console on the bridge went dark.

"What's happening?" roared someone. "Aren't shields up?"

"Yes, but all systems are failing!" The officer pounded his board in futility as he floated off his seat.

Realizing there was no time to save the Pakled crew, Wesley focused anew and brought himself to Fristan's cell. It was already dark, but he could see the vague outline of the battered prisoner floating in the gloom.

"It's come!" he whispered. "I told you!" The Androssi cackled insanely and began to sing.

"We're not staying to meet it!" shouted Wesley, grabbing the slender humanoid and hauling him twenty kilometers into the boneyard.

The frightened salvager clung to him like a monkey and stared wild-eyed at the space rubble and dusty derelicts surrounding them. "I don't understand," he muttered.

Wesley felt defeated and wondering if it was his fault for tripping the buoy . . . only to draw the monster to them.

The Traveler pointed into the distance. The fragile Androssi followed with his eyes and saw two identical Pakled cruisers. Their shiny newness glistened in the junkyard like jewels among brass. From this distance, Wes couldn't tell which one was real and which was the shapeshifter. They had the appearance of art-deco bookends holding a field of stars between them.

"How am I standing in space?" asked Fristan, sounding very rational.

"I'll tell you later," said the Traveler. He glanced down to see that his tricorder was still dead; even his senses felt dulled, as if he had almost passed out. "Let me take you somewhere you'll be safe."

"Safe?" asked Fristan with a chuckle. "You are funny, human. *Safe* he says!"

The Androssi was still tittering when they showed up on the *Enterprise* bridge, where Riker was in deep discussion with Troi and his mother. They looked at him and his traveling companion with curiosity and broke off their conversation.

"I like it," said Fristan, looking around the sumptuous bridge. "Won't help . . . but cheerful."

"Captain," said Wesley, trying not to sound as panicked as he felt. "I've seen it out there—the replicating ship. It . . . it attacked a Pakled vessel. That's where I rescued Fristan."

"Can we reach them in time?" asked Riker, striding forward.

"Yes, but I don't know if we should," answered Wes. "I mean, we don't really know what to do with this thing. However, we could track it from a distance." He moved toward Data at the conn.

Fristan hooted. "Yes, you should chase it! You *must*. It likes to play tag, it does!"

While Wesley gave Data the coordinates, Riker turned to Deanna and said, "Counselor, will you please make our visitor more comfortable."

"Certainly," said Troi with her most cheerful smile. Wesley didn't pay much attention to their conversation, but Troi was quickly able to win Fristan over and conduct him off the bridge.

"Captain," said Data from the conn, "these coordinates are on the other side of Rashanar. The best available path we can take will get us there in forty-two minutes. The *Skegge* is closer and could take a more direct route, reaching the site in half that time."

"And what could the *Skegge* do?" asked Beverly Crusher.

"They've got a cloak," answered Wes. "They might be able to trail the demon ship, but we'll have to come back in time to meet the Androssi."

"Don't take any chances," warned Riker, looking sternly at the young man. "You can escape from almost anything; however, I don't want to lose Picard and Vale."

"Wesley," asked his mom, "did you feel as if you were affected by the presence of this thing?"

He nodded slowly. "Yes. I felt as if I needed the focus of all my fellow Travelers in order to escape."

"Then you stay away from it," ordered his mother in no uncertain terms. "When you go off by yourself, you're all alone out there. There's no one to help you or to even tell us that you need help. Use the *Skegge,* but don't go after this entity on your own. Will you promise me that?"

The young man gulped, realizing he had been taking a substantial risk, especially with the presence of wild antimatter. He turned to the android. "Data, here's a tricorder I used to monitor the anomaly. It died, but maybe you can get something off it. We'll check in from the *Skegge* and tell you our status." Without waiting for a response, the Traveler vanished from the bridge of the *Enterprise.*

Jean-Luc Picard poured himself another cup of tea and tried to keep from pacing across the cabin of the *Skegge.* He held up the pot, offering some to Christine Vale, but she politely declined and turned to view the distant light show intermittently illuminating the hulking wrecks and clouds of glitter.

"I dislike waiting," said the captain, employing a smile to make his statement sound less like a complaint. "I would prefer to be on the offensive. Of course, we need more information. Maybe this Fristan can give it to us." Thoughtfully he sipped his tea, wishing they had a bona fide plan.

"Well, I slept very well," bragged Lieutenant Vale, "better than I have in months. This is kind of a peaceful place, as long as you're hiding out."

"It's not peaceful anymore," said a somber voice.

They both turned around to see Wesley in the bow of the craft, entering coordinates into the conn.

"Wesley!" said Picard with relief. "We were wondering what the next move should be."

"Captain, I've seen the mimic ship." Crusher never looked up from his grim task. "It's out there right now, replicating a Pakled cruiser. Allow me to take the controls."

"Make it so. Will the cloak help us?"

"I don't know," answered Wesley, dropping into the pilot's seat. "I don't intend to get close enough to be in danger. The *Enterprise* can't get there as fast as we can, because we have to go right through the center."

"You can't use the cloak and the engines at the same time," Vale reminded them. "What about the Androssi?"

"I rescued Fristan from the Pakleds, so dealing with them is pointless—unless we turn Fristan over to them in exchange for the cloaking device." Taking the trimpot controls in hand, he piloted the little tug out from under the *Hickock*'s saucer section and sputtered away into the haunted darkness.

After they were under way, he brought Picard and Vale up to date on what he had seen. "I know it's real now, Captain. I know I'm in danger too. Everything made of matter is in danger."

Picard sat in the seat nearest his old comrade. "What do you think it is, Wesley?"

The young man frowned and finally said, "The nearest I can suggest is that it uses matter-antimatter conversion. It's almost more biological than mechanical. Converting into matter, it has to have a form, so it picks the closest living spaceship and replicates it, the way a cancer cell mimics a healthy cell and feeds off it. Maybe it's not a force weapon, but a kind of succubus. It sucks the life out of them. I'm sure it's attracted by a distress signal, which I unwittingly set off."

"That makes sense," answered Picard. "On our previous trip, the first Ontailian ship we saw expelling antimatter—they also set off a distress signal. Later the Ontailians denied that their ship had even been in the area."

"Things started going downhill after that," added Vale.

"You know," said Wes, "there's a theory that antimatter can't exist in such small amounts as we find it or create it. There has to be a whole antimatter universe equivalent to ours, existing right beside us. Perhaps there is some seepage between the two—or a doorway. If there can be living matter, why can't there be living antimatter?"

Vale sighed. "Now you're starting to scare me, Wes. The Travelers don't even know about this?"

"They didn't before, but they do now." The young man made a course adjustment to skirt around a scorched Jem'Hadar derelict, then continued zooming toward the flashes of light in the center of the graveyard. "Like Data, I've seen it up close, but I can't tell you what it is."

"I hear Cabot's voice in my mind," muttered Picard, "saying that if it's a living thing we shouldn't destroy it."

"Yeah, I know how she feels," answered a frustrated Wes. "But I don't agree, not after seeing it. Maybe this thing is not malevolent, but it kills us the way you would step on an insect."

"If this is the Ontailians' demon flyer," said Picard, "then it's also been around for hundreds of years."

"And they've been feeding it, appeasing it." Wes narrowed his eyes, concentrating on his flying. They were reaching a dangerous part of the boneyard, near the center, where the gravity sink had drawn lots of company in swirling, crashing orbits. Picard folded his hands, watching Crusher, thinking that maturity and experience had only magnified his old skills. Wes almost never checked their position; he seemed to be piloting by instinct. If he weren't a

Traveler, wondered Picard, would he be able to fly like this?

The captain peered out the convex viewport at the debris that sparkled off their shields; he flinched as larger, more dangerous chunks barely missed hitting them. Wes had nerves of titanium with an admirable sense of purpose, but Picard could feel their quarry slipping away. Maybe it was the young man's urgency that convinced him that they may have missed their opportunity.

As they neared their destination, Wes's shoulders slumped. He began to check his coordinates and sensors. He stopped when they spotted a sleek, fairly modern starship rotating slowly in the middle of some sparkly rubble. It was a new addition to the forlorn shipwrecks, but it looked as if it belonged.

"A Pakled overcruiser," said Picard. "Not much of a salvage craft but good for maintaining order."

"There's only one," replied Wes, stating the obvious. "The duplicate is gone."

"Caution," warned the captain. "We don't know how far away it went. There's not enough debris for the cruiser to have been destroyed. You say the demon ship should look like that?"

"Yes," answered Wes, sounding relieved that his captain believed him. "Exactly like that."

Vale cleared her throat and asked, "I thought this thing destroyed the ship it turned into?"

"It can't do only that," answered Picard, "or every

ship in Rashanar would be space dust. The *Vuxhal* and the *Calypso* were both destroyed, but this one was left. Why?"

"I'll have to go aboard," said Wes grimly.

The captain put his hand on the Traveler's shoulder. "*We* will have to go aboard, but not until we make sure this one won't explode, too. Vale, take my seat and send a status report to the *Enterprise* via subspace. If they want to make their way here, that's fine. Tell them we'll be cloaked."

"Aye, sir."

"I'm changing into my EV suit," said Picard.

"You don't need that, not if you're with me," Wes offered.

"Mr. Crusher," said the captain, "I'm very glad to have you back, and I do marvel at your abilities. However, we can't continue to depend on them—we have to wean ourselves off them. Perhaps you do, too."

The young man was quiet for a moment. "How close do you want to get, Captain?"

"Get close enough for sensors to return useful data. Let's monitor the Pakled ship for a few minutes. For all we know, *that* could be the duplicate. If it's not, at least now we know how to attract it."

They stared at the dark Pakled cruiser revolving slowly in the glittering emptiness of space. Ghostly wrecks surrounded the clearing, forming a silent audience of dead witnesses.

* * *

Deanna Troi sat in her favorite chair in her office, where she saw most of her patients, and studied the elder Androssi who was asleep on her couch. She had taken Fristan to sickbay, where Ogawa had cleaned him up and given him a brief examination. Except for his obvious bruises, contusions, and signs of abuse, he seemed to be in normal physical health. However, his mental state was a different story.

She didn't wish to wake him, but they only had fourteen hours before their away team was due to turn him over to his fellow Androssi. If there was anything to be learned from Fristan, if there were any breakthroughs to be made, they had a finite time in which to do it.

"Why does everybody want you?" she asked rhetorically, more to herself. "You don't look all that impressive."

"Neither does that human of yours who can race through space without a ship or a spacesuit," said Fristan, who didn't move or open his eyes. "But he is impressive."

"Wesley," replied Deanna with a smile. "So why do they all want to hold you prisoner?"

He shrugged. "Fristan is valuable, he is. Not for what he does . . . but for what he knows." He pointed to his skull and laughed.

"Do you want us to turn you over to Overseer Jacer? They want you back."

"Why? *Why!*" he shouted, growing agitated.

"I didn't tell them my secrets before, and I not tell now! Jacer not my friend . . . Wesley is my friend."

"Calm down," she whispered, gently touching his shoulder. "You're safe with us. If you don't want to go back to Jacer and your own people, where do you want to go?"

The Androssi sat up. "I want my ship, my crew. But all dead. Thieves took it all from me, because I won't tell. They beat me, torture me—they don't find the cache." Acting as if he had said too much, Fristan rolled over on the couch and turned his back to Deanna.

"Aren't you afraid of what's out there?" she asked. "The demon ship?"

"Ha-ha!" he crowed. "The Avenger will find my enemies. I pray for it to come, I do."

"Just remember, we're not your enemies." Her combadge beeped. "Troi here."

"It's me," said Riker. "How is our guest doing?"

She rose from her chair, then walked to the opposite end of her office, keeping her voice down. "He seems convinced that he knows something everybody in Rashanar wants to find out."

"If he knows anything, he's ahead of us," said Riker. "We're about to arrive at the *Skegge*'s position near the Pakled cruiser."

"I thought the Pakled ship was destroyed."

That brought a cackle of joy from Fristan. "Destroyed! All of them destroyed!"

"Evidently not," Riker acknowledged. "I could use you on the bridge."

She glanced back at the Androssi, who was humming in a raspy singsong voice. "I'll have to bring my patient—I want to keep an eye on him."

"All right. I'll have security here to help you keep an eye on him. Riker out."

Just then her door chimed. She pressed the panel on her desk to open it, and Colleen Cabot sauntered in.

"Hello, Counselor." She eyed Fristan curiously, who looked back at her with interest. "I'm sorry, I didn't mean to disturb you."

"Aren't you supposed to be in sickbay?" asked Troi.

"I couldn't lie down any longer. I was getting bedsores. Besides, I hear we're supposed to rendezvous with the *Skegge*. I want to get back to *my* patient."

"Ah," said Troi knowingly. "You're hoping I'll back you up in your effort to return to duty."

"Something like that," admitted Colleen. "I'm fine now, really."

Fristan jumped off the couch and cautiously approached the young woman, who gave him a placid professional smile. "Who are you?" she asked.

He peered at her. "Fristan I am. Are you a goddess?"

"Only in my own mind. Why are you here?"

"Wesley saved me. He's my friend." Reverently

the Androssi touched Colleen's flowing blond hair. To her credit, she didn't flinch a muscle.

"He's my special friend," whispered Cabot. She held out her arm. "Come on, shall we go to the bridge and talk to Captain Riker?"

The scrawny Androssi grinned, showing a mouthful of missing teeth, and gleefully took Cabot's arm. Troi sighed, knowing she had just lost a patient.

"You go ahead," Troi told them. "I want to check on the Ontailians in the brig before I go there."

"Ontailians?" Fristan started, turning in the doorway. "You have captured Ontailians?"

"Yes," Deanna answered hopefully. "Can you tell me anything about them?"

"Be careful." He wagged a finger at her. "Martyrs they be! Don't turn your back on them. Martyrs all . . . and fools."

"Thanks," said Deanna doubtfully. Cabot led him into the corridor, no doubt discussing Wesley. The Androssi's words disturbed Troi; in fact, so did Rashanar and this whole mission. As much as she loved Will, it wasn't right for anyone but Picard to be captain of the *Enterprise*.

The counselor was still in a worrisome mood when she reached the brig, which was guarded by only one security officer. However, she found Beverly Crusher standing in front of the forcefield barrier that separated them from the only occupants of the cells. The multitude of Ontailians had ample food, water, and trellises suited to their taste, but these amenities were untouched. The gravity was normal for the *Enterprise,* so they could move. Still the slender, long-armed, slothlike creatures lay huddled on the deck, looking more dead than alive.

Beverly had a medical tricorder in her hand, and she finished taking her readings. "Hello, Deanna. I was just trying to figure out what would be the best way to start feeding our guests."

"Leave them be," the Betazoid replied. "This is what they chose for themselves."

"That sounds awfully coldhearted. It wouldn't be that much trouble to force-feed them."

"They won't crawl half a meter to get food," said Troi. "I'm beginning to understand them and this is what they want."

Crusher sighed. "They can't go without water in our gravity more than two more days. If no other solution presents itself, I start beaming them out before they die."

"Just be careful with them," Troi warned. "I've got it on a good source."

Crusher looked intently at her, but Deanna didn't avert her dark eyes. "All right," said the doctor. "But you start thinking of an alternative to letting them die."

"By the way," remarked the counselor, "your other patient is running around up on the bridge, with my patient, Fristan, who is now enamored of her. Will you please let her go back to the *Skegge?*"

Beverly tapped her combadge. "Crusher to bridge."

"Riker here," came an exasperated voice. "I'm glad it's you. I've got Colleen Cabot in my face, and she demands to go back to the *Skegge* or . . . you know what she'll do. She says she'll take Fristan with her, and now he wants to go as well."

"Tell them to report to sickbay," replied Crusher. "I want to look at both her and Fristan one more time. If they pass, I'll release them."

"Thank you, Doctor, Riker out."

As they walked out of the brig, Troi glanced over her shoulder at the eerie sight of the lethargic Ontailians. It was disturbing to think that prisoners were committing suicide on the *Enterprise*. They had no way to even return them home. She was also worried that Fristan was right, and this was all a ruse to lull the captors into making a mistake. Either way, the Ontailians would die as martyrs or succeed as heroes. *In a way,* she decided, *that's what we're doing.*

Captain Picard waited patiently outside a gangplank on the belly of the Pakled cruiser while his companion opened it from inside. Although he had insisted that Wesley wear a spacesuit when he went inside the derelict cruiser, he let him go inside using his special ability. They could have drilled or blasted their way in, but that would have sucked out any air. They still had hope that some of the Pakleds were alive. It was too dangerous to use a transporter, even if the *Skegge* had one. Picard bore his jet pack and bulky suit but felt better having some autonomy from Crusher. If they had a Traveler at their disposal all the time, they would soon forget how to dock or send a subspace message.

The hatch finally popped open and hung below the struts. This design indicated that the overcruiser could make surface landings. Picard maneuvered close enough to reach the Traveler's outstretched hand, and Wes pulled him into the weightless airlock. Here Picard was thankful for his magnetized boots, which allowed him to walk slowly. It was dark except for the beams on their helmets, and Picard turned on a hand light as well.

Crusher closed the outer hatch and waited a few seconds. "Life-support, gravity, everything is dead," he pointed out, his voice sounding hollow in Picard's headgear. "I don't want to risk losing any air."

"Understood," said the captain, although the possibility of any of the crew being alive was remote.

"I noticed that their buoy was destroyed," said the Traveler. "There's debris which may account for it. That's where the distress signal came from."

"Is that why this ship was spared?" asked Picard. "It wasn't the source of the distress signal?"

"I don't know." The young man pulled a lever and had to manually release the inner hatch that led into the corridor. He stepped through, seemingly walking on air, as Picard clomped after him.

Listening to each other's breathing, Picard and Crusher slowly made their way down the narrow corridor. Their wavering beams cast intermittent streaks of light against the bulkheads, but the darkness remained thick. Wes stopped at an open access panel and tried to close it to get past; instead a bulky object floated out of the compartment. Picard realized it was a body. The bloated Pakled stared at them with unseeing eyes as he bobbed in their crossed beams, drops of blood floating from his flared nostrils. His face had blisters and boils as if it had ruptured from within. Without flinching, Wesley pushed the corpse into the next compartment, which seemed to be a central hub with a ladder leading up a broad access tube.

"Can you tell how he died?" asked Picard.

"Radiation poisoning, I would guess," answered Wes. "The tricorder readings don't make a lot of sense." He looked around, his light illuminating dark corners of the disabled ship. "I was on this cruiser twice before. There's a torpedo room beyond this hatch, a brig back on the deck above us, and the bridge two decks above us."

"Let's go to the bridge," said the captain.

Effortlessly, Wes flew into the access tube above their heads, while Picard had to turn off his boots and jump to reach the opening. Wesley caught him by the wrist, guiding his gloved hand to the rung. After that, Picard was able to pull himself easily in the zero gravity, despite his bulky suit.

"This ship had a big crew," said Wes. "I expect to find a lot of bodies."

"Where is the engine room?" Picard inquired as they glided upward.

"I was never there. Is there something in particular you're looking for?"

"Yes, the matter-antimatter reactor."

"We'll find it," promised the Traveler.

When they reached the bridge, it looked like a holiday parade with a dozen large balloons tethered to floats. Only these weren't festive balloons but dead Pakleds. Like the first one, they appeared to have burns and blisters on their skin. Starlight spilled in through the large viewport, and the grim scene was brightly illuminated by energy bolts in the distance. Solemnly they moved enough of the floating bodies to check the dark consoles and unresponsive controls. *Without refurbishing the Pakled cruiser, there is nothing to be learned from this collection of dead circuits,* thought Picard.

Wesley found a plaque with a cross-section of the cruiser embossed upon it, and he shined his light across the image. "The engine room takes up all three decks in the stern," he pointed out.

"Let's go."

Although they could have arrived there in the

blink of an eye with the Traveler's powers, Picard wanted to move by normal albeit ponderous means, giving them time to look around at the dead ship. He didn't know what he expected to find, except for the eerie similarities between this newly murdered ship and the hulks that had been haunting Rashanar for some time. The captain couldn't help but wonder how far away the demon ship had gotten. They were too late to chase their quarry, but there would be a next time. They would make sure of that.

This is an entity which willingly hunts and kills with no remorse and no more thought than a human takes a breath, decided the captain. *Its reign of terror has to end.*

Plodding along through the depressing corridors and tubes, Picard could barely keep Wesley in sight ahead of him. The Traveler's light often glimmered dimly far ahead, until the young man stopped to take tricorder readings or move a bloated corpse.

In due time, they reached the engine room, and Wesley had turned his torch into a lantern to give them more light to study it. Like the rest of the ship, it was remarkably clean and intact, but completely lifeless. Dead crewmembers had gathered in a corner; Picard wondered if momentum or air currents had carried them there. The captain fumbled for his tricorder, but he saw that Wes was taking readings near the reactor core and other parts of the propulsion system. Picard trudged across the deck, thinking that this ship had been a vibrant cocoon for a collection of living beings only half an hour ago. Now it was just a shiny mausoleum.

"Odd," Wesley remarked. "There's no antimatter in the reactor. There should be. This ship has conventional warp drive."

"If we thought this ship had been through a battle like the other derelicts, we wouldn't be concerned with an absence of antimatter. We would assume it had been dispersed in a hull rupture or a core breach."

"How did this antimatter get out?" asked Wes.

"I would look for a minute breach somewhere," answered the captain. "Maybe a crack in the conduits that carry antimatter from the storage units or in the venting units. You know, when all systems fail, so do the antigrav containment fields that keep the antimatter stable."

Even through his clear faceplate, Wes's face registered surprise, then dawning realization. "That would be enough to blow up a ship as a side effect. If this thing is stealing antimatter from its prey . . . that's like delicately poking a hole in an eggshell and sucking out what's inside. One small slip and boom."

"If you were this predator, how would you learn the workings of a ship well enough to take its antimatter in such a manner?"

"By scanning it and replicating it," answered

Wes grimly. "Almost biological reverse-engineering. If a captured craft had no antimatter, like the *Calypso*, destruction would be the result of this probing."

The young man heaved his shoulders in his heavy suit. "Too bad we don't have any proof of this. We would need a team to go over this ship with a fine-toothed comb, and they would need plenty of time and luck. Are you saying this creature is the same as an antimatter asteroid?"

The captain shook his head. "I don't know. But it must have a natural form when it's not imitating its prey. You saw it."

"I'm not sure *what* I saw. All I know is I'm not anxious to see it again. You know, Captain, we're only going to get one chance at this thing."

"We'd better be ready," said Picard through clenched teeth. Suddenly static filled his headgear. He groaned in pain, until he thought he heard a voice trying to break through the interference.

Wes also bent over as if in pain, and he gripped the captain's arm. "Excuse me, I have to go. Just for a second."

With that, the Traveler disappeared, leaving Captain Picard alone in the shiny crypt. The dead beings marooned in the corner seemed to be smiling at him, wanting to welcome him to their ghostly crew. The human couldn't ever recall being abandoned in a more macabre place than this, and was quite relieved when Wesley reappeared a moment later.

With urgency, Wes grabbed his arm. "Captain, a Pakled cruiser like this one is headed right toward us. There's no time—"

"Get us back!" Under the circumstances, Picard didn't resist using the uncanny abilities of a Traveler to escape. He only hoped they could flee before the predator condemned the *Skegge* to this appalling fate.

Chapter Eleven

CAPTAIN PICARD STUMBLED in the cabin of the *Skegge,* and was surprised when Colleen Cabot caught him. A giggle caused him to look up and see an unfamiliar, rather scurvy-looking Androssi staring at him. Wesley popped magically out of his suit and stood beside it as it collapsed to the floor.

Christine Vale sat in the pilot's seat, fearlessly manning the *Skegge's* controls. "I'm doing what I told everyone not to do," she announced. "We're retreating with the cloak still on."

"Make it so," barked Picard. With Cabot's help, he pulled off his helmet and asked, "What about the *Enterprise?*"

"We were cloaked," answered Wesley. "The Pakled ship is making directly for the *Enterprise.*

They've got no place to hide, and they can't outrun the cruiser in the graveyard."

The lights dimmed, and the artificial gravity seemed to lessen, making Picard feel light-footed as Colleen helped him out of his EV suit. "I take it you got a clean bill of health," he said to the counselor.

"Yep, and it looks like I made it back just in time." They were clearly moving and none too soon, because a Pakled overcruiser identical to the first one was bearing down on their position. Wesley dropped into the secondary-console seat and started running sensor scans.

Picard took a step behind the young Traveler. "Are those two ships really the same?" he asked.

"That's what I'm trying to figure out. These sensors aren't precise enough. It's definitely the same class. Now I'm losing the data entirely."

Under Vale's piloting, they were pulling away so fast from the approaching duplicate that the sensors became useless—they were back to relying on their eyes alone.

"What's the *Enterprise* doing?" asked Picard worriedly.

"They're holding their ground," answered Vale, "but there's really nowhere for them to run. They could be hailing each other on subspace, and we wouldn't know."

Wes turned to look at the captain. "I could check on them."

Picard was considering that option when Colleen stepped between them. "No, Wes," she insisted. "You're on *this* crew. You can't make a whole starship disappear, so what can you do to protect them?"

"I agree," Picard said firmly. "Stay with us until we know what the danger is."

The old Androssi in the rear suddenly concurred. "Stay with me, Wesley! Don't leave me!"

A bright flash from the graveyard almost blinded them. At first Picard feared that they'd been hit by an errant bolt of energy. Vale struggled with the controls for a moment, then she slowed down and cut engines to let their momentum carry them.

With relief in his voice, Wesley reported, "The Pakleds have fired phasers! No damage to the *Enterprise*."

The captain let out a pent-up breath and turned to his counselor and their Androssi visitor. "You must be Fristan," he remarked. He waggled his finger at the elder. "Behave yourself and we'll keep you safe."

Fristan made a mock salute. "*Safe* he says! Hoo-hoo! Another one who wants to die."

Picard tried to shake off that unexpected and disturbing response.

"Vale," ordered the captain, "take us to maximum visual range and keep them both in sight. Maintain cloak, then send subspace to the *Enter-*

prise that we're all right. As soon as we know they're out of danger, I want to get back to the *Hickock.* I want to be early for our rendezvous with the Androssi. If we're going to conquer this thing, we need to start getting some cooperation from our neighbors."

"What are we going to tell the Androssi about Fristan?" asked Wes in a low voice. "They're not expecting him to be here."

Picard glanced over his shoulder at the deranged former prisoner and the dedicated counselor who was trying to comfort him. "I don't know," he admitted. "Maybe they'll look at him and realize he's not worth fighting over."

"Those damned idiots," muttered Riker under his breath, leaning forward in the command chair. "Shooting off phasers in the middle of Rashanar? They're not the sharpest knives in the cupboard. Mr. Erwin, send them another subspace message that we didn't kill their comrades, we tried to rescue them."

"They didn't answer the last one," said the Bolian. "But I will resend."

"Shields are holding," said Data as another phaser blast gently jarred them. "To continue this one-sided bombardment will risk plasma discharges and energy arcs. If we run, we may come close to the derelicts and make it easy for them to destroy us."

"I know," answered Riker, jumping out of his chair. He glanced at Deanna.

"They are very angry," she said unhelpfully.

Riker fumed. "I'm glad the away team is cloaked."

"Captain!" called Erwin, intently studying his board. "Coming in on subspace . . . the *Skegge* reports normal, code one."

"Data, take over the weapons systems. Target the incapacitated ship with pinpoint phaser and take off a nacelle. Ignore the one firing at us."

"Aye, sir. Targeting complete."

"Fire."

A narrow beam, hardly visible, streaked across the blackness in the surreal confines of Rashanar and struck the crippled ship, shearing off the port nacelle in an impressive display of marksmanship.

"That got a response out of them, sir," said Lieutenant Erwin. "They say we are cowards and heathens because we're trifling with their dead."

"Tell them we'll *vaporize* their dead if they don't stop firing at us," ordered Riker. "Conn, take us closer to the crippled cruiser—try to get it between them and us."

"Yes, sir," answered Kell Perim. They made a careful circuit around a few pockets of rubble in order to get a good shot at both cruisers, while making it difficult for the active one to fire at them without hitting their fallen comrades. At any rate, the Pakleds had stopped firing.

The situation under control, Riker straightened his tunic, stepping back toward his command chair. "Mr. Erwin, tell the Pakleds to inspect their damaged ship and conduct their inquiry. They'll find that it wasn't us. We will welcome contact with them later. However, we're leaving now. If we're followed, we'll destroy both of their ships. Have you got all that?"

"Yes, sir," answered the Bolian. "Transmitting."

"Mr. Perim, plot a course back to the vicinity of the *Hickock,* safest route."

"Yes, sir." They watched the Pakled cruiser while beating a slow retreat into the graveyard. When they neared the closest derelict, they were extra vigilant, fearing the Pakleds might fire wildly in hope of starting a deadly chain reaction. But their foe had apparently decided to let them leave, since they were busy trying to dock with the disabled vessel. The *Enterprise* crew remained cautious until the Pakleds were a distant blur among the rest of the bones in the yard.

"We are out of effective sensor range with the Pakled cruiser," announced Data. "They would have difficulty following us. No sign of any other vessels of the same class."

"Good," breathed Riker. "Mr. Erwin, send subspace to the *Skegge* and tell them that we've escaped from our friends. We're taking our time going back."

"Very good, sir."

More to himself than anyone else, Riker said, "We need a plan or we'll be chasing our own tails . . . until something bad happens again."

He stared glumly at the viewscreen, watching distant eruptions illuminate the ghostly silhouettes of Rashanar. After a moment, Will detected a pleasant fragrance and a welcome presence to his right. Deanna put a hand on his shoulder and gave him an encouraging smile.

"We haven't been here very long," she said. "We'll figure out the right way to handle this."

"Those cruisers aren't salvage vessels," Riker admitted. "What are the Pakleds doing here?"

"We know they've been kidnapping people, collecting ransom, making deals, running a tavern, and acting like gangsters. With the Federation vessels officially gone from Rashanar, the scavengers are getting bolder and better organized. They've formed syndicates which need protection from other competitors. Hence, the need for warships and rougher tactics."

"You're probably right," muttered Riker. "And the Ontailians seem to be preoccupied with keeping everyone *inside* the graveyard. You can check in, but you can't check out."

"Like the battle of Rashanar all over again," said Troi softly, her brow knitted in thought. "What if they did this during the original battle? What if the Ontailians surrounded the site, letting no one get out . . . for fear of letting *it* out?"

"Let's hope the outcome is different this time." Something bright splattered against their forward shields, and he added, "Slow and steady, Lieutenant."

"Yes, sir," answered Kell Perim.

"You see, Wes, I'm definitely needed on this mission," said Colleen with a coy smile. "The *Skegge* may be a small craft, but I've already got two patients. That's half the crew."

Crusher shifted uneasily on the deck, where he was sitting cross-legged as there were no more chairs left. The traumatized Fristan was asleep on the bunk, exhaustion finally taking its toll on him. Colleen was seated at the rear station. While Vale piloted and Picard navigated, she was trying to cheer Wes up; he had been subdued ever since seeing the Pakled cruiser fall prey to the mimic ship.

"It's not your fault," she said, taking his hand in hers. "You touched a buoy. That's what you're supposed to do here—investigate. You were meant to see its transformation and tell us about it. Do you think it's a living creature?"

"That's a good question. And don't tell me we've got to capture it alive. If you ever saw this thing up close, you would realize that we don't have a cage big enough to hold it."

"Fristan claims he can control it," whispered Colleen, pointing to the snoozing Androssi. "He calls it his Avenger."

Wes looked skeptical. "Does he? If it weren't for me, his little pet would have killed him along with everyone else on that cruiser. Little by little, we're learning about it. With every bit of knowledge comes a chance to beat it."

Colleen sat beside him on the deck and put her head on his shoulder. "I don't suppose we can sneak off somewhere for an hour or so?" she whispered.

He laughed. "I thought you said my place was here on the *Skegge*. Besides, I'm afraid Rashanar doesn't have any romantic getaway spots."

"We could make one," she suggested.

"Look alive," said Picard. "The Androssi are at the *Hickock*, waiting for us."

Wes jumped to his feet, then helped Colleen to hers. "I thought our meeting wasn't for another six hours."

"Apparently it's been moved up," answered Picard. Their cloaking had been turned off ever since they made their escape from the grieving, angry Pakleds, so they couldn't hide their presence.

Colleen glanced at the sleeping Fristan, telling herself that she wouldn't let the captain give the Androssi up. The demon ship was the only thing Picard wanted, and she doubted whether Overseer Jacer and his colleagues could produce the scourge of Rashanar. She crossed her arms and watched while Christine Vale carefully piloted them to their unofficial home port under the battered saucer section of the *Hickock*. The Androssi salvage ship immediately maneuvered under their bow, looking to dock. The counselor couldn't see any real place to hide Fristan.

"How are we going to explain Wesley?" she pointed out. "He wasn't here any of the times we met with them."

"I can make myself scarce," responded Wesley.

Picard quickly realized that once again, quite against his better judgment, he was going to have to use the Traveler's special abilities. Colleen was beginning to understand the captain better. He was such a straight arrow without any ulterior motives, except when it came to protecting his ship and crew; then he was almost obsessed. They heard a clanking sound beneath their feet. No one had to tell them that Overseer Jacer had docked with the *Skegge*.

"Wesley, you should stay," said Picard finally. "The Androssi have more than one ship here, as do the Pakleds, Orions, and everyone else. We picked up some help—there's nothing wrong with that."

"If they even believe we're Maquis," remarked Cabot. "I'm not sure they do."

"That's immaterial," said Picard. "No one around here is particularly honest." They heard a knocking on the hatch. The captain himself went to open it.

Jacer stuck his bearded head through the opening and smiled with pleasure at his fellow thieves, immediately noticing the extra crew member, Wesley.

"Jean," he said, taking Picard's hand and letting the captain pull him onto the deck. "I was beginning to worry about you."

"Our meeting is not for six more hours," said Picard.

The Androssi stared at Wesley, who kept a blank expression on his face. "Somehow you added to your crew. How did you manage that?"

"We had an advance spotter here," answered Picard. "I believe the Androssi have been known to do that, too."

"True," replied Jacer with a nod. "You can never have too many eyes in Rashanar. So are you ready to do our negotiation for us?"

"We would be, but it's unnecessary. That Pakled cruiser was destroyed by the demon ship . . . with almost all hands lost."

"No!" exclaimed Jacer, sounding shocked. "Are you sure?"

"We'll be happy to give you the coordinates," said Picard. "Another Pakled cruiser is there, investigating, so I'd be careful."

The Androssi looked honestly stumped. "Then I suppose our deal is broken. You'll have to give us back the cloaking device, unless you have something of value."

"We have Fristan. We liberated him before the demon ship got there."

Jacer was smiling, as he wagged a slender finger at the captain. "Jean, I have always heard that humans were the most devious race in the quadrant, but I always thought that was jealous Ferengi talk. How can I believe that you have Fristan?"

Picard motioned to Colleen. "Show him."

She dutifully stepped aside to reveal the slight, snoring Androssi asleep on the lower bunk. When Jacer's hand moved toward his weapon, Christine Vale produced a phaser, pointing it directly at the Androssi scavenger. "Don't make a move," she warned.

Jacer let out a breath, smiled again, and moved his hand away. "Well, it seems that you are in a very good bargaining position. I suppose you want the ransom that we were going to pay the Pakleds, in addition to the cloaking device you already have."

"We haven't decided to give him up," answered Picard. "If he's so valuable, I'd like to know why."

Now Jacer's face darkened, and he pointed a long-nailed finger at Captain Picard. "Jean, I have you and everyone else outnumbered."

"Rashanar is a house of cards built on a volcano. Everyone is scrambling to steal as much as they can before they get killed." Picard scoffed. "You know there's something bad out there. Why do you think the Ontailians and Starfleet fled? The demon ship got the Pakleds. It will get you, me, and everyone else in this graveyard unless we stop it."

That thought sobered the Androssi. He pursed his lips, trying to think of a coherent response. Colleen motioned to Picard that he was on the right track.

"Fristan can help us find it, can't he?" asked Picard.

Overseer Jacer narrowed his golden eyes at the human. "You tossed out the deal we made, stole what was ours behind our backs, and now you're making demands. How do I know we can trust you?"

"We want to kill the entity that endangers Rashanar," said Picard with steel in his eyes. "It's a grudge, I admit. If you help us do that, we'll help you with your task, whatever it is."

"We need Fristan to do that," insisted the Androssi. "He's the one who knows—"

"He doesn't know," Colleen broke in. "The Pakleds tried everything possible to get it out of him. They never discovered this so-called cache of antimatter. They were looking for the same thing we are. Whatever Fristan found, he lost, and this includes his mind. He can't tell you anything, or maybe you just wanted to make sure of that."

The Androssi captain glowered, but the counselor figured she had scored a hit. Sticking out her chin, she said, "We'll arrange an exchange of hostages. We'll keep Fristan on this tug, and I'll go with you on your craft."

She almost laughed at the horrified looks Wesley

and Picard flashed at her, but the Androssi gave the offer serious consideration. "That is acceptable," replied Jacer.

"I'd rather have you take Wes here," said Picard, pointing to the Traveler.

Jacer chuckled. "I'm sure you would. The woman made the offer, or don't you let your crew have free will? Is she your slave?"

"He'll agree," replied Colleen with a smile. "Jean doesn't tell me what to do. But let's get a plan, shall we, before we do any splitting up. Jacer, does your ship have cloaking?"

"Yes."

"Then we set a trap." She smiled slyly at Wesley, who squirmed noticeably under her gaze.

On the bridge of the *Enterprise*, Will Riker took a rather scorched and beat-up tricorder from Geordi La Forge. A wire trailed off to a gel power pack, since it had been deactivated by the mimic ship.

"I got a little data off this," explained La Forge. "It was all collected before it got fried. In its natural state, the demon flyer could be mistaken for the antimatter asteroid we've seen, although it's not. In fact, that may be just another mimic mechanism. Just before it died, the reading shows increased antimatter and traces of neptunium, which we've seen near the gravity sink. I can't claim these anomalies are all related, but there may be some connections.

Also, the power was drained through a tiny fissure in the tricorder, which we don't think existed there before."

He handed the captain a digital magnifying glass and turned the tricorder to a taped marking on its side. Riker was amazed to see a precision cut of several centimeters that wasn't visible to the naked eye. "We need to look over the shuttlecraft where you and Data—"

La Forge shook his head. "It's back in San Francisco, evidence that was never used in the court-martial that never was."

"Yeah," said Riker. "Now that we know what to look for, we don't have it."

"Captain, there's a subspace message from the *Skegge,*" announced Lieutenant Erwin. "It's code five, saying the weather is calm but hot back home."

Riker rose from his command chair, pacing in front of the viewscreen, which showed him nothing but emptiness and waste. "That means they're on the move, possibly hunting the mimic ship, and they're not alone. The Androssi must be with them. I wish we could get more information out of these crude codes."

He turned to Data on ops. "Do we still have the *Skegge* on sensors?"

"Just barely. Once they cloak or leave the *Hickock,* we will lose them. If we change position, we risk showing up on the Androssi's sensors."

"Then we're stuck," said Riker. "It's their move." He stepped toward the viewscreen, staring at the vast graveyard, where death seemed to have everyone outnumbered and outmaneuvered.

"How can you know so much about the Ontailians?" asked Overseer Jacer suspiciously as he leaned over Wesley's shoulder. Everyone was watching as the young human programmed the distress-signal emitter of the *Skegge,* being very careful not to set it off.

"I've studied them," he answered defensively. "That only makes sense, if you're going to be in Rashanar."

"And how is this going to work without us all getting killed?" asked the Androssi doubtfully.

"We'll pick a remote marker buoy, then use its subspace relay to send out the distress signal. I can patch it in from here, programming it to repeat indefinitely. All we'll be risking is the buoy. Starfleet left plenty of them around Rashanar."

Jacer cocked a golden eyebrow. "And how do you know so much about Starfleet?"

"My parents were in it," said Wes truthfully. "I'm not Starfleet, believe me." He glanced at Colleen, who gave him a saucy smile, but he didn't return it. He was mad at her for volunteering to go with the Androssi. Wes didn't trust them; also, he hated being separated from her, unless she was back on the *Enterprise* where she belonged.

"I know a likely buoy not too far from here," answered Jacer. "Are you almost done?"

"I'm done," stated Wes. "We could use some tests, but we don't have time for that."

"No, we don't." The Androssi turned to Colleen. "Are you prepared?"

"Yes. Please give me a moment with my colleagues. Go on to your ship. I'll be right there."

The Androssi scanned the human faces in the cramped cabin, then looked at Fristan in the bunk. "If there is any trickery, we will hunt you down and destroy you. We leave as soon as she comes aboard. When you see us leave, you follow." With that, the slender scavenger dropped down into the hold and crawled back into his own ship.

Picard, Crusher, and Vale all looked at Cabot with concern. "I wish there could have been another way," muttered Picard.

"You don't gain the trust of thieves easily," answered the counselor. "You have to make broad gestures and clear sacrifices, which they understand. Besides, I have a guardian angel."

She looked at Wes, and he said, "It's not easy for me to come and go in these little scows. I'll be worried about you."

"Worried about me?" she replied with a laugh. "Here in this delightful place, what could happen to me?"

Without warning, Wes took her in his arms and hugged her fiercely. Picard and Vale looked away, trying to give the illusion of privacy, but there was no place to hide in the little tug. Words failed both of them and the lovers clung to each other, until they heard sniffling from the back of the cabin.

She turned to see Fristan, sitting up in the bunk. "It's so sad, you leaving," he said hoarsely. "You risk your neck to save mine, yes you do. Beware them *turguts*—Jacer and his lot. Take Wesley with you."

"I'm hoping he'll check in with me," answered Colleen, holding back tears. She gently pushed the Traveler away from her and descended into the hold. His reason to exist seemed to vanish with her.

Wes felt a hand on his shoulder and turned to see a sympathetic Picard. "We won't let her get far away," vowed the captain. His tone was sharper with their Androssi passenger. "Fristan, you can see that we protected you, even risking Counselor Cabot. If you've got anything useful to tell us before we hunt your Avenger, now would be a good time."

"It stores it, it does," said Fristan mysteriously. "Only *I* know where its larder is."

Picard glowered at him and turned back to Christine Vale. "What are they doing?"

"The Androssi ship has just disengaged and is firing thrusters," answered the lieutenant from the pilot's seat. "There she goes."

From beneath their belly, a similar cobbled-together craft darted into space and paused long enough to let the *Skegge* fire engines. Picard jumped into the auxiliary chair. "Go ahead, I'll help navigate."

With Vale manning the control, the *Skegge* streaked after the Androssi tug. For several minutes, the two small craft played tag among the hulking wrecks and fiery energy bolts. Wesley sat beside Fristan on the bunk.

"Listen," he whsipered, "if anything happens to her, I'm going to hold *you* responsible. You could help us, but, so far, you refuse to do so."

"This is my livelihood, *turgut!*" snapped Fristan. "You are looking out for me, says you, but how do I know? You stole me before someone else could steal me—doesn't make you honest, no, no! If you kill the Avenger, you kill my secret along with my livelihood."

"So it's like a bee—it collects antimatter and takes it somewhere. And you know where."

"A bee?" asked Fristan, puzzled.

"An insect. It collects nectar from flowers."

"Like a *turgut!*" Fristan cackled and slapped his knee; then he began one of his garbled songs. As the Androssi warbled off-key, he rocked back and forth, closing his eyes. Wes saw no further reason to talk to him, so he stood and paced nervously in the rear of the cabin.

"They're slowing down near buoy thirty-two," announced Vale. "That must be our destination. How close do we have to be to patch in?"

"Ten meters should do," answered Wes. "Even with the interference, the signal should be strong enough from there. Excuse me, Captain."

Picard rose from the auxiliary console. "Is this going to work?"

The young man shrugged. "A distress signal is an open invitation. You never know who will respond."

As soon as Vale killed the thrusters and stopped the craft close to the buoy, Wes sat down and began to go to work. After several minutes, he reported, "I've dumped the signal to the relay. It's repeating."

For proof, he turned on the audio speaker in his console, and they listened to the urgent chirps of an Ontailian distress signal. Vale said, "The Androssi have backed off to three kilometers."

"Go to our position," Picard ordered, stepping behind his pilot. They watched silently as Vale brought them to a distance of three kilometers from the buoy, across from the Androssi vessel. Now they had the buoy bracketed. The Androssi vanished from sight, leaving only rubble and a man-sized buoy shimmering in the graveyard.

"They've put up their cloak," said Vale.

"So will we." Picard moved to the rear console, where he manually activated the jerry-rigged cloaking device. It was all that hung between them and destruction if the mimic ship showed up as planned.

Wes knew that he could make the difference in any encounter, but all he could think about was Colleen aboard that ragtag Androssi scow. *What's she doing? How are they treating her?* It was maddening not to be able to check on her, even for a moment. He realized that her bold offer had won the scavengers over and allowed the *Skegge* to keep their cloak. How much good was Androssi aid? How much good was a cloak going to be against . . . what he had seen?

"Mr. Crusher, watch those sensors," warned Picard. "I know they're not always accurate; however, they might spot a ship coming toward us."

"Of course, sir." Wes felt remiss about being caught daydreaming. There was no sign of any living ship, not even the Androssi scow.

He looked out the viewport and saw a hulking Klingon battle cruiser that had been split in two. Startling ruptures like that were such a common sight in Rashanar that he hadn't thought much about them until now. No starship ought to be broken in half like that by normal weaponry. Had the Klingon vessel cracked while the mimic ship was trying to extract its antimatter?

The Traveler looked at the eerie expanse of space, broken by dark mountains of twisted metal and glittering clouds of debris. He seriously doubted they could ever tame this war-torn wilderness. His senses told him where the Androssi scow was hiding, even though neither he nor the scanners could see it. He could tell where Colleen was, but not what they were doing to her.

I hope you're all right, Colleen. I hope they're not making you do anything against your will.

Colleen Cabot stood behind a phalanx of slender Androssi; it seemed to take six of them to man the three stations on the Androssi bridge. Even though the Androssi vessel was only a bit larger than the *Skegge,* its crew had to number at least twelve. In fact, it was shoulder-to-shoulder, standing-room-only in the main cabin. She noticed that some of them were heavily armed.

"They have put up their cloak," she heard one of them say.

Overseer Jacer glanced uneasily at her and said, "This plan is not likely to succeed."

"I realize that," she answered. "In fact, I don't want to destroy it at all. This demon ship is the perfect tool to find all the antimatter in Rashanar. It's better than Fristan, who's lost his mind. We should follow it and capture it."

"You want to betray your comrades? They're expecting us to destroy it."

"If the demon flyer lives," said Colleen, "just remember that it's not over. As long as we're cloaked, we may have other means to control it . . . like artificial gravity, magnetic fields! There are ways to control antimatter."

"In small amounts." Jacer countered. "We would require a starship for that."

"I know where we can get one. Not a dead one either."

He lifted an amber eyebrow. "That Starfleet vessel . . . or a facsimile of a Starfleet vessel."

"She would be big enough to control it, wouldn't she?" Colleen gave him an encouraging smile.

"Overseer!" called a voice. "Pakled overcruiser closing on the buoy. They're eight lengths away and slowing."

Jacer looked at Colleen. "That is the shape it had before."

"Yes, but there are also real Pakled cruisers around here."

"Prepare to engage tractor beam," ordered Jacer, lifting his finger to signal.

Despite the crowd in the Androssi scow, Colleen could hear her own breath as they watched the Pakled cruiser drift to within half a kilometer of the buoy. A standard communications frequency suddenly crackled with interference, and the Androssi pilot said, "I think they're trying to hail the Ontailian ship, because they can't see it anywhere. They must not realize it's the buoy that's putting out the signal."

Overseer Jacer lowered his hand. "Then it must be real Pakleds."

The tactical officer agreed. "It would seem so . . . except I'm not certain the hail is coming from them."

Colleen saw a moving reflection in the viewport at about one hundred and fifty degrees to starboard. She gripped Jacer's wiry arm and pointed. "There! What's that?"

His biceps tensed with fear as another Pakled cruiser became visible in the swirl of wreckage just below them. Jacer asked hoarsely, "Can sensors tell us which one is real?"

"No, sir," answered the tactical officer.

Colleen felt a press at her back as the other Androssi pushed forward to see. It was clear that they couldn't move or drop their cloak, because Pakled cruisers or the mimic ship were equally deadly. They had no choice but to hold their breath, watch, and see how the two cruisers reacted to each other.

The closest ship suddenly elongated like an eel, shooting straight toward the farther one off starboard. The silvery wad oozed around a wreck like a glob of mercury, resumed its former shape, and streaked toward its new prey.

"Run!" shouted Colleen to no one in particular. "Tell them to run!"

"Hails are no good," the tactical officer reported. "Too much interference. They're still within tractor-beam range, Overseer."

Jacer hesitated, but Captain Picard didn't. The *Skegge* became visible as a blip in the chaotic firmament, and its tractor beam grazed the rushing demon flyer. A slice was skimmed off, and exploded with a chain reaction of searing pops. Colleen was momentarily blinded, and when she could focus again, she quickly saw that none of this had any effect on the entity, which streaked toward its prey like a bolt of lightning.

"Save them, Wesley!" begged Colleen.

"What?" asked Jacer, thinking she was talking to him.

The woman blinked at the Androssi and said, "Follow the demon ship! Keep the cloak on. Hurry!"

Jacer hesitated only for a moment. "Follow it. Cloak and shields up."

"Yes, Overseer." Colleen could see the alien's larynx bobbing nervously in the alien's skinny neck, but she felt exhilarated by the chase.

Chapter Twelve

A SHOCKWAVE RIPPLED all the way back along their tractor beam, then slammed the *Skegge*, shaking them like a rag, blowing out the main console, and plunging the tiny craft into silent darkness. Wesley felt himself lifting off the deck, and focused until he could move as normal without gravity. He caught Captain Picard, helping him gently back into his seat. As he peered out the viewport, trying to find the Androssi ship, Fristan was screaming and sobbing in fear behind him, while Vale fought the fire in her console, smothering burning embers with a stream of foam.

"Did the Androssi come out of cloak?" asked Wesley.

"I didn't see them." Picard was still a little shaken.

The lights flickered back on, and the gradual return of gravity put them more at ease. "Do we have engines?"

Vale looked up with concern. "I don't have a console anymore!"

"I'll check the secondary." While the captain tried to switch helm control over to the remaining console in their damaged craft, Wes paced nervously in the rear of the cabin. Fristan wailed at him and beat his forehead.

"She's gone, she is! You let her get away," screeched the Androssi. "It's your fault—the Avenger has her!"

"Shut up!" snapped Wes, whirling on the old fool. He instantly regretted his harsh words. "I'm sorry . . . we'll get her back."

Picard pounded his console to no avail. "We've still got life-support, but we're dead in space. Wes, check and see if the cloaking works."

Seizing the opportunity to do something useful, Wes turned to the controls in the stern. Nothing seemed to happen, after forcing the lever several times. "Negative."

"Both cruisers are out of sensor range and visual range. We have no idea what's happening," said Picard.

"The mimic ship may not be done with us," added Vale.

Wes knelt to face Picard at the only working console. "Captain, I've got to go find her."

"First you've got to tell the *Enterprise* what's happened to us. Give them our coordinates. Then you can do what you need to do." He pointed to their sobbing visitor. "Take Fristan back to the *Enterprise* with you."

"No, no, I will stay!" insisted the Androssi, getting control of himself. "This is my new ship, you my new crew, so says Fristan!"

"I'll be faster without him," declared Wes. He was not going to lose Colleen now, after waiting all his life to find someone like her.

A moment later, he was gone.

Colleen Cabot gripped the back of the pilot's chair. It seemed as if the scow were a comet as it careened between the wrecks of Rashanar, following the Pakled cruiser that was no more than a sprite of light in the distance. The other Pakled vessel had escaped, showing that they were learning from their mistakes. Their prey looked like a spacecraft, but it was not flying like one—it moved more like a dragonfly shooting across the waters of a swamp.

"We're getting closer to the center of the zone," reported the Androssi pilot. Colleen let go of the chair and stretched her arms.

Captain Jacer glared at her. "I don't like this. It's dangerous in here. Do you have a plan for when it stops?"

"It can't see us if we're cloaked," she replied.

"We want to find its hive, right?" At his blank expression, she added, "Where the bee stores its honey."

"It has stopped," reported the pilot, "only two lengths from the vortex around the gravity sink. Overseer, we cannot get too close. It will be difficult enough to maintain our position with the gravity pull."

"Start drifting now," ordered Jacer. "Keep the cloak up. When we have to correct our course, we will."

Colleen stared in awe at the maelstrom of crushed starships, racing around an unseen force in the middle of the void. Despite the chaos, one shimmering ornament floated like the moon in a swirl of storm clouds—the demon ship. This unearthly beacon suddenly elongated into a serpentine chrome tube, which penetrated the teeming vortex and burned a fiery path into its heart. Debris that struck this glowing tentacle was obliterated in a flash of white light. Everyone on the bridge of the Androssi ship had stopped breathing at the sight of this fearsome spectacle.

"It's not a gravity sink at all," said Colleen with realization. "It's a rift—from here to an alternate universe made of antimatter. The vortex is the intelligence behind it, and the demon flyer is an entity which gathers and returns antimatter that has escaped from that other realm. This ship has photon torpedoes, doesn't it?"

The Androssi stared at her with wide golden eyes. "We will not attack either one of them. I have no idea how Fristan got any antimatter from that whirlpool, but I will not risk an attempt."

"Now when it's off-loading," she whispered, "it's vulnerable. Overseer, this anomaly is destroying Rashanar and making it very dangerous to work here. How much better would it be if you didn't have to worry about the demon ship or gravity crushing your profits before you can get to them?"

"We do need to be rid of this gravity sink. The shipwrecks would stop their orbit and float outward, making Rashanar larger."

"Hit it now," she urged, "while there's still time."

The Androssi captain straightened his shoulders. "Tactical, target a torpedo on the Pakled cruiser in front of the vortex."

"Yes, Overseer," answered the officer with a worried wince. After working his board for a moment, he said, "Targeting complete."

"Fire torpedo."

The scow came out of cloak just long enough to launch it. The torpedo streaked a relatively short distance into the misshapen Pakled cruiser, which looked to be attached to the havoc like the stem of a child's pinwheel. At first, Colleen didn't think the weapon had any effect, until she saw a blazing hole begin to expand from within the blackness, crawling outward.

The entity exploded, unleashing a rippling wave of charged particles that flowed outward and ignited the debris. Suddenly, the entire center of Rashanar erupted as matter and antimatter annihilated each other with all the force of a sun being born.

The Androssi salvage ship was flipped and spun around. Something black and heaving coalesced all around them. Colleen could hear her Androssi shipmates scream in terrified death throes, but strong arms wrapped around her and pulled her out of the malevolent presence that had suddenly overtaken them.

"Wes," she sighed as she was carried through space. They raced against the explosion as it expanded outward, which made it seem as if they were witnessing the dawn of the universe. "So . . . beautiful."

"Hush," he whispered, gripping her tighter. She could feel his strength and resolve. They paused at a safe distance.

Wordlessly, they watched it finally die down to a silent, ever-expanding fireworks show. While her head seeped blood, Colleen felt as if she were in a dream. A dark and ominous force seemed to collect from the edges of space and slowly metamorphose into something metallic.

"Damn," muttered Wes, his voice sounding like nonexistent breeze in her stunned ears. "What the hell did you do? We've got to get back to the *Skegge*. How do you feel?"

"Great . . . now that you're here." She patted his arm, and he tearfully nuzzled her neck.

"I love you," rasped Wesley.

"Me too." She tried to shake herself back to her senses, despite the fact that she was floating in space. Once again, it looked like a very active battle-field.

The Traveler focused, and a moment later he and Colleen were back on the *Skegge*. Only the cabin was empty—no Picard or Vale. No one was at the controls, no one was drinking tea and pacing impatiently, but otherwise the tug seemed normal.

"Did the *Enterprise* rescue them?" asked Wes, setting Colleen on the deck. She stumbled for a moment, but he held her up. The hackles on his neck rose just as he heard the whisper of the curtains opening.

"Nooo!" he yelled, whirling around, but it was too late. A disruptor blast shot from the bunk behind the curtain, ripping Colleen across her midsection. She stared at him wild-eyed as her blasted body slumped to the deck, and more disruptor fire raked the place where Wesley stood.

He stood for a moment before he bent over her body, numbed by shock and grief. "Noooo!" he roared at the top of his lungs. He bent down and hugged her bloody form even as another salvo blew out the viewport and allowed most of the air and loose articles to explode outward into space. He let go of her body, and watched it fly from his arms into the void. She was dead, beyond even his powers—and nothing could bring her back.

His vision blurred with grief and rage, the Traveler felt as if he was outside of his body. He could see himself flying to the curtain even as two Orions in spacesuits stumbled off the bed, disruptors still blazing. He instantly had a fist in each Orion's chest and was squeezing their massive hearts as they bellowed and kicked. Wes could feel their desperate need to get back to their ship, and he heard their death squeals. His body was encompassed in a transporter beam that was obviously intended to save the assassins, and he let himself be dematerialized.

The human materialized in a small transporter room on the Orion vessel, and he sprang off the transporter pad even as two guards tried to aim their weapons at him. Before they could pull a trigger, he grabbed both of the green-skinned brutes by their sashes and whisked them off the ship into space. He flung them into the cold blackness and watched them flail in agony. A second later, Wes was on the bridge, where it was already pandemonium. Through burning tears and heartfelt sobs, the berserk Traveler singled out each Orion and either collapsed his windpipe, stopped his heart, or dragged him kicking and screaming into the graveyard.

The horrible massacre went on for only a matter of seconds, although it must have seemed an eternity for the poor survivors who scuttled from the bridge like green rats. Wes hunted them down and found each Orion cowering somewhere on the wretched craft. "Why? *Why her?*" he shrieked as he snuffed out their miserable lives.

Only none of it happened, except in his mind. In reality, two Orion assassins stumbled from the curtains, disruptors blazing, but the beams passed through the Traveler and only made the hole in the bow bigger. It took about a second before the escaping air blew them out the cavity into the graveyard where Colleen had vanished a moment earlier. Wesley had wanted to rip them apart, and he could have . . . but his training and basic nature restricted the bloody vengeance to his mind, leaving him only the grief. The two Orions were in spacesuits, he told himself, and they had associates nearby.

The scavenger ship did not have as large a crew as his feverish imagination had conjured. Their bridge was empty, and he found the sole remaining Orion in the hold, guarding a cell that contained Captain Picard, Lieutenant Vale, and Fristan. The guard made the mistake of firing at him. In the blink of an eye, the Traveler streaked across the room, and the Orion found the disruptor in his midsection.

"Stop!" shouted Picard through the bars of his cell. "Wesley, don't kill him!"

The words broke into Wesley's consciousness, and he took several calming breaths and dropped the trembling Orion onto the deck. He stood there, red-eyed, panting. Hoarsely he said, "They murdered Colleen. They were lying in wait for us on the *Skegge*."

"Yes, I know," answered Picard, lowering his head. "They were hoping to get revenge on us, and they thought you were a shapeshifter. They weren't going to take any chances with you, no matter what we told them. They just wanted to kill you."

Wesley rubbed his eyes with his fists and grunted. "They only killed Colleen. They were blown into space along with her."

"Wes!" called Christine Vale, looking miserable. "I'm sorry for you. We all grew to like her, and we'll miss her . . . but your anger won't bring her back."

"It was in the line of duty," said the captain, "and we all owe her a lot. Shake it off, Wes, concentrate on the mission, and grieve later. Guard, let us out of here!"

"Don't hurt me!" begged the cowering Orion, fumbling in his pocket for some old-fashioned keys. "I can show you how to run our ship."

"Just hurry," urged Picard.

"Yes, sir! Yes, Captain Jean!" The sole survivor quickly opened the cell door and ushered his new masters out, keeping a wary eye on the Traveler.

Wes dropped to the deck and began to weep. He

couldn't think about anything but the lifeless body he had held in his arms. That could not be the woman he loved, the woman he thought he had saved. Instead he had swept her into harm's way, and she had died instead of him. *I was meant to die for misusing my powers! I went too far. Because of my arrogance, Colleen is dead.*

It seemed as if both of his lives were over. He wept for all he had lost . . . Colleen, his father, then his mother for several years, Starfleet, the faith of his fellow Travelers, and his innocence.

He felt a gentle hand on his shoulder, and he looked up to see Captain Picard. "Wes, I'm sorry. The Orions came after us as soon as you left. We were dead in space. They used transporters—we had no chance to resist. You take some time to recover, but try to collect yourself. Vale and I are going to the bridge to contact the *Enterprise*. Are they on their way here?"

The young man nodded.

"What shape is the *Skegge* in?" asked Picard.

"It's destroyed," answered Wesley, forcing himself to think of his comrades and not just his loss. "Listen, Captain, something else has happened. The Androssi followed the mimic ship to the vortex. I'll have to sort out what I saw, but the demon ship seemed to be transferring antimatter into the gravity sink. It may be a rift that leads to an antimatter dimension, I don't know. The Androssi fired on it. The gravity dump and the vortex were caught up in a chain reaction. The demon ship is still out there, still dangerous but without any purpose."

Wes realized it. It sounded as if he was talking about himself.

The captain's face darkened. "It seems as if matters have come to a head. We'll be on the bridge."

"I don't know where I'll be," said Wesley, his voice cracking.

Although a dozen emotions crossed Picard's face, he looked as if he couldn't find any words to express them. He waved his arm, and Vale and the cooperative Orion followed him out of the brig. Fristan slumped down beside the young man and hummed silently.

"Everything dies in Rashanar, they do," said the Androssi sympathetically. "No one ever leaves. No one, no they don't."

Wes sniffed back a stream of mucus and rubbed his reddened eyes. "Everything dies but the damn demon ship. The Androssi blew up its nest, but how can we kill that murderous entity?"

Fristan scratched his stubbled chin, nodding in thought. "You still have the fire of revenge burning in your belly, you do. That will eat you alive, says I."

"Spare me the lecture," grumbled Wesley. "Just tell me how to kill it."

Fristan looked perfectly sane as he mulled over the request. "When it *becomes* its prey, it must have the weaknesses of its prey. Do you not think so?"

"Yeah," said Wesley, still feeling as if he wanted to break into tears. The emptiness in his heart was searing, and the only event he could compare it to was his father's death. But that had happened when he was a little boy. As a man, he had never experienced the loss of someone like Colleen Cabot. It had been true love, however brief. He had a feeling he would have been good for her, a calming influence in her life. Now he would never know.

One fact of being a Traveler that failed me, he decided, *is that I can't be in two places at once.* That's why the Travelers had banded together to see and experience as much as they could by multiprocessing. Any individual Traveler who tried to use his powers to influence events, as Wesley had, was doomed to failure. In the end, he would always be limited by operating alone.

"I'll have to find it," Wes told Fristan, "because I'm the only one who can."

The broken-down Androssi patted his shoulder. "The Avenger is just like you, it is. All the roots have been torn up, and it's alone. Yes, perhaps now is the time for it to die, like poor Colleen."

His tears welling up again, Wes jumped to his feet and paced to the center of the brig. "I've got to be by myself. My arrogance killed her. It attracted her, then killed her."

"Listen, young man, take me back to the *Enterprise,* I beg you!" Fristan croaked. "I want to see Counselor Troi again. I want to help them."

Wes lowered his head and swallowed hard. "I can't face . . . any of them."

"You don't have to stay," insisted Fristan. "Just drop me off and disappear. I'm ready to help them."

The Traveler frowned and gulped back another lump in his throat. "All right, I'll drop you off."

When Deanna Troi entered the brig on the *Enterprise,* she expected to find Beverly Crusher there. But she didn't anticipate the Ontailian prisoners leaping and crawling all over their trellises while chirping frantically. Despite this seeming improvement in their condition, the doctor didn't look happy. Her tricorder apparently wasn't telling her much either.

"Beverly, your patients are up and about, looking much better."

"They're agitated, not better. See their food—they still haven't eaten. It happened all of a sudden. I don't even know how they have the energy to carry on like this. What does it mean?"

"Can we use the universal translator?" asked Troi.

"It's on," muttered Crusher. "I'm afraid it just puts out gibberish. I've got a call in to La Forge, but they're shorthanded down there. Do the Ontailians look frightened to you?"

The Betazoid stepped closer to the frantic activity in the enclosure and was bombarded by alien emotions. "Anxious and alarmed . . . almost panicked. Resignation more than fear."

Beverly sighed. "Do they know something we don't? Is this what they do before they die? I'm thinking about stunning them all and starting intravenous care, especially if any of them drop into unconsciousness. If only they would drink some water."

They heard the door whoosh open, and both of them turned to see Will Riker walk in. Deanna was glad to see him, but she instantly realized from his eyes that something was wrong.

Riker couldn't help but be distracted by all the thrashing and howling going on in the cell. "What is this, exercise period?"

"We don't know," answered Beverly with concern. She briefly explained that the prisoners had gone from total lethargy into this frenzy in a matter of seconds. "If you've come down here to ask what we're doing with them, that's a good question. I want to talk to you about it."

"That's fine," replied Riker solemnly, "but that's not why I've come to see you. We've gotten a message from the *Skegge*."

Beverly looked stricken. "Wesley?"

"They're all right, except for Colleen Cabot. She was killed in an ambush by some Orion salvagers. I don't have the details. Wes has apparently taken it very hard, but he single-handedly captured the Orion ship after this happened. The away team is trying to fly it."

"Where is my son now?" asked Beverly, turning off her tricorder.

"They don't know. If he shows up, we're supposed to keep him here." The acting captain added, "They didn't say *how* we were supposed to do this. I guess it will have to be by asking nicely."

The doctor seemed to break. Her shoulders slumped as she cried softly for a few moments. Deanna put her arm around her friend's shoulder, and gave Will a nod of dismissal. He hesitantly walked to the door. Beverly had eight years of pent-up worry to release, but she didn't use this moment to do it. As the whooping and hollering of the Ontailians grew louder, the doctor abruptly dried her eyes.

She sniffed. "I grieve for that young woman and my son, too. You want your children to excel, but you also want them to have a normal life . . . to be happy. He's blessed, but I know he isn't immune to heartache. Will I lose him again?"

Troi had no answer to the anguished question. The two women stood close to each other, lost in a myriad of thoughts. After a few moments, the counselor noticed a difference in the room—the Ontailians were quieter. She saw a few of them huddled by the water dispenser and the trays of greens and grain.

"Beverly," she said, prodding the doctor's arm. "Look!"

The doctor looked up to see that her patients had opted to live rather than waste away.

On the bridge of the Orion salvage ship, Picard scanned the cluttered region of space for the two missing Orions and Colleen Cabot's body, but interference from the boneyard made the job impossible. The surviving Orion, Taluk, stood nearby, his hands behind his back and a look of contrition on his rugged face. Knowing what he did of Orions, the captain assumed that their prisoner had decided he was now their slave, and his fear of Wesley Crusher would keep him in line.

The captain frowned at the confusing sensor readings, while Lieutenant Vale familiarized herself with the navigation controls. According to Taluk, the Orion scow was called the *Green Goddess,* and it appeared to be a serviceable craft that could replace the *Skegge* in their plans. Still, Picard was happy to know that the *Enterprise* was en route to their position, and Fristan was safely in Counselor Troi's custody.

Suddenly Vale turned to him and said, "Captain, one of those big Ontailian warships is off our stern. I think it's the *Yoxced.*"

"Did they hail us?"

"No. They're just sitting there, trying to scan us. Our shields are up."

Picard turned to their host. "Taluk, did this ship have any dealings with the Ontailians?"

The big Orion shrugged. "They chased us a few times. We bought them off."

"How?"

"Antimatter. They were always willing to buy it, but we didn't salvage it. We brought it with us, which is why the Ontailians let us in. We just wanted the slave trade and a piece of the profits."

"I want to talk more about this, but later," said Picard. He peered out the viewport, but saw only a few glittering chunks of debris. Less than a hundred meters away, a scorched Cardassian hulk slipped past them, but there was no active ship in sight.

"The Ontailians were there," said Vale, puzzled, "but now I can't find them."

"What's the matter with the wreckage?" asked the Orion. "It's coming so close to us."

"Without the gravity sink in the center," answered Picard, "the wrecks are losing their orbits and drifting wherever their momentum takes them. Rashanar is going to change now."

"Ship to starboard!" called Vale as a monstrous silver apparition glided in front of them, taking up the whole viewport. Picard's hands were on the weapons console, but he let out a sigh and removed his fingers from the unfamiliar controls.

"The *Enterprise*," he breathed as the sleek lines of the *Sovereign*-class starship cruised past them, thrusters firing to bring the graceful ship to a halt. "Perhaps that's why the Ontailians left so abruptly. Lieutenant, send the *Enterprise* subspace and tell them to keep their shields up, because Ontailians are nearby."

"Yes, sir."

The captain turned to the Orion. "Do you know what the Ontailians did with that antimatter you sold them?"

"No. Why should we care?"

"They expelled it here in Rashanar," answered Picard. "We don't know if it was to appease the demon ship or to attack it."

"Or perhaps to poison it," said the Orion with a nervous chuckle. "Ontailian assassins are well known in certain circles. They always use poison to weaken their quarry, then they strangle them. Or so I've heard."

The captain scratched his chin, unable to refute that theory any more than he could a dozen others connected with this lethal anomaly. One thing he now knew: The shapeshifting mass was not of this universe. Now the Androssi had closed its escape hatch.

"Captain," said Vale warily, "I'm getting a subspace message."

"From the *Enterprise?*"

"No, sir. From the Ontailian warship *Yoxced.*" She worked her board hesitantly. "It's on an open Starfleet channel, so I assume the *Enterprise* is receiving it too. I don't know how the Orions' universal translator works."

"Allow me," said Taluk helpfully. He took over the console, and a moment later they heard the subspace message translated into a series of languages by an authoritative computer voice.

"Federation ship, Orion ship, you are in grave danger," began the message. "A demon is loose now in Rashanar. She is enraged because the rift was destroyed. Before she had but one purpose, but now she is erratic. We fear she will escape from Rashanar."

The voice concluded ominously, "So now you will do as we say."

In the bowels of the *Enterprise,* Fristan hummed an off-key ditty as he approached the doors of the brig. The guard glanced at him through the window, saw who it was, and opened it. Fristan had come down here before to see the Ontailian prisoners, although he had always been with other people.

"You're by yourself?" asked the guard.

The hunched Androssi shrugged and shuffled inside. "Oh, they're all so busy, they are. Protecting the universe. How are my fellow passengers?"

"Fine," answered the young security guard. "They're eating, drinking, even making merry. Or wrestling, I'm not sure which."

"Ah." Fristan pulled two apples from his pocket and chomped into one of them. "I just discovered these remarkable fruits, what do you call them?"

"Apples."

"Mmm-mmm, they're good, says I. Would you like this extra one?"

The guard shook his head. "No, thanks."

"I will not tell anyone," promised Fristan cheerfully. He moved closer to the guard, holding up a scarlet orb with one hand.

"I really shouldn't," the guard said.

In a flash, Fristan injected the guard with the hypospray he'd palmed in his other hand.

The human did dropped to the deck, unconscious. Fristan went immediately to the cell and deactivated the forcefield, allowing the host of Ontailians to scamper out on their long arms, chittering with anticipation.

"Get moving," urged Fristan, running to open the door for them. "There are only a few humans on the bridge. I must get to a spare console."

Chittering and snorting, the Ontailians scurried over the limp body of the guard and into the corridor, where they swung themselves into the Jefferies tubes and access panels.

"Hurry!" barked the Androssi. "I've waited a long time to be paid!"

Chapter Thirteen

STRIDING ACROSS THE BRIDGE of the *Enterprise*, Riker knew the situation had finally come to a head. "An ultimatum from the Ontailians. What do you think?"

"I do not see how they can force us to do their will," answered Data. "The *Yoxced* cannot destroy us by herself. To fire now would be foolish. After losing their orbits around the gravity sink, the trajectories of the derelicts have become very unpredictable. My suggestion is that we make our way to the outer belt as soon as possible."

"They're worried about the mimic ship escaping from Rashanar," said Troi.

Riker tapped his combadge. "Bridge to transporter room one."

"Erwin here," answered the Bolian, who had returned to his regular post.

"Have you locked on to Picard and Vale yet? They're on that Orion ship."

"I'm trying. Perhaps if we could get a little closer, or they used a signal booster at their end. Even so, I don't recommend transporting in here."

"I know," answered Riker, "I don't want to drop shields either. This is our desperation plan. Keep trying and notify me if you lock on to them. Riker out."

"If only Wesley were here," said Beverly Crusher. She immediately bit her lip.

"We'll find a way to help him," promised Deanna.

"Captain," said Data with a curious look on his face. "There is no response from the brig, and . . . someone is accessing the life-support systems."

A second later, the gravity completely cut out, and everyone began floating from the deck, flailing their arms. "Computer!" shouted Riker. "Restore gravity!"

"Life-support is frozen," reported Data, just as access hatches and Jefferies tubes all over the bridge flew open. The liberated Ontailian prisoners flung themselves from the hatches, and furry streaks flew across the weightless expanse to attack the crew once again, wrapping around necks and legs. In zero gravity, Riker was unable to get any leverage in his fight against them. Com signals were beeping, but none of them would be answered during this life-and-death melee.

Data floated out of his seat. Even he was having trouble with a dozen or so Ontailians crawling all over him, trying to open his access ports. As soon as the android forcefully peeled one off, two more would take its place, restricting his grip.

"Don't kill them," said a reedy voice. "We need them to pilot this ship."

Riker craned his neck around and saw Fristan floating out of a Jefferies tube with a phaser in his hand. He made a strange clicking-cooing sound out of the side of his mouth. The Ontailians reduced their murderous assault.

"Don't struggle, I beg you," said Fristan. "You'll only die. Surrender your ship, if you want to live. If you don't give up, we kill you and take your ship anyway."

Riker saw Deanna gasping for breath and beating her fists helplessly on the appendages around her neck. "Let everyone live. You can have the ship. Why are you doing this after we saved your life?"

The Androssi wheezed a laugh. "You didn't save me, Wesley did. And he's not here, nowhere I can see. Let them breathe, my friends!" He again made sounds in their own language.

The wiry creatures loosened their grips minutely. Riker tried not to show his fear as he demanded, "What the hell is going on here?"

"I'm an agent for the Ontailains," explained Fristan. "Why do you think everyone in Rashanar wanted to question me? No matter, I run the *Enterprise* now. You'll do as we say, or pretties will die." He pointed to Deanna and Beverly, who floated in the crushing grip of the Ontailians.

"Order your android to return to his seat and fly to our coordinates," Fristan continued. "We know he can pilot this vessel alone. We don't need you. Need only android."

Feeling helpless, Riker acknowledged his first officer. "Do as they say."

"I am unable to move," reported Data.

Drifting in the middle of the bridge, Data had no way to get back down until the Ontailians crawled from his torso to his legs and feet. There they extended their long limbs and formed a chain reaching the console and pulling the android down into his chair. It was an impressive display of teamwork, thought Riker, but it did nothing to lessen the death grip the beasts had on his own neck.

"Oh, yes," said Fristan thoughtfully, "what about our friends on the Orion craft?"

"I am sending them a message telling them to flee," answered Data, working his board. "There, subspace message sent."

"Why the blazes did you do that?" Fristan snarled.

"Because I wish to protect their lives," responded Data simply. "If you kill any of my shipmates, I will refuse to help you. I can propel myself faster across this bridge than the Ontailians. A phaser will not stop me."

"Oh, no sense to be dramatic," replied the Androssi with a nervous chuckle. "Of course, we've made a deal, we have, and we'll abide by the terms of it. Yes, yes! Now be so kind to send a subspace to the *Yoxced,* and tell them Fristan is in charge. They will send you the coordinates of the demon flyer, they will."

"You know where it is?" asked Riker with surprise.

"We're trailing it as we speak," answered Fristan. "How else are we going to stop it from escaping Rashanar?"

"You didn't need to hijack our ship to do that," grumbled Riker. "We would have helped you."

Fristan smiled slyly. "Would you sacrifice your ship to stop it? The Ontailians will."

"I have the coordinates," reported Data, working his board in a blur of quick movements. "I will take the most direct route, but our progress may be slow as I must estimate the new trajectories of the derelicts we pass."

"Best get moving." Fristan waved his phaser. Riker spied Deanna, who looked like an old tintype of a woman wrapped in fox furs. She gave him the most encouraging smile she could muster, but Riker didn't feel much like returning it. He could only hope that La Forge could do something to help the situation from engineering.

As if reading his mind, Fristan made a strange

chirping noise out the side of his mouth, and one or two Ontailians broke off from each of the prisoners. They slithered over their fellows, the equipment, and furniture until they reached the Jefferies tube, where Fristan ushered them into the opening. The cagey Androssi gave the captain a wry grin, as if to show he was still thinking ahead of him.

"The computer won't let us into life-support," complained one of La Forge's subordinates in engineering. He slapped his console with one hand as he hung on to his chair with the other. "We still can't restore the gravity."

"All right," said La Forge. "None of my hails to the bridge are getting through, so we've got to assume that something bad has happened. Garsee, do we still have forcefields and emergency containment in engineering?"

"Yes, sir."

"Put them on, full red alert," ordered the chief engineer. When the klaxons sounded and the emergency red lighting came on, he added, "Now nothing is getting in or out of here."

"Sir, we're moving," reported Garsee from his console, "one-quarter impulse. Data is logged in at the conn."

La Forge tapped his combadge again. "Engineering to transporter room one."

"Erwin here!" came a breathless voice. "I just got back to my console. Sir, what's happening?"

"As you've figured out, the bridge crew is not responding, even though we're under way. Somebody did a very specific job of sabotage on our artificial gravity, and the only ones who would benefit from that are the Ontailians. Do a direct-beam to the brig and see if the Ontailians are still there."

"Aye, sir. Stand by." La Forge gritted his teeth and tried to calm himself as he waited for the results of this little experiment. After what seemed like a long time, Erwin came back. "No Ontailians left in the brig. Do you want me to lock on to the captain or someone else on the bridge?"

"Hold off on that for now. I don't want to cause any ruckus while we're trying to maneuver through this minefield. Stand by. La Forge out." He flailed helplessly in the air, trying to catch hold of something, anything, but his hands missed every edge and handle within sight. "Garsee, let's do an override to patch directly from the stator pulse grid into the gravity generators in the engineering subsection. We'll cut out the shipwide system entirely."

The young ensign lifted his hands hesitantly from the console. "Where should I start?"

"Start by tying yourself into the chair," La Forge ordered. "You're going to need both hands since you're going to be there awhile."

"I think I'm getting a handle on flying this ship," said Vale as she slowly piloted the Orion vessel through the shifting graveyard. Even so, Picard was glad that the Orion craft had strong shields and was in relatively good condition for a Rashanar salvage ship. Their Orion prisoner snored quietly in the corner, apparently glad just to be alive.

Of more concern to the captain was the cryptic subspace message from Data, urging them to flee. Subsequent communications requesting more information had gone unanswered, and Picard had to fear the worst.

They had, however, caught sight of the big Ontailian flagship, which had been forced to plow slowly through the changing panoply of burnt hulks and swirling debris. They were following the *Yoxced* toward the outer ring of the boneyard, which suited Picard's sense of urgency. The Ontailians believed that the uprooted replicant ship would be trying to escape, and he had no reason to doubt them. If it reached Federation shipping lanes, the loss of life could be staggering.

Whatever danger the *Enterprise* was in, he had to put that worry out of his mind for the moment. With Counselor Cabot's death, his own status was also in limbo, and he could easily be remanded back to Starfleet Medical Mental Health. But he had to ignore all repercussions for the moment. *I came back here to get the mimic ship, and until that's done, no other problem matters.*

They were rocked by a plasma burst with such

fury that Taluk woke up. "Are we there?" muttered the Orion.

"Are we where?" responded Picard.

"Wherever we're going." The big Orion yawned loudly and looked around.

Picard turned to Vale and said, "Don't lose the Ontailians."

"Don't worry, sir. They're leading me through here, and I'm grateful for that. Rashanar is a real mess now."

Picard laughed grimly at the irony of her statement. "It was an organized mess before," he said, "and now it's a disorganized mess."

He gazed out the viewport just as they swerved around an old Jem'Hadar relic, with a jagged hole in its bow that looked like a mouthful of sharp teeth. Picard wished there were some sort of cosmic cremation they could perform on all the old wrecks, unrecovered bodies, and unexorcised ghosts of Rashanar, putting them all to rest at one time. In his current mood, he would like to see the whole battle site turned into a haze of gray ashes.

"Uh oh!" exclaimed Vale, yanking the captain out of his grisly reverie. "The *Yoxced* is stopping."

The lieutenant barely had time to slow down before they crashed into the massive Ontailian starship. The salvage vessel swerved off, barely missing the giant silver fin. Picard worried that they would be fired upon, that was until he saw another ship closing fast upon their stern, plus two more Ontailian starships off the port bow.

Phasers and beamed weapons flashed across the blackness. He braced himself for impact. But the Ontailians weren't firing at the Orion scow. They were firing at the ship that had been closing on their tail. Picard moved to an auxiliary console to get a better look at the frantic action, and he realized the ship that was attracting the fire was a Pakled over-cruiser. *Which cruiser,* he wondered, *the real one or the replicant?* All three Ontailian ships were shooting mercilessly at the vessel, tearing into it with all they had.

His question was answered a moment later, when the overcruiser blew up in a blazing eruption of twisted metal and shimmering debris. On a hunch, the captain ordered, "Vale, get us away from the Ontailians. Evasive maneuvers."

His advice came not a moment too soon, as they turned their attention and their weapons upon the Orion salvager. But Vale had gotten enough of a head start to duck back into the turmoil of Rashanar before the Ontailians could focus their firepower. Their beams went amiss, raking already dead hulks, which helped to cover the escape of the Orion craft. Vale brought them perilously close to a Vulcan heavy cruiser; then they slipped into its shadow as Picard ordered, "Cut power and drift. Let's play dead."

They'd had so much practice with this in Rashanar that it was almost second nature. With the lights out, the two humans and the Orion stood motionless, barely breathing, as Ontailian vessels scooted by them in the darkness.

"What are those crazy bastards doing?" muttered Taluk. "We're their *allies!*"

"It looks like they're after every vessel that tries to escape from Rashanar," answered Picard. "They're not sure which one is the mimic ship, so they'll destroy them all."

"What are we going to do?" asked Vale.

The captain's lips thinned. "What can we do? Sit tight and wait." He stared into the murky starscape of blasted wrecks and ghostly clouds of rubble, wondering if any of them would get out of this hell alive.

With relief, Geordi La Forge set his feet back on the deck in engineering and immediately dashed to Ensign Garsee's position. "Good job," he said, patting the young man on the back. "I'll take over here. You get over to the warp core and run diagnostics. Make sure we have warp drive if we need it."

"Warp drive?" asked Garsee doubtfully. "In the boneyard?"

"Going to warp would put our gravity back to normal," explained La Forge. "The velocities are so high that artifical gravity is maintained by the warp subsystem, so it's a natural bypass of the affected circuits."

They heard a banging on the bulkhead somewhere above their heads, and looked uneasily at one another. Unseen attackers, probably Ontailians, had been trying to break into engineering for the last half hour, and sounded as if they were getting closer. Unfortunately, La Forge's crew was trapped in their workspace as long as they had to keep containment measures going.

"Determined buggers, aren't they?" asked La Forge. "Well, the same goes for me. The way we're picking up speed, I think we're headed out of Rashanar. Once we get into open space, I'm kicking it into warp manually . . . but going a very short distance."

Geordi heard more commotion, and saw that his handful of engineers were getting accustomed to walking again. "Everyone," he called, "go to the weapons locker and get a phaser! I have a feeling we're going to need them."

The furry appendages that were wrapped around Riker's nose and mouth were beginning to stink, and more than anything he yearned to tear those foul limbs off his face and break them in half. But he doubted whether any of his bridge crew would survive a battle to the death with the Ontailians in zero gravity. Fristan kept his phaser trained on Riker, when he didn't have it pointed at Data, who calmly piloted them through the deadly obstacle course of Rashanar.

From what he could see on the viewscreen, it was clear that they were in the outskirts of the graveyard, which was now expanding rapidly since the demise of the gravity source at the center. He supposed they should be thankful that the Ontailians hadn't destroyed them outright after taking over the ship. Still it was maddening to be in command of the *Enterprise,* then have it stolen out from under him. Then to see his crew trussed up made him angrier . . . more determined to get revenge. True, the Ontailians were headed out of Rashanar, but they had better turn them loose after that—or Will Riker would extract his pound of flesh from these treacherous thieves, especially Fristan.

They zoomed past scorched hulks drifting a safe distance away. Riker could see at least two of the narrow silver Androssi ships waiting for them. A moment later the flagship *Yoxced* cruised into view, and it seemed as if the gang was all here.

"We have reached the edge of Rashanar," said Data.

"Yes, yes!" crowed Fristan happily as he gripped the hatch of the Jefferies tube in order to keep from floating away. "Now turn on your distress signal."

That caused the android to whirl in his chair. "Turning on the distress signal will attract the demon flyer."

"Yes, we know," answered the Androssi, lifting his phaser. "Get ready to expel your antimatter too. Do it, android, or I'll vaporize you, I swear I will!"

"For either of those actions, I would need a direct order from my commander," replied Data, placing his hands in his lap.

Fristan chittered and whistled to his Ontailian conspirators, and they finally released Riker's mouth and face. Without hesitation, Will shouted, "I'm not going to let any of my crew get killed! Before you use this ship as bait, I want them all evacuated."

"Says you!" scoffed Fristan. "I can't restore gravity and let your crew run loose. They'd fight us."

"Not if I ordered them off the ship," declared Riker. "Let us cooperate with you. It isn't necessary to do it this way."

Fristan seemed to mull it over; then he waved his phaser menacingly. "No, I have my orders! No one leaves the ship but me. Data, turn on the distress signal."

Riker noticed that Data cocked his head in a quizzical fashion, as if seeing something very unusual on his board. A moment later, there came an odd tingling. The viewscreen blurred. Riker went plummeting from the air to the deck. Fortunately, the Ontailians wrapped around him broke his fall, and they had already loosened their grip around his head.

With both hands, he gripped the octopus-like head of a slippery Ontailian and choked it with all his strength. Writhing and lashing him, the thing struggled until it went limp.

Fristan tried to shoot, but the sudden gravity doubled him over. The beam barely missed Data. The android dashed from his seat and kicked the Androssi in the mouth. Fristan dropped into the Jefferies tube. They heard his bloodcurdling screams all the way down. The door of the turbolift flew open, and La Forge led a charge of armed engineers onto the bridge, firing phasers. The low stun setting had little effect on the humans; however, the Ontailians curled up in sleep whenever a beam struck them. Within a matter of seconds, order had been restored to the bridge.

Riker staggered to his feet and wiped the fur from his face and hands. Then he helped Troi while Beverly Crusher checked a gash on Kell Perim's forehead. "Geordi, you got here not a moment too soon," panted Riker. "I don't know what you did, but good job."

"We're not out of the woods yet," said La Forge at his engineering console. "Because they're members of the Federation, the Ontailians know a lot about our systems. They did a number on our life-support."

Suddenly a bright flash ricocheted off their bow, and the ship bucked.

"Shields are holding," reported Data.

"Captain, we still haven't got full computer control," said La Forge. "We can't outrun them or outfight them."

"All right." Riker made the difficult decision. "Data, put on the distress signal. Let's try to convince the ones on the ships that Fristan is still in charge."

"Yes, sir."

"If we've got to go down fighting this thing," said Riker, "let's do it with minimum losses." He gave Deanna a hug. She looked curiously at him as he let go of her shoulders and walked to his command chair.

Riker tapped the companel on the arm of the chair and announced, "Attention, all hands, this is the captain. All personnel not currently on bridge or engineering duty are ordered to report immediately to the shuttlebay to evacuate the ship. And I mean *all* personnel. Riker out."

"Captain," said Dr. Crusher, swabbing blood from Perim's forehead, "Lieutenant Perim should be evacuated, too."

"Please take her to the shuttlebay," ordered Riker. "Do what you can to organize the evacuation. You're going with them, Doctor."

"But Wes . . . and Jean-Luc?" she asked hesitantly.

"Since they're not here, we'll have to proceed as if they're not coming back." Riker grimaced as one of the Ontailians began to squirm on the deck. He pinned the creature with the heel of his boot and tapped his combadge. "All security officers report to the bridge immediately. Bring rope and nets with you."

"Captain," said Data, "the Ontailian vessels have backed off two-point-five kilometers from our position."

"La Forge, I want full control soon."

"I'm working on it," promised the engineer. "I could use Data's help."

The android looked at his captain, and Riker nodded. Soon both of them were working at adjoining consoles. Deanna Troi took Data's vacated seat.

"I'm not leaving your side," she declared.

Riker gave his *Imzadi* a loving smile. "I never thought you would."

"I'm picking up a distress signal," reported Christine Vale at the helm of the Orion salvage ship. Her eyes widened, and she looked at Captain Picard with horror. "It's the *Enterprise.*"

"Take us there," ordered the captain.

"But the Ontailians?"

Picard's jaw clenched, and his lips thinned. "If the *Enterprise* is in trouble—or trying to attract the demon ship—we need to be there."

Slowly the Orion scow pulled out from the cover of the Vulcan derelict, making its way toward the edge of the graveyard. Finding the *Enterprise* was no difficulty, especially when her shuttlebay doors were wide open, disgorging a steady stream of small ships. Every shuttlecraft, shuttlepod, and escape pod was apparently launching; Picard even spotted their spare salvage tug pulling away from the mammoth starship.

"They must be evacuating," said Picard. "The Ontailians don't seem to be interfering."

"No, they don't, sir," answered Vale. "They have three ships in weapons range, but they're just watching."

"In all that shuttle traffic, I think we could slip aboard. Lieutenant, pull close to the stern, then wait for a chance to enter the shuttlebay."

"Yes, sir." Vale plied her controls.

Wesley Crusher hovered in space, partially obscured by a glittering mass of rubble. From his unique perch, he watched the demon flyer slowly rebuild its strength by absorbing the antimatter from the remains of the Androssi salvage ship. There was nothing left for the entity to mimic. It seemed content just to rest and recuperate in the vast field of death and destruction . . . still maintaining the vague outlines of the Pakled overcruiser, but having lost its yen for perfection.

Like me, thought the Traveler, *still possessed of all its powers but aimless and pointless. Its reason to exist is gone.*

He couldn't tell for sure, but he had an uneasy

feeling that it knew he was there. In the past, it had destroyed anything it couldn't use. Now mere survival was the only instinct it had left, and the Traveler was no threat to it. Both of them were relics of some grand design that had ceased to be important.

The young man lowered his head and felt like crying. His heart, which had been full of love and hope, was as dark and empty as the graveyard around him. He wondered if he would ever leave this place, or would he just languish until his powers left him? Maybe godlike beings didn't die; they just faded away.

Suddenly the running lights on the phantom ship blinked on, and neon stripes ran down the length of its sleek hull. Lights glimmered on the empty bridge. Replicated impulse engines fired in the stern, as if testing. *The entity is going to go back on the hunt,* thought Wesley. What would lift this monster out of its lethargy? *A distress signal from a starship full of antimatter.*

Wes groaned, because this could only mean carnage, and he didn't really think he could stand to see any more of that. However, when the reenergized replicraft took off, the Traveler followed a safe distance behind. There weren't many vessels among the scavengers and traitors in Rashanar who really deserved saving. He figured he should see if this was one of them.

The Traveler was surprised when the demon ship reached the outer layer of wrecks in Rashanar without finding what it sought, and even more so when the lethal look-alike actually left the boneyard. *This is not good. There is not a lot I can do about it.*

Instinctively he looked for the *Enterprise*. His eyes found her before his acute Traveler senses. The majestic starship was waiting in the void outside the newly freed herd of derelicts, her shuttlebay door open, an escape pod shooting off from her saucer section, and distress signal blaring. The ship was helpless as the demon flyer swooped down upon her.

Chapter Fourteen

CAPTAIN PICARD STEPPED off the turbolift with Christine Vale right behind him onto the bridge of the *Enterprise*. They were met with shocked expressions, then smiles, although only Riker, Troi, La Forge, and Data were present.

"Captain, good to see you," hailed Riker as his attention was diverted to the viewscreen in front of him. "Is that a ship bearing down on us?"

Deanna Troi gasped and pointed beyond Picard. "Wesley!"

Picard whirled around to see Wesley Crusher in his gray Traveler's garb, looking ten years older. Before anybody could gather their wits, blinding beams of energy flashed across their bow. Everyone scurried to their positions. Vale went to tactical. Troi jumped up to give the conn to Data. La Forge stuck to his engineering console.

"Captain," reported Data, studying his board, "there's a Pakled cruiser bearing down on us, but the Ontailian ships are firing at it. The cruiser has been slowed but not diverted."

"Close shuttlebay, shields up," ordered Riker. "Evasive maneuvers."

"That's the mimic ship," said Wesley. "Head to deep space."

"We don't have warp," La Forge warned them. "It's already affecting our antimatter stream in the reaction chamber. We still have impulse."

"Get us out of here, Data," barked Riker. "Full impulse."

"Yes, sir." The starship banked gracefully to escape from the new battle zone outside Rashanar. It looked to Picard as if the Ontailian bombardment was having no effect on the mimic ship.

"Captain," asked Riker, "would you like your command back now?"

"Not especially," he answered. "You're doing fine, Number One. It was a good idea to evacuate."

Wesley stepped between them. "Listen, we only have a few seconds. The Ontailians won't stop it. I can think of only one way to destroy the mimic ship. Fristan gave me the answer. If it duplicated the *Enterprise* at the exact moment we were going through an autodestruct sequence, perhaps that would be duplicated as well. It's during that scanning/replicating phase that it's vulnerable. But someone will have to go on board the mimic ship to make sure that it doesn't have a chance to destroy the real *Enterprise*. The only one who can do that is me. Even Data would be deactivated. The rest of you have to get off the *Enterprise*."

Riker was not pleased. "Is this really the only way?"

"I've watched it . . . I think I understand it."

"Captain Riker," said Data, "two Ontailian vessels have been destroyed by the mimic ship. The third has broken off the fight. The false Pakled cruiser is in pursuit of us."

"You've got to leave now," insisted Crusher.

"Wes, there's a problem," said Riker. "You need both me and Data to initiate the destruct sequence."

Picard broke in, "It's all right. The Orion salvage ship has a transporter, which we can now use. We'll get you off, Number One. I think Wesley has given us the only possible way to kill it."

"However," said Data, looking up from his console, "we have seen that the entity can be scattered into bits of antimatter. These may coalesce into a new entity as before, unless there is sufficient matter present to annihilate them."

La Forge snapped his fingers and said, "We can blow hydrogen out the ramscoop. Wes, you can do that."

"Yes," agreed the young man. "Please, Captain Picard, you've got to go. Take everyone but Riker,

Data, and me. Transport them as soon as we signal you."

"If we're wrong about this—" Picard warned.

"Everybody will be safe but me," countered Wes. He pointed to a blip on the viewscreen. It was the only object on the screen that was gradually getting larger as it escaped from the swirling morass of Rashanar. "If we don't stop that thing now and it gets into Federation space—"

"All right, Mr. Crusher," said Picard, mustering an encouraging smile. "It's your show. We'll have to send Riker back to stop the destruct sequence."

"No, sir, autodestruct will shut down when all the other systems go down. I'm counting on that. When I get inside the duplicate, I'll set a core overload in addition to the self-destruct. As soon as you see the mimic ship explode, Captain Riker will have to get back to this bridge, although it may be dead."

"If need be, the Orion tug can tow the *Enterprise*," said Picard.

Wes asked sheepishly, "Does anyone know where my mom is?"

"She was leading the evacuation," answered Troi. "I know where we can find her when we get done. I'm worried . . . if there's a problem locking on with the transporter—"

"I'll drop the commanders off on my way to the mimic ship," answered Wes. "Now all of you must get going." He glanced at Riker. "Except for you and Data, sir."

"I sure picked a good week to be captain of the *Enterprise*," joked Riker. He gave Deanna a hug, as she tried unsuccessfully to hide her emotions.

"Vale, Troi, La Forge, you're with me," said Picard, heading for the turbolift. As he saw Wesley slip into the conn station, he wondered if this desperate plan would work. Pausing in front of the turbolift, the captain turned to see the silver object in the viewscreen zooming closer. He could almost make out the faux outlines of a Pakled cruiser.

Wes is right. There is no escape—we'll have to make a stand here.

"Initiate autodestruct sequence," said the captain, pressing his palm to the dermal recognition pad. "Riker, authorization alpha-alpha-zero-theta-nine."

"Riker identified," said the computer.

Now Data put his hand on the pad, although the android stole a glance at the viewscreen, where they could see the Pakled cruiser firing thrusters to stop. "Data, authorization alpha-alpha-two-gamma-six."

"Data identified," repeated the computer.

"Set autodestruct sequence, five minute delay," ordered Riker. "Commence countdown now."

"Autodestruct sequence set," replied the computer calmly. "Four minutes fifty-nine seconds and counting. Four minutes fifty-eight seconds. Four minutes fifty-seven seconds."

"Expelling hydrogen from the ramscoop," reported Wes as he worked the ops console. The computer droned on. The lights began to flicker on the *Enterprise* bridge. The young man hit the com panel and barked, "Crusher to Picard, energize now!"

"Good luck," said Riker as his solid form began to dissolve into a column of sparkling molecules. Data nodded encouragement as well. Wesley felt great relief when his shipmates were finally whisked off the bridge, leaving him alone. He didn't want to face this threat by himself, but he was the only one who could.

His feet floated off the deck as artificial gravity died, quickly followed by the rest of the ship's systems. The computer's voice wound down like a phonograph record losing speed. Wesley began to feel light-headed. He willed himself some distance away from the mimic ship and its large, helpless prey. The entity was already folding inward and outward, like a deck of cards shuffling itself and expanding as it did.

Moving like a Traveler was starting to come hard for Wes again, as it had when he feared he was losing the support of his fellowship. There was only one more jump he had to make—into the silver-blue jewel that was blossoming to match the immense size of the *Enterprise*. Gradually its rough edges became smooth to approximate the graceful lines of the starship. *Please include the autodestruct sequence,* he begged the powers of the universe. If it didn't, his job would be twice as hard.

From his vantage point in space, the Traveler marveled at the transformation of an elemental force into one of metal, bolts, and resin. Colleen had been right—the dreaded demon flyer was truly one of the wonders of the galaxy. If they could have captured it, it would have been a prize unique in the quadrant, one that might open up new doors of understanding, even to the Travelers. But somehow he didn't think it would survive in captivity, nor would any cage hold it.

I'm sorry I have to kill you.

Wesley checked the chronograph on his wrist, seeing that he had three minutes left before the countdown ended. The mimic ship might not have every bulkhead and conduit of the *Enterprise* down to perfection by then, but it would be very close. The Traveler closed his eyes, trying to envision himself inside the glistening duplicate that was molding itself before his eyes.

Moving toward it was like swimming through quicksand. He feared that he couldn't penetrate the hull of the anomaly. *One more time,* he told himself. *Let me focus the lens one more time.*

With an effort that left him exhausted, the Traveler sprawled onto the bridge of what might have been the *Enterprise,* except that parts of it were liquid, like paint. The deck solidified around him, and he staggered to his feet, feeling nauseated.

To his great relief, a voice echoed in the emptiness: "Two minutes forty-eight seconds, two minutes forty-seven seconds."

The countdown was still on. First he had to make

sure it didn't destroy the real *Enterprise*. Wes staggered to the closest console, dropped into the seat, then tried to bring up the weapons systems on the computer. The readouts behaved as he expected, but he was shocked to see that phasers were charging for a full burst. He quickly took them offline and switched to readings from engineering. As expected, the antimatter storage pods, the reactor, and every conduit were rapidly filling with antimatter. Wes caught his breath, because he knew this was the stage where some of the prey ships exploded just from the unexpected stress.

But there was no battle going on, there were no stray plasma bursts, so Wes hoped the real *Enterprise* would remain intact through this ordeal. Behind him, a voice announced, "One minute fifty-nine seconds." He cranked up the plasma-injection system, flooding the reactor, which was already filled with antimatter. Now an overload was bound to happen to this counterfeit starship, self-destruct sequence or no.

Wes felt a horrible pain in his stomach. He groaned and doubled over. He knew he had to get off the mimic ship immediately, or he might pass out. The Traveler had done everything he could. The demon flyer was clearly not geared to combat anyone who could survive its initial assault and proceed to board her. To the naked eye, this *was* the *Enterprise,* but it felt all wrong to his body.

He tried to focus—to will himself into space—but

he couldn't even get a clear sense of what it would be like to float in the void. It was as if he once knew a foreign language but had somehow forgotten it . . . in the blink of an eye! He staggered across the deck, barely getting his legs to carry his body, which seemed to have the mass of a small moon. *I'm going to die. I'm no longer a Traveler.*

"Fifty-nine seconds," intoned the computer.

"Computer," he grunted, "automate operations in transporter room one. Direct-beam me to transporter room one."

"Fifty-two seconds," said the computer, ignoring him.

With survival instincts taking over, Wes lunged to his feet and bolted to the turbolift, hoping against hope that it would operate as expected. The door at least slid open. He tottered inside. Wes gave a wretched dry heave and collapsed to the floor, summoning just enough strength to say, "Transporter room one."

"Acknowledged. Autodestruct in forty-five seconds. All personnel are advised to leave the ship."

"I'm trying," he groaned, feeling as if his insides were about to rip open.

By the time the door opened and he stumbled into the corridor, klaxons were blaring and emergency lights were flashing throughout the ship. "Autodestruct in thirty seconds," reported the computer. "Twenty-nine, twenty-eight."

Everything around him was surreal, nightmarish, and he wondered whether the corridor was actually glowing and writhing or whether his condition had brought on hallucinations. Wesley beat upon every door as he lunged down the hall, finally discovering the double doors for the transporter room, which slid open.

"Twenty-two seconds, twenty-one seconds," intoned the computer over the blaring klaxons.

Despite a feverish headache, Wes rushed to the transporter console and tried to remember the coordinates of the Orion salvage ship. He couldn't recall, but the duplicate still had operating sensors. A quick scan of the area located the closest vessel—the *Enterprise* floating dead in space.

"Autodestruct sequence in progress," said the computer. "Abort now impossible. Five seconds, four seconds—"

Every muscle in his body seemed to contract as he shuffled to the transporter platform and hurled himself upon a pad. Mercifully, he felt the familiar tingle of the beam as it spirited him away from the doomed demon ship.

Now Wes floated helplessly on a darkened bridge, his gut still tied in knots. Twisting around, he caught sight of the other *Enterprise* through a small port to the left of the dark viewscreen. It looked like a toy vessel floating upon the black water. As he reached for it, the starship detonated in a monstrous fireball, spewing glittering rubble into the far corners of his vision. This sparkling mass met the cloud of hydrogen he had released minutes ago. The starscape turned into bright daylight for a few seconds, and finally the flashes and pops died down.

With a start, Wesley realized this was the scene he had witnessed in the Pool of Prophecy after being born as a Traveler. All of that was over now . . . all of it, especially being a Traveler. Wes believed he saw an Ontailian ship cruise past the viewport, but he passed out before he could confirm it.

Chapter Fifteen

WESLEY CRUSHER STIRRED from what seemed like the deepest sleep of his life, and found that his joints were all sore, along with his back. He also noticed an intravenous tube in his arm, feeding him nutrients. He looked around, and there was his mother, striding toward him with a big grin on her face.

"Ah," she said with satisfaction, "I thought you would wake up today." The doctor peered with interest at the readouts on the screen over his bed.

"Today?" he asked with confusion. "How long have I been out?"

"Almost three days," she answered, fondly brushing the hair off his forehead. "You almost died, Wesley. Neptunium and gamma poisoning. I don't think anyone else could have survived inside the mimic ship. You'll be weak for several more days."

"Was it destroyed?" he asked hopefully.

"Yes. You did it."

He closed his eyes and slumped back in his bed. "I lost my powers, Mom. I'm not a Traveler anymore."

"Maybe that will keep you home and out of trouble. I have to notify the captain—he wants to see you. I'll be right back."

The young man drifted in and out of sleep for a while, until he heard voices. He opened his eyes to see Picard, Riker, Troi, and La Forge, all beaming at him. His mother bustled around the room, checking machines and his intravenous tubes.

"Well done, Mr. Crusher," said Picard with pride. "Data and the rest of the crew all wanted to see you, but they'll have to visit in shifts. Your mother says we almost lost you, which would have been very unjust, after everything you did for us and the Ontailians."

"The Ontailians aren't mad at us anymore?" asked Wes.

"No, just the opposite," answered the captain. "The Ontailians were a big help getting the *Enterprise* operational again. They replenished our antimatter, and supplied spare parts and technical support. It's not official, but they told us they would stay in the Federation and allow Starfleet back into Rashanar. Of course, there's nothing for them to be secretive about anymore. I believe they had a love-hate relationship with the demon ship. They had appeased it as best they could for five hundred years."

"Does that mean your name is cleared?" asked Wes.

Picard sighed. "Not exactly. Oh, Nechayev and Ross know what we've done, but the case won't be reopened. We can't revisit it, because we might have to find the Ontailians culpable for the destruction of the *Juno*. They don't want to go into the whole matter of the demon ship. Things happened with the scavengers that none of us are anxious to discuss. The Ontailians are quite embarrassed and grateful. It's more important that we keep them in the Federation fold than saddle them with blame. Think of all the reports we *won't* have to write."

"It's still not right," muttered La Forge. "And Data still doesn't have his emotion chip. They say they need to give it more testing."

Picard raised his hand in a conciliatory gesture. "We knew the ground rules going into this mission. It was undercover and unofficial. Whether we were successful or not, there would be no exoneration and no public record. Let's be thankful we were so successful. We made Rashanar a much safer place than it was before. The *Enterprise* will just have to erase this black spot on our record by our future actions."

"But Jean-Luc will be captain of the *Enterprise* again," added Beverly. "As soon as we get back, it will become official. Also there will be a memorial service for Colleen Cabot. I'll present her parents with a commendation from Starfleet Medical."

"Remarkably," added Riker, "Cabot was the only crew member we lost on this mission, although it took us a day to round up everyone who evacuated the ship." He lowered his head. "We're all really sorry for your loss, Wes. She was something else."

Wes nodded his thanks.

"But we're glad to have you back," said Troi, patting him on the shoulder. "When you're stronger, we should get together and talk about everything that's happened to you."

"All right, Counselor," agreed Wesley. He didn't know how much good talking would do, but he knew he had issues that had to be discussed.

"What was it like over there?" asked La Forge. "On the mimic ship."

Wes shook his head, thinking that those three minutes were a blur, like an old dream one can't recall clearly. "I was in pain most of the time," he admitted, "but it *was* the *Enterprise*. You know, I had a feeling it was ready to die . . . that it knew it had outlived its purpose."

"That's enough conversation for now," insisted his protective mother. "We'll be home tomorrow, and you can entertain visitors all day long."

"You get well," said Riker as Beverly ushered them toward the door.

"I'm glad to be back," called Wesley weakly. "With my friends."

When sickbay was again quiet, his mother returned to check his vital signs one last time. "You're lucky you're young," she said finally. "Or that would have been your last mission."

"It may be my last one, anyway," Wes murmured to himself, feeling very drowsy. A moment later, he was asleep.

As they strolled out of the chapel on the grounds of Starfleet Academy, both Wes and Beverly were still wiping their eyes. It had been a very beautiful service for Colleen Cabot. The usually stoic Admiral Nakamura had broken into tears during his eulogy. Nobody could quite explain how Colleen had died on a routine training mission, but her family wasn't asking embarrassing questions. The outpouring of affection and respect for the counselor had impressed everybody. Many had stayed behind to share anecdotes about her.

Even so, Wes hadn't wanted to engage in small talk about Colleen. He was content to stroll through the lush gardens of Starfleet Academy with his mother, saying very little. It was a gorgeous sunny afternoon, with birds chirping in the trees; the breeze rustled through the flowers, carrying their delicious scents across the walkway. Wes felt recovered physically, but he felt enormous emptiness. He had lost a great love, plus the life to which he had devoted himself for the last several years. The young man had no idea how he could replace either one.

As they passed a bench, he asked, "Can we sit for a moment, Mom?"

"Sure."

Wes watched a bee toiling tirelessly among the blossoms. So far he had avoided all questions on the topic of "What will you do now?" but he realized that he would have to answer that question sooner or later. He could sense his mom wanting to ask, but resisting the impulse. She had been wonderfully understanding about everything. It was then that he realized how lucky he was to have this dynamic woman as his mother. The way everyone treated her, it was clear that Dr. Crusher would someday be running Starfleet Medical again. Maybe that was the question that preoccupied her as she sat silently beside him on the bench.

"You're looking fit," said a male voice, breaking into their quiet reverie.

Wes looked up and was dumbfounded. There stood his old comrade, the Traveler, smiling beneficently at him. His mother stiffened her back, as if she wouldn't let this interloper take away her son again.

The young man rose hesitantly to his feet. "I . . . I didn't think I would ever see you again."

"You almost didn't," answered the Traveler. "Your mother had to work hard to save you."

"And I'm going to work hard to keep him," she vowed.

"I don't need him for long," answered the Traveler, growing serious, "but I do need him to go with me."

Wes shook his head in confusion. "But you revoked my powers."

"I haven't got time to go into that now," said the Traveler. "Let's just say you passed your final test."

Wesley turned to his mother and took her hands in his. "I have to go with him," he said. "I can't give this up when there's still so much I don't understand. But I promise that I'll visit you often, wherever you are. I won't forget my friends in Starfleet."

Tears welled in Beverly's eyes, but she managed a pained smile. "Just take time to have children someday, so that you'll know how awful it is when they leave. At least now we know you can fall in love. That still makes you human."

Before he could change his mind, Wes gave his mom a quick hug, then grabbed the Traveler's arm. As they strolled down the sidewalk, the flowers and trees faded to blackness sprinkled with distant stars, and the Travelers eased gently through space.

"There's someone I would like to bring into the fellowship," Wes said excitedly. "He's not humanoid—he's a Medusan—but I *know* he would make a great Traveler."

"Your first apprentice would have to be unusual," replied his comrade pleasantly. "Commodore Korgan will be welcome. And I must say, it is good to see you again, Traveler."

ABOUT THE AUTHOR

John Vornholt is the acclaimed author of numerous *Star Trek*® novels, including *Genesis Force, The Genesis Wave* Books One through Three, *Gemworld* Books One and Two, *Sanctuary, Mind Meld, Masks, Contamination, Antimatter, Rogue Saucer,* and *The Dominion War* Books One and Three. He lives in Arizona with his wife and two sons.

The saga continues in April 2004 with

STAR TREK®
A TIME TO SOW

by
Dayton Ward & Kevin Dilmore

Turn the page for an electrifying
preview of *A Time to Sow*. . . .

"I am Zahanzei, first minister to the people of the planet Dokaal. I speak to you as the leader of a people in desperate need of assistance from anyone who might hear this message."

Though he had watched the recording twice already, Jean-Luc Picard once again found himself drawn by Zahanzei's appeal as if seeing it for the first time.

"Catastrophic seismic forces are tearing our world apart, and our most experienced scientists believe that total destruction is inevitable. Our planet is the only one in our solar system capable of sustaining life, and we do not possess the resources to evacuate our people to a suitable world in another system. We have only just recently discovered a means of propulsion that would allow us to complete an interstellar journey, but our level of technology is limited. Our calculations tell us that there is insufficient time to build vessels capable of carrying a sufficient number of our people to safety in order to insure the preservation of our race."

Standing before a window offering a picturesque

view of a thriving city, the Dokaalan leader's visage was noble and thoughtful, as would befit a person in his position. Tall and thin, he was humanoid in appearance. His skin, possessing a light blue tinge, was free of any blemishes that Picard could see. Deep maroon eyes peered out from beneath a prominent brow, while only small holes represented where the ears and nose might be on a human's head. Completely devoid of hair, his skull tapered to an almost arrow-shaped chin. Despite his stately bearing, Zahanzei still seemed to possess a vulnerability held only barely in check by the need to carry out the duties of his office for the benefit of those he governed.

"Therefore, I ordered the creation of these three small probes, one of which has traveled to you and carries with it my plea on behalf of my people and my world: Please help us."

As the recording completed and the *Enterprise*'s senior staff turned back to the conference table and one another, Picard knew that already their minds had set to work. He could almost see them ordering their individual lists of responsibilities to support a rescue operation on the scale they believed was coming.

"How soon do we get under way, sir?" asked Commander William Riker from where he sat to Picard's right, giving voice to the concern and determination that was evident on the faces of the others.

As Picard regarded those faces, however, he felt a twinge of regret, knowing that it fell to him to dash those plans and remind them of the reality of their current lot in life.

"Three weeks ago," Picard said, "the *U.S.S. Crazy Horse* discovered a small probe of unfamiliar design adrift near the Jeluryn Sector. It had suffered massive damage during its rather lengthy voyage, and engineers aboard the *Crazy Horse* weren't able to retrieve anything of value from its onboard computer system. What they did discover, however, was that this was not the first object encountered from these people. According to Federation databanks, another such device was encountered by a Vulcan ship more than two centuries ago."

"Two centuries?" said Deanna Troi, seated next to Riker and sporting a confused expression. "We're just now learning about it?"

Picard nodded, resisting the urge to smile at the counselor's confusion. "The Vulcan Science Directorate spent several months analyzing data retrieved from the first probe. They concluded that the planetary disaster described by First Minister Zahanzei occurred decades before the first probe's discovery, and well before Starfleet possessed any sort of deep-space exploration capability. The Vulcans advised against sending a ship to investigate, and the matter was closed."

"Earth was taking a lot of advice from the Vulcans in those days," said Lieutenant Commander Geordi La Forge, "but it's hard to believe that anyone in Starfleet could resist the urge to find out where that probe had come from. It sounds like just the mission to give to one of those first long-range ships."

Seated next to La Forge, Lieutenant Commander Data replied, "It was a very active, almost chaotic, period in Earth history, Geordi. With only a single vessel of sufficient capability available for such a task, Starfleet's priorities did not allow for a mission of extended duration at that time. By the time such resources were available, Earth found itself embroiled in conflicts with both the Xindi and the Romulans."

In response to the android's words, Picard could not help but glance to the rear wall of the observation lounge and its array of replicas portraying the lineage of starships named *Enterprise* dating back more than two centuries. Grimly, he reminded himself that in addition to the promise of peaceful exploration, the replicas also represented decades of conflict, both victorious and damaging.

Picard almost smiled as he watched the exchange between the two colleagues. Even in the face of what was shaping up to be little more than a milk run, La Forge and Data were trading information both relevant and trivial, just as they would if they were attempting to solve a looming crisis. *Some things will never change.*

"Once the Federation was founded," he said, "and with a whole host of new friends, to say nothing of enemies, Starfleet's charter and mission initiatives took them in other directions. After a time, verifying the fate of a single planet which was already believed destroyed for years was lost in the shuffle of larger concerns."

A student of history, Picard was intimately familiar with that period in Earth's evolution from a single civilization to one of the founding parties of what was now a Federation of more than one-hundred-and-fifty worlds. Such a feat, carried out in the space of little more than two centuries and accompanied by all manner of ancillary accomplishments and setbacks along the way, would have been more than enough to obscure any desire to investigate the presumed destruction of one planet.

Leaning forward in his chair until his forearms rested on the conference table, Riker said, "I don't understand. If there's nothing we can do for these people, then why show us the message at all?"

"It seems," Picard replied, "that Starfleet Command wishes us to chart the area of space where the probes are believed to have originated, and see if we can determine what exactly happened to the Dokaalan and their world."

"Sir," said Lieutenant Christine Vale, the *Enterprise*'s security chief, from where she sat at the far end of the table, "wouldn't an actual science ship be better equipped for such an assignment?"

Tugging on the lower edge of his uniform jacket, Picard replied, "Perhaps, Lieutenant, but Admiral Nechayev believes that under the current circumstances, the *Enterprise* is the perfect ship to head up this mission."

A bitter aftertaste remained even as he spoke the words, but Picard vowed he would reveal none of that irritation or disappointment to his subordinates. Vale's point about sending a science vessel in search of the Dokaalan was a valid observation, but there was also the simple matter that no science vessel, or captain of same, was currently believed to be a hindrance to Starfleet. . . .

Don't miss

STAR TREK®
A TIME TO SOW

Available April 2004 wherever paperback books are sold!

KNOW NO BOUNDARIES

Explore the Star Trek™
Universe with Star Trek™
Communicator, The Magazine of
the Official Star Trek Fan Club.

Subscription to Communicator is
only $29.95 per year (plus shipping and handling)
and entitles you to:

- 6 issues of STAR TREK Communicator

- Membership in the official STAR TREK™ Fan Club

- An exclusive full-color lithograph

- 10% discount on all merchandise purchased at
  www.startrekfanclub.com

- Advance purchase preference on select items
  exclusive to the fan club

- ...and more benefits to come!

So don't get left behind! Subscribe to STAR TREK™
Communicator now at www.startrekfanclub.com

www.decipher.com

DECIPHER®
The Art of Great Games®

A VIACOM COMPANY
www.startrek.com
STFC

STAR TREK

STARGAZER: THREE

MICHAEL JAN FRIEDMAN

WHEN A TRANSPORTER MISHAP DEPOSITS A BEAUTIFUL WOMAN FROM ANOTHER UNIVERSE ON THE *STARGAZER*, GERDA ASMOND SUSPECTS THE ALIEN OF TREACHERY.

BUT SHE HAS TO WONDER—IS SHE FOLLOWING HER KLINGON INSTINCTS OR SUCCUMBING TO SIMPLE JEALOUSY?

GERDA NEEDS TO FIND OUT—OR PICARD AND HIS CREW MAY PAY FOR THEIR GENEROSITY WITH THEIR LIVES.

AVAILABLE NOW

STAR TREK

STARGAZER: OBLIVION

MICHAEL JAN FRIEDMAN

IN 1893, A TIME-TRAVELING JEAN-LUC PICARD ENCOUNTERED A LONG-LIVED ALIEN NAMED GUINAN, WHO WAS POSING AS A HUMAN TO LEARN EARTH'S CUSTOMS.

THIS IS THE STORY OF A GUINAN VERY DIFFERENT FROM THE WOMAN WE THINK WE KNOW.

A GUINAN WHO YEARNS FOR OBLIVION.

AVAILABLE NOW

STAR TREK